BEATRICE BRADSHAW

Love on the
Scottish
Spring Isle

Part 2 in the 'Escape to Scotland'-Series

She got cold feet – now a hot Scot is melting her heart...

An American runaway bride, a Scottish player with a guarded heart, and a love like a tidal wave.

April flees her own wedding and lands on a remote island in Scotland, seeking solace and escape. She's done with predictable, safe choices, yearning for liberation and self-discovery. Enter Euan, the isle's charming surfer, bartender, and expert in female orgasms with a past he's keen to forget.

April's insatiable desire for liberation clashes with Euan's fear of getting too close, igniting a fiery yet precarious love affair. When April's past finally catches up, and Euan's secrets surface, their newfound romance is put to the ultimate test.

Will they be brave enough to become more than a vacation fling?

Content Note

This book uses British spelling and expressions. However, since the main female character is American, there are some US expressions in here as well – that's her character voice.

Please be aware: this story contains explicit open-door sex and quite a bit of profanity. It also references topics that could trigger certain audiences, such as abandonment, divorce, and alcoholism. Most of it is in the backstories of the characters, but it's best to be prepared.

Your mental health matters. <3

To all the fearless girls who embrace their desires without shame – even though they were taught not to. Own your sexuality with pride.

Prologue

I *don't think I can do this.*
This was the worst possible moment. April clutched her bouquet, knuckles whitening around the stems.

Just breathe.

Except the stupid dress wouldn't let her. Part of her wished she could rip the silly bodice and watch the pearls spew everywhere. Her gaze was fixed on the polished chapel floor. Out of the corner of her eye, she saw the shiny tips of her father's leather shoes. Today, he was forced to notice her for a moment.

This was her big day, after all.

April's heart drummed a staccato beat as she half-lifted her head, looking at the closed wooden doors in front of her. In less than one minute, they would creak open. In less than one minute, she'd begin the slow march down the aisle in her ivory lace gown. Past rows of two hundred distinguished guests. Happy and smiling with glistening eyes. And in less than five minutes, she'd pledge forever to the only man she'd ever known, the only one she'd ever…

Loved?

April blinked hard, swallowing around a lump in her

throat. After ten years together, shouldn't love come easily? Shouldn't she ache to run into Dick's comforting arms and never leave? Shouldn't she rejoice at the prospect of ceasing to be April Virginia Smith and becoming Mrs Richard Williams III?

Yet all she felt was overwhelming nausea.

What's wrong with me?

She usually did the right thing. The sensible thing. Whatever was expected of her. She wasn't much of a rebel, that had always been her brothers' privilege.

The organist played the first chords of the wedding march and the doors groaned open. April's breath caught as the guests rose and all eyes turned to her silhouetted in the doorway. There were audible gasps and sighs.

Dick stood at the altar. So handsome. The tux accentuated his shoulders. The perfect guy and ideal husband. Kind and generous. Gentle and caring. Financially stable. A good man. Everybody here wanted them to get married. To be happy.

But as April took her first step, a violent sob welled in her chest. She paused, the lace train of her gown whispering around her ankles. A ripple of confusion swept through the guests.

'What's going on, April?' her father hissed over the deafening music. Tugging discreetly on her left arm.

She couldn't move.

All April saw was a grim future of polite smiles, nice cuddles, and the annual obligatory sexual intercourse to create more babies. A slow suffocation of her spirit. Was the price of marrying a good man to have no sex, no passion, no real intimacy? And was she willing to pay it?

She blinked at the altar, at Dick's furrowed brow and pursed lips. She loved him, but—

I can't do this.

The realisation shot through April like a million volts. Each fibre of her being was screaming. As if she had spent the past years in a foggy cocoon and now everything came into sharp focus.

Marry your best friend, they said. But April didn't want to marry her best friend. And was he even her best friend? She didn't want to spend the rest of her life with a man who didn't desire her. Whose response to 'Don't you think we should talk about our sex life?' was always 'Don't be silly, honey'.

She couldn't lie there every twelve months and wait for Dick to soundlessly do the deed in the dark – only to hide in the bathroom for half an hour afterwards, suppressing her sobs by biting into her fist. She couldn't be that lonely with someone. She couldn't live a half-life until she died.

It wasn't too late.

As if in slow motion, she saw her cramped fingers open and the bouquet – red and white roses with baby's breath – tumble to the floor before the hem of her dress.

As the organ music stopped, as distraught murmurs and her mother's pointed cry echoed through the chapel, April turned on her heels and ran.

'To the airport!' she shouted at the cab driver as she tossed her suitcase onto the backseat and slid in, pulse racing.

'Sure? Aren't you missing someone?' The driver inspected her wedding dress in the rear-view mirror.

'Kansas City International. Now. Fast as you can!'

'All right, all right. Jesus!' He stepped on the gas.

She dug through her purse for her phone and sent a text to her mother.

APRIL (12.18 PM) I'm so, so sorry. But don't worry.
I'll be okay. Explain later. A.

And another to Dick.

> *APRIL (12.19 PM) I'm sorry that I couldn't marry*
> *you. But this is not the life either of us deserved.*
> *Be happy with someone else. Talk later.*

Then she switched it off without checking the dozens of messages and voicemails flooding in and tossed it back into her bag. With a groan, she folded her body over and buried her face in her hands. Her breathing was fast and shallow.

This dress is killing me.

Lauren Williams, her almost-mother-in-law, had chosen it for her. April would have picked something much simpler, more comfortable. But when she tried it on, Lauren had gushed, 'You're so glamorous in it, doll. Simply stunning. This is it!'

Of course, it had been incredibly generous of Dick's parents to pay for it. But from the second she tried it on, April had felt like an extravagant cake decoration. With an exasperated groan, she straightened up and fumbled the veil out of her updo with sweaty fingers.

'Bad day?' the driver asked.

'Oh, you think?'

His eyes flashed amiably in the rear-view mirror. 'Don't have to be a genius to see that something went wrong.'

'Almost made a mistake today,' she said. 'Until I didn't.'

He smiled at her. 'You'll figure it out. Where're you going?'

'No idea. Far, far away from here.'

This was the moment when it dawned on April that, for the first time in her comparatively uneventful life, she hadn't thought it through. She hadn't thought at all. Her dress felt tighter still. She couldn't wait to get out of this pearly prison.

Luckily, their packed suitcases had been at the venue. The plan – Dick's plan, as per usual – had been to fly directly to Mexico after their wedding party in the country club next to the chapel. To spend their honeymoon in Tulum.

The one place April was definitely not going to. But where else?

A place where no one will ever find me. Wouldn't mind being swallowed whole by the earth. Where's the abyss when you need one?

She pressed her temple to the cool glass of the window and took a deep, steadying breath. Tears filled her eyes. Impossible to even begin thinking about all the people she had failed and let down today.

Most of all Dick.

The good guy. The nice guy. So few edges that everyone liked him. Without exception. And she had jilted him at the altar like an ungrateful jerk-face. She should be feeling gut-wrenching guilt, despair, self-hatred.

And yeah, she did.

Yet there was also an unstoppable liberation seeping through her like molasses, interrupted by short heaves of panic. A faint aroma of freedom with an aftertaste of bitterness. Excitement and fear were having an MMA fight inside her ribcage as the cab sped down the highway towards the airport and into the unknown.

But wherever she would end up, it would be the right place. Simply because it wasn't here.

She pushed the little button, let the window down, and threw her veil out.

This was madness, wasn't it? Or this could be a chance to discover what she wanted in life. After having very publicly declared what she did *not* want. An opportunity to find out who she truly was, beneath the polite smile she'd worn for so long.

No, she didn't have a plan.

But she did have her freedom. Sort of.

When the cab pulled up to the airport, April dug her card from her wallet.

'Listen,' said the driver as he handed her the receipt. 'No idea what happened today. None of my business. But you'll be fine. I got a feeling.'

'Thanks,' she said with a quivering voice. 'I hope you're right. At least it can't get any worse.'

Chapter One

P eople were staring at her. Of course they were. It wasn't
    every day that they saw a messed-up runaway bride.

April stood at the entrance of the terminal with her suitcase, sporting her wedding dress. Puffy, red eyes from crying.
A teenage girl whispered something to her mother, who in
turn glanced away to avoid any sign of discomfiture. An
older couple stared with sympathy written over their faces.
April's gaze was pinned ahead, never meeting the curious
stares of those around her. Her practical side took over. First
mission: taking off the gown. Second mission: finding a spot
to hide for the foreseeable future.

With shaky legs, April took a step forward. Into the great
mystery that was her life now.

A detour to the restroom to get rid of the suffocating dress
of doom. It took her a good ten minutes to wrangle and
wrestle herself out of a gazillion layers of lace, tulle, and
taffeta. She opened her suitcase, filled with summer clothes,
and picked out a pair of comfy leggings, her black Chucks, a
white t-shirt, and a denim jacket.

When she was done, April stumbled back and leaned
against the wall. She could breathe again. Felt good. Overdue.

After washing her hands and face, she stared back into a hollow pair of dull green eyes in the mirror. A few strands had come loose from her hairdo and stuck to her sweaty cheeks.

Who are you?

April blew out a breath. She'd find out soon enough. She stuffed the ivory fabric into her suitcase, put the heels next to the sink, and left the ladies' room.

As she entered the terminal, a video advertisement on a large illuminated billboard caught her eye.

A crescent moon of sand and dune nestled between arms of rugged rock. The ocean was a gradient from clear crystal to deep azure. Where the land met the water, thrift blossoms stood in defiance of the salty winds. Grasses clung to dunes that rose and rolled like slumbering giants beneath a blanket of sand. Beyond were green hills, their peaks draped in mist. A place where the soul responded to the call of the wild. April was magnetically pulled into the scenery. It looked like everything she needed. Serenity, peace, quiet. But raw and true, not easy and artificial. A landscape that whispered its old tales to those who would listen – the solitude of the beach, the stoicism of the mountains, and the endlessness of the ocean. The next frame of the video showed the same stunning place, this time with a large whisky bottle and the text: 'Isle of Saorsa. The taste of freedom and Scotland'.

Scotland?

Somewhere in the depth of her soul, a hidden, secret part began to rouse. A remote Scottish island was the textbook definition of far, far away. Slap bang in the middle of nowhere. Nobody could find her there. Or even look for her.

It was perfect.

April's heart raged with each step, beneath the panic and confusion wound an undeniable thread of excitement.

Off to Scotland then.

. . .

Sitting on the long-haul flight from Chicago to London a few hours later, she had plenty of time to drink and think. About her life. Her relationship with Dick. His proposal and her acceptance. A wave of sadness washed over her and the icy air stream from the vents made her shiver. The engines' hum hid the sound of her sniffles.

Where did it go so terribly wrong?

She met Dick at the end of her first year of college, only eighteen. Dick was the first boy who ever noticed her. Her first boyfriend.

Her *only* boyfriend.

They never fought. It took a dedicated and prolonged effort to fight with Dick. After graduation, they moved in together. Days turned into weeks, months, a year, then ten.

It didn't matter much that his parents were wealthy and her parents weren't. That his parents had a picture book marriage and her parents had the polar opposite. Dick had always made her feel safe. As they grew older, they occasionally talked about getting married. Just like everybody did. Dick wanted to wait until he was settled in his father's firm. During the past two years, he had spent more and more time at work. She often joked that he should put up a cot in his office.

Now was the time, he had said last Christmas, and stuck an engagement ring on her finger. They were both thirty, ready for the next phase. Their life's path had been laid out before them: two or three children, one or two dogs, sex once a year. Maybe. Large house, country club, mommy Insta account, beige baby clothes.

Cosy and stable.

Infinitely smothering.

'Would you like something to drink?' The flight attendant looked at her, not at all fazed by April's weepy face.

'Can I have a tomato juice, please?' Then April called

herself to her senses. 'Make that a Bloody Mary. No, make it two.'

Why had she said yes to him?

Probably because it had been the next logical step. Superficially, Dick was a good catch. Attractive, kind, dependable. Someone who would never abandon her. And it wasn't that he didn't love her. He just didn't do it with his body.

The problem was: April yearned for precisely that. With every part of her entire self. She wanted to be desired and accepted for who she was and what she wanted, not merely tolerated for fulfilling a role in someone's life plan.

A flame of guilt and shame seared in her thorax. This mess was her fault. If she'd been honest with herself for five minutes during those past ten years, she would have heard herself scream on the inside. She would have understood what was missing. Done something other than trying to seduce him, trying to talk to him, and eventually giving up…

She would have spared a lot of people a lot of pain and anger. Including herself.

Nope. She didn't want to deal with the aftermath of today. At all. At some point, she would have to. When she was ready. Which she wasn't. Not by a long shot.

At least, Dick's father, Richard William II, had paid handsomely for the party. She hoped everybody got decently smashed on his account.

God knows they deserved it.

She slurped the last drop of her second Bloody Mary from the bottom of the plastic cup. As she leaned back in her seat, the realisation that she had wasted ten years of her life with Dick wrapped itself around her heart, squeezing. Tears gathered in the corners of her eyes, silent throbs heaved in her chest. It hurt. But neither of them deserved the stale life that they would have had together. Living like ghosts. Eternally side by side, but never together.

April had always been reasonable, everything planned

out. Now she was flying by the seat of her pants. Things were going to be uncomfortable after this stunt. Terrifying, even. She needed time and space to clear her head, to hide and lick her wounds, to muster up the courage to face the consequences of her escape. To find out what she wanted in life without distractions. To make her own choices without pressures or influences steering her in one direction or another.

The vodka, the exhaustion, and the hum of the turbines lulled her into a shallow sleep. When the wheels touched the ground on the tarmac at Heathrow hours later, April was still dreaming of untamed Scottish landscapes.

Chapter Two

Morning sunlight filtered through the windows of his VW camper van as Euan stretched under the crumpled sheets. He woke slowly, surfacing from sleep like a diver coming up for air. For a second he was disoriented, confused by the warmth pressed against his side. Then it came back to him in a rush – his shift at the pub, the thrill of a new connection, stumbling into the back of his van, all eager hands and groans and hungry mouths.

The usual.

He yawned and opened his eyes. Next to him – Poppy? Ruby? – stirred, the sheet slipping to reveal the curve of her hip. Memories of last night flashed in his mind. Nice memories. Her breathy moans, the taste of salt on her skin. The scent of sweat and sex still lingered on the sheets, blending into the smell of musty wood and petrol.

'Morning', she mumbled, rolling onto her back. Her full breasts peeked from under the sheet, rosy nipples stiff in the chill air. This was the Hebrides in May, not Alicante in August.

'Morning.' He propped himself up on an elbow, tracing a finger along her arm. 'Sleep well?'

A slow smile spread across her face. 'Mhm. And you?'

'Can't complain.'

'Good. I'd like to think I did make you tired.' She let out a contented sigh.

Euan grinned and shifted closer. 'Aye, you did.'

Was it too late to ask for her name? Best to keep the conversation to a minimum. Less potential for…misunderstandings. Euan brushed his lips against hers, lingering for a moment, looking at her. Eyeliner smudged, faint lines around her sleepy eyes, her long, dark hair dishevelled. Girl was rocking that bed head. Lovely woman. They all were.

'Thank you for last night,' he murmured against her lips. They both knew that such encounters weren't meant to last. One-night stands were unique moments of shared passion. Nothing more. A brief respite from the natural loneliness of humans. Pure, honest pleasure. Like a good dram. Precisely why he liked them. That was also how he liked his women: mature, full-bodied, and, most importantly, gone after a few sips. And Euan was always upfront about it. He was a one-night only event. No need to hurt or trick anybody. No need to play stupid games. Not among adults.

'If anything, I have to thank *you*!' She laughed, bright as a bell. 'I came here for a break with the girls and look what I found,' she yawned, 'a sexy surf instructor and many orgasms. Lucky me. Too bad I'm leaving this afternoon.'

Euan got the hint. He let his hand wander up her thigh in a gentle caress, barely grazing her skin. Classic move. 'Want another one?'

She reached across the narrow space between them, finding him already hard. 'Wouldn't say no to a parting gift.'

Music to his ears.

Euan eased away from the sleeping – Poppy? Ruby? – mindful not to wake her. He slid the van door open, almost noiselessly. After all, he had plenty of practice with his 'shag mobile', as his sister called it. Euan shook his head. He loved her, but Morag lived a completely different life.

The sun was climbing higher in the sky over Saorsa. It was past seven now. Euan cast one last glance at his night guest. She looked peaceful. He had made her happy for a few moments. She would smile whenever she remembered her trip to Saorsa after her return to…Dorset. Or was it Dover? Doncaster? Definitely England.

Am I happy?

The question popped up in Euan's sleepy mind. Hard to say. At least he wasn't actively *un*happy. He was healthy and got to do what he liked. Had the surf school and his van. The job behind the bar at the Old Barn and his writing. Morag, Allan, and their bairns. A stream of people – yes, women – from everywhere during summer. But most importantly he was here. On the isle where he was born. His home. Eilean na Saorsa, the island of freedom.

Yep. Could be worse.

The chill morning air cleared his head. His board was propped against the van. Euan ran a hand along the fibre-glass, feeling the dings that marked the years. It had been with him through it all. He had flashier ones at the surf school, but this was his favourite. His first. A gift from Morag when he had turned fourteen and discovered his passion for the waves. Almost seventeen years now. Shortly after… Well, a long time ago.

With practised movements, Euan slipped into his wetsuit. He grabbed his board and headed out to the beach. The sand was cool beneath his feet, not yet warmed by the sun. How beautiful it was, the water crystal-clear turquoise. A few diehard surfers sprinkled the shore, scanning the horizon for the first set of swells.

Morag had always taken care of him. If it wasn't for her… She was the reason he was able to stay in Saorsa when their parents got a divorce and moved to different cities on the

Scottish mainland. It couldn't have been easy for her to raise a teenager, only in her mid-twenties herself. Euan would forever be indebted to her.

Aye, he'd let her give his van any silly nickname she liked.

As he swam out, the first wave was approaching. A wall of cyan water that promised a solid ride. Euan turned his board to shore. When the wave was about to break, he whipped around and began paddling hard. The acceleration sent a thrill through his veins. He stood up on his board, the hiss of the water filling his ears. The world narrowed to him and the sea. It had been his solace for as long as he could remember. Out here, he didn't have to think or feel or want for something he couldn't have. He could simply be. This was freedom. This was life.

Euan grinned as the wave spit him out, heading straight back out for another.

By the time he returned to his van – muscles pleasantly worn, mind empty, heart free – Poppy was gone. He felt a pang of relief. No need for small talk, thank God. Relationships were like waves. Transient and temporary, coming and going. There was always another wave out there, just as there was always a new connection to explore. The most exciting one was always the next. No point in looking back.

As he made himself a coffee, he saw Ruby had left him a note on the counter. Scribbled onto a napkin.

Thanks, Euan. You're a star.
XOXO
Jen

He shrugged. Hard to get it right each time.

· · ·

Euan drove his rumbling camper up the single-track road to his sister's house, engine roaring. As soon as he had passed the last hill, the familiar whitewashed walls and slate roof came into view. The former crofter's cottage fit perfectly into its rugged surroundings next to the shore, a stone's throw from the pub. Minuscule yellow flowers were blooming on the low, mossy dry-stone wall at the front. Every time he saw the cottage, Euan admired Allan's skill. He had essentially rebuilt the MacDonald/MacLeod home from the ground up. Euan could barely fix his van. Woodwork, building, construction – handiwork wasn't where his talents lay. Even though he helped Allan here and there with construction during the winter.

No, his hands were better suited to handling delicate material.

Euan pulled into the parking space next to the house, gravel crunching under his van's tyres. Morag, Allan, and their three kids lived in the top-floor flat; in the middle were the four rooms of their bed and breakfast. The ground floor had the kitchen, breakfast room, and a tiny studio flat with a separate entrance. During spring and summer, they rented it out as an Airbnb. During the winter, it was where Euan went into hibernation and wrote. When it was too cold and dank in this van. Due to the high demand in holiday houses, it was virtually impossible to find a permanent home in Saorsa. Unless it was an inheritance like Allan's. This wee house on the edge of the isle was Euan's half-home.

He pushed the van door shut with a dull clang and walked through the creaky back entrance. No key needed. The people of Saorsa only ever locked up during the two weeks of the music festival in August, when the entire isle was overflowing with tourists. Commonly known among locals as 'the invasion'.

The smell of bacon and eggs filled the breakfast room. Instead of several small tables, it had a long and large wooden table at the centre. That way, the guests had to talk to each other. Feel more at home, like family. At least that's what Morag always said. Euan wasn't too sure about that.

'Well, well, well…if it isn't my philandering baby brother. Breakfast?' Morag asked, turning from the stove with a smile.

He hugged her. 'Always. But I'll take a quick shower first.'

She arched an eyebrow. 'Washing off last night?'

'More the salt water of this morning. But aye, that, too.' He grinned.

'Euan,' Morag said, waving her spatula in the air, 'I seriously don't understand what you're doing. Honestly, your van needs a revolving door.'

He snatched a strip of bacon from her pan. 'You don't have to understand me. You just have to love me.'

'Och, you know I do.' She rolled her eyes fondly. 'But I want you to be happy and find something lasting. Calm doon a wee bit. Settle a little. You're almost thirty-two, for goodness' sake.'

'Still in my prime. Unlike you. Ten years make such a difference.' Euan ducked from her spatula.

Morag shook her head. 'Still on your own. Only you and your rusty little hump truck. People are talking, you know?'

'Let them. At least I give them something interesting to talk about.' He nibbled on the last bit of his bacon. 'Where's Allan?'

'He's taking the kids swimming and then he'll be working at the petrol station.'

'They're still not done with construction there?' Euan asked while taking off his jumper. As the only contractor, Allan was very much in demand and involved in everything that was built, torn down, flipped, renovated, and repaired in Saorsa. Meanwhile, Morag was running the small family business. She had a first-class honours degree in literature. But tourism was the principal source of income here. More or less the only one. It hadn't always been like that. Their grandfather had been the last islander to own a distillery in Saorsa. But that had been in the 1970s and 1980s. Much had changed. But then, as now and always, island life wasn't easy. It demanded and moulded a certain personality.

'Two more weeks. Apparently. We'll see.' Morag sighed audibly as she poured the eggs into another pan. 'Hey, I had a last-minute cancellation today. You can sleep in your room if you wish.'

Euan frowned. As tempting as that sounded, he had another shift in the pub tonight. And who knew what – or who – would happen. Better to leave his options open. He was to spend more than enough time in here from October until March. 'Naw, I'll sleep in the van.'

'Course you will.' She gave a snort. 'You and your bang bus. Aside from anything else, that stupid thing is a traffic hazard. I *heard* you coming up that hill a mile away. It's falling apart, Euan.'

'Not quite. It still has some life left in it.'

'That's a miracle, considering how the poor old chassis is constantly being rattled.' She shook her head, but returned his smile.

Euan laughed. Morag wasn't judgemental. It was her way of looking out for him.

And although it was annoying at times, part of him was glad that someone actually, truly did.

Chapter Three

White-capped waves broke against the curved shore. April peered out the airplane window at the golden rays catching on the sea, heart leaping. Saorsa looked exactly like the video ad. Serene, with its distant rocky hills disappearing into the mist. The ocean's surface was a rippling patchwork of blues and greens. Scattered seaweed-clad rocks emerged from the water. Sparse houses dotted the landscape, their lights twinkling in the glow of the fading sun. The small plane rattled as it descended onto the makeshift runway on the beach, skidding to a stop on the sand.

The pilot turned around. 'Welcome to the Isle of Saorsa. Local time eight forty-five, temperature fifteen degrees Celsius. And, in case you haven't noticed, it's wet. The airport is that shed over there,' she nudged her head to the left, 'that's where you'll find your bags in a minute. Thank you for flying with DeanAir and all that. Good night.'

There were only five other passengers who had boarded the tiny twin-engine aircraft in Glasgow roughly forty minutes ago. April was the last to step onto the sand, the wet chill seeping through her Chucks.

This was the world's end.

Her new beginning.

She sauntered into the small airport hut, which was roughly the same size as her old classroom. She had loved teaching, loved the kids. But earlier this year, she and Dick decided it made sense for her to stop working, especially with him taking over his dad's firm. April couldn't figure out why she'd agreed. It was as if the logic of her old life was drifting further away with each minute.

'Oi, lass. Yer first time in Saorsa?' There was a deep Scottish burr behind her. When she turned around, a massive guy stood behind a panelled counter. He was tall and broad-chested, with a belly like a barrel. His round face was framed by a curly, copper-coloured beard and equally red mane. *A younger, ginger-haired Santa Claus.*

April gave a short laugh at the thought, exhaustion bordering on hysteria.

Something akin to concern appeared in his eyes. No wonder. She had been awake for almost forty hours. And if she looked anything like she felt, concern was the appropriate reaction.

'Is somebody pickin' ye up? Ye seem a wee bit lost. And ye're no wearing much for the weather,' he said and frowned.

'Yeah, it's my first time in Scotland,' April explained. 'I was supposed to go to Mexico. But then…I changed my mind.'

'Mexico ye say?' He laughed, and it sounded like rolling thunder. 'Mexico! Now that's as far from here as ye can get. Changed yer mind? Let's hope ye won't regret it!'

'Fingers and stub toes crossed. Do you know where I can find my luggage?'

'I ken, aye.' He flipped up a section of the counter and came out from behind. 'It's outside, just round the corner. I'll show ye.'

The baggage claim on the side of the minuscule airport

was a simple aluminium extension that looked like a bus stop, with suitcases on a single low shelf, not a long conveyor belt. It was sufficient, there had barely been enough room for the people on the plane. They had already left. April picked up her black trolley. Everything she owned now. Mostly. Luckily, she still had her own bank account and savings.

'Where are ye stayin', love? Do ye have transport?'

'Don't know.' She shook her head. 'I haven't booked a hotel. Maybe I can get a taxi and find a place in town?'

'In *town*? A *taxi*? Ye Americans are funny, I gie ye that.' He laughed so heartily that his belly wobbled. Then he looked at her again and stopped. 'Ye're serious? That's bold, love. It's May. The season has started. Everywhere's gonnae be booked tae the brim.'

April's sternum wanted to pull inwards. It dawned on her that the main problem with not making a plan was the general lack of a plan.

'Do you know a place? Any place? Just for the night. I'll take a tent in a front yard.' Memories of mirthless camping trips with her dad and her three older brothers rose. April pushed them back down where they belonged.

'Let me text the wife. If there's anything, she'll know.' With two huge thumbs, he tapped surprisingly nimbly on his smartphone screen.

April took in her surroundings. In the twilight, the clouds glowed in vibrant oranges and pinks with streaks of magenta, as if the heavens caught fire. The colours were receding into the water that encircled the island, the sun kissing the ocean good night. It was breathtaking.

No, that's wrong, she thought. *It's breathgiving*.

'So the wife says that Morag MacDonald had a cancellation. But that's in Cuanag, right at the southern end of the isle. A forty-minute walk. Nae taxi or bus, I'm afraid.'

April shrugged. 'That's okay. I can't sleep at the airport now, can I?'

'Naw, that ye can't.'

He then called that woman named Morag, apparently they knew each other, and asked if she could come to fetch April. But this Morag and her husband had both had a bit too much wine. Somebody's birthday.

'No problem. Honestly. I can walk', April said to the Scottish Santa Claus, tightening her shoulders to instil confidence in herself. 'Thank you so much for your help.'

'Nae problem. I would drive ye myself. But I can't leave yet. Take my number in case anything happens and ye need something. Name's Angus.'

He wrote the digits on a small flyer for a whale watching trip. She folded it into her wallet. Then she clasped the plastic handle of her wheeled suitcase. Time to walk five hundred miles.

April trudged along the single-track road as rain drizzled down, gradually soaking her hair. Road was an exaggeration. It was a carelessly poured strip of asphalt with no footpath on either side, only narrow ribbons of grass and ditches. This was the main road – the *only* road – subtly ascending and descending and winding, hugging the island's uneven topography. Saorsa's sky had changed to azure as the sun dipped into the sea, the silhouette of the land quiet in the last streaks of daylight. The air was heavy, smelling of brine, moist grass, and dung.

Her feet were hurting. These thin fabric shoes weren't made for long, strenuous marches. April had no idea how far she was from Morag's B&B. No phone reception meant no map, not that she wanted to switch it on anyway.

There were no road signs and not a single person had passed since she had begun walking thirty minutes ago. Only cows and sheep, lots of them. Other than the wheels of her suitcase hissing on the asphalt, the only sound was the sea lapping against the shore.

And the increasingly fast pitter-patter of raindrops.

I need warmer clothes. And boots. And a raincoat. And an umbrella.

But even the sturdiest umbrella couldn't have saved her.

Within minutes, that pitter-patter turned into a downpour, soaking her to the bone. The rain was sharp and cold and everywhere. Droplets stabbed at April's face and hands like evil icy needles. It was coming down so hard it looked like white streaks against the darkening sky, making it difficult for her to see more than a few yards. With each step, her feet were pelted with stinging rain, as if she was standing beneath a waterfall. The saturated fabric of her denim jacket clung to her skin. *What was I thinking, fleeing my own wedding, coming to this remote place with no plan and no place? And no umbrella?*

Too late for regrets. She was here, for better or worse, on this tiny Hebridean island with no way to leave for at least another day. And relentless rain battering her. April stopped. She was truly on her own for the first time in her life. In the middle of nowhere. Alone. Drenched and exposed. Planless and powerless. There was no point, nothing she could do.

Something inside her dissolved.

She threw her head back and laughed into the rain. It was more of a howl, really. April Virginia Smith surrendered. To the rain, to life. Something wild was beginning to twitch inside her. She closed her eyes, spread her arms into a T, and spun in a circle. The rain didn't matter anymore. She was a part of it now.

Well, that and definitely sleep deprived.

When she opened her eyes again and the dizziness faded, she could just about make out a sign on the side of the road: Cuanag, 1/2 mile. Nearly there. April clutched the grip of her suitcase and quickened her pace, her Chucks squelching through the hiss of the rain on the ground.

She wouldn't mind a whisky now.

Euan worked quickly, pulling each tap handle and filling the glasses to the brim before passing them down the bar. The clinking of glassware and hum of conversation echoed around the room. Most of the people who stayed within a two-mile radius, or lived near Cuanag, found themselves at the Old Barn at night. Lorna's place was the only pub at the southern end of the isle. Euan had started working for her a good twelve years ago, after a brief stint in Glasgow. He could do the job in his sleep. Nothing ever changed here.

Not that it was a bad thing.

The walls of the Old Barn were made of rough-hewn stone, the same kind this isle was made of. Old fishing nets hung from the ceiling, real ones that had been used by Saorsa's fishermen. The long wall opposite the wood-panelled bar was covered in framed photographs of crofters, fishermen, and their families. The serious faces of proud and resilient island folks. Their stories were still being told, their names known around here, carried by those frequenting the Old Barn. They were ancestors, not decorations. Euan's own grandda was in two of those pictures. A young, energetic man in a suit with sideburns, the owner, and keeper of Saorsa's traditional distillery.

Before he had to sell. Before it all went to shite.

The stinging old grudge was welling up in Euan's throat. Intergenerational anger – it was a thing.

Most of the patrons, some locals, some tourists, sat on well-worn wooden chairs at reclaimed whisky casks. They were from the decommissioned MacLeod distillery and now used as tables. There was a whiff of salt and Scotch in the air, along with the hoppy scent from freshly poured pints. If any of those isle folks from the old pictures travelled in time and walked through the door, they would be right at home.

Said door opened and something caught Euan's attention.

A woman stood in the doorframe, looking like a ship-wreck survivor. Wet strands of blonde hair had escaped her bun and were plastered to her pink face. Her eyes were wild and bright, as if she had just had an epiphany. She was shivering, but she didn't seem to be cold.

If Euan believed in the old folk tales of the selkies – mythical beings that transformed from seals into humans by shedding their skin – this was how he imagined them.

Over the years, Euan had watched hundreds of women come through the door of the Old Barn. He let his seasoned gaze roam over her. She was short and petite. Not in a skinny way, more an hour-glass. Her heart-shaped face was that of a person any child instantly placed their trust in. She was cute alright. But he wasn't into those well-behaved, doll-faced, tame girls. He liked them older, edgier. Confident and carefree women who knew what they wanted. This one seemed sensitive and serious. With expressive green eyes full of questions. The tears-and-trouble type. Definitely not his. Not even for one night.

But he kept watching as she made her way to the bar, pulling her sodden suitcase behind her. Each step cast drops onto the wooden floorboards. She didn't notice the looks of pity or bemusement from the other patrons. As she came nearer, Euan saw the exhaustion on her face. She still managed to smile at him. And lightened up the whole room.

'Hi. Um…I'm looking for Morag's place? I was told it's nearby.'

Her voice shot a jolt to his belly. It wasn't what he'd expected. Deep, smooth, raspy. Like honey on toast. Her accent was American, his least favourite kind of tourist. Not her fault, just too much ancient family history.

But something about her demeanour…she carried her

miserably drenched state with a natural dignity. As if she had escaped her home, the sea, and was popping into the land of humans to see what the fuss was all about.

He only realised he hadn't let go of the tap when beer flowed over his hand.

Chapter Four

'Morag's my sister. Her house is next door.' The Scottish barkeeper put the tea towel down and pointed towards the door. 'Turn left, then it's the second on the right.' His rolled 'r' and the cadence of his vowels did a teasing slow dance in April's ears.

He looked like one of those guys from a nineties denim commercial. His hair a tousled mane of hazelnut brown, thick with a natural wave that many would spend hours trying to replicate. Light stubble on a firm jawline and a playful hint around his mouth. He wore a knitted grey hoodie and jeans. The kind of man who put on his clothes as an afterthought and still appeared photoshoot ready. Definitely not someone you'd expect behind a tiny bar on a remote Scottish island. And most definitely too cool and confident for his own good.

Exhaustion flowed through her veins like liquid lead. She needed a warm and dry bed. Maybe a nightcap first, then a bed. So she just nodded, droplets landing on the bar.

'Drink?' he asked.

'Immediately.'

He was reading her mind. But that didn't require much skill. 'Whisky, please.'

'Any preference?'

April slanted her head. 'A glass would be useful.' Rain trickled down her neck and she rubbed her arms.

'Honestly? You look like you could do with an entire bottle.' He flashed her a grin. 'I got an idea. What about a hot toddy?'

She hoisted herself onto a stool, using her suitcase and the rim of the bar as handholds. 'Hot sounds fantastic. But who's Toddy?' Even to her own ears, her attempt at a joke sounded lame.

'Not me. I'm Euan.' He gave her another broad, semi-flir-tatious smile. It worked. At least according to the jitters in her tummy. Although that was most likely hunger, she hadn't eaten outside an airport for ages. Her last proper meal had been her wedding breakfast. Something sharp lurched at the back of her throat.

'A hot toddy is a warm whisky with honey and lemon. Good for colds,' he explained. 'And, no offence, but I think you need one.'

'Hi, I'm April. And I agree.'

'April you say? But it's May.'

Clearly, his jokes weren't any better than hers. 'If I got a dollar each time I hear that,' she said, 'I could buy myself a raincoat, a hundred bottles of whisky, *and* a set of parents with better taste.'

His deep laugh made her ears tingle almost as much as the melodic cadence of his Scottish accent. She was caught off guard by the itch to make him laugh again.

'Here, have a wee drink of water.' He put a glass in front of her, then he poured a generous sip of whisky into a mug and went to the back. 'I'll only be a minute.'

April let her gaze wander. Brass taps lined the bar and the shelves behind were stocked with bottles in fifty shades of amber. Obviously a whisky joint. The pub was bustling with patrons. This was probably the only place for miles, making it the go-to spot. As Angus had said, the season was kicking off.

The door swung open and a bunch of dudes stumbled in. They wore matching shirts, each with their own sash: 'groom', 'usher', 'best man', 'plus one', 'someone's brother'. Bloodshot eyes, noisy and rowdy – a small stag party. And, as far as April could tell, already pretty drunk. The last thing she needed tonight. A stinging reminder of her own broken-off wedding. April and her best friend had spent a day in the spa; Dick's stag party had been a round of golf with his buddies. A part of her wished they'd had booked a stripper. But no. Just wasn't his thing.

The barkeeper came back with her drink. He looked over to the group of five with a frown and said to her, 'Same old. Trashing an Airbnb here before one of them ties the knot. Like their lives are over forever and they have to let it out one last time. But in a place where nobody knows them. Where no one can hold them accountable. Stupid.' A muscle wormed in his jaw. 'Why anyone wants to get married in the first place is beyond me.'

April lifted her hot toddy with a slanted smile. 'Yeah. Cheers to that!'

There was a hint of wariness glinting in his grey eyes. Beautiful, deep eyes that made her forget about the wet and the cold. *Since when were men allowed to have such long lashes?*

'I don't buy into this "till death do us part" shite,' he continued. 'I don't think humans are meant to be together forever.'

But before April could open her mouth to reply, the big guy with the 'groom' sash and the plastic tiara shoved one of his companions and spat out a threat. 'Say that again and I'll rip your stupid head off!' He shook his fist at a shorter, redheaded guy, the 'plus one'.

'Best man' stepped between them. 'Calm doon, pal. He was just jokin'.'

'Shut up, you fuckin' arsehole! What do you know about it, huh?' The groom's cheeks were splotchy red, his eyes bleary. He swayed on his feet.

With a sideways glance, April noticed the barkeeper slowly moving from behind the counter. 'Plus one' was cackling and clearly not reading the room. 'I bet you can't get her off with your tiny tadger!'

'Fuck you!' The groom lunged for the redhead again; only this time he knocked over one of the cask tables instead of throwing punches. Guests jumped off their chairs and scattered out of the rioting stag party's way. The 'usher' and 'best man' tried to stop their large and raging friend, but they staggered. That's when April's instinct kicked in, honed over nearly two decades of living with three unchecked, spoiled older brothers and years of being a teacher. She hopped off the stool and stepped between the guys.

'Oi! Stop it! Right now!'

But the riled-up, plastered groom didn't pay her any heed. Clenching his jaw, he was gearing up for a fight. A real fight. What April needed was a distraction. Something of a shock, a stick in the wheel. That's what she always had to do. She had been too young and too small to be taken seriously or even heeded by her brothers.

Without hesitating, she grabbed her water and splashed it right in the groom's bearded face.

The coldness startled him. He stumbled against a chair, lost his balance and fell into April. With the full force of his over two hundred pounds, he rammed her sideways.

She felt the impact before she realised what was happening. The barkeeper reached her, arms opening wide to catch her mid-fall. Her body slammed against his torso, and her hands grabbed onto his shoulders. The heat of his body emanated through his sweater, accompanied by the rapid beat of his heart. He was tall and surprisingly strong. And his scent...

salty, warm, fresh. Like a day on the beach. A *naked* day on the beach. Her body buzzed in this closeness. His chest rose and fell against hers, mirrors of each other. Blood rushed to her face and then swiftly migrated south. When he wrapped his arms around her, her body reacted to his on a visceral level. Despite the chaos around them, a calmness spread in her, alongside this insane, pulsating fire. She felt safe and aroused at the same time. It took everything not to press her cheek against his chest and *purr*. She realised she had stopped breathing.

Oh no.

This was the *very* last thing she needed.

Euan didn't know what hit him, it happened so fast. April squalled when she was smashed into him, her hands clutching his shoulders for balance. She was so small and so soft. Her t-shirt and denim jacket were still wet. Euan's eyes met hers, green and huge and stunned. She looked as shocked as he felt. More than that...she looked bewildered, pupils dilated, lips parted. Pillow-like lips. He was all too aware of her breasts pushing against him as her sweet fragrance flooded his senses. There was an odd ache inside his chest. The noise of the brawl faded away, and Euan's arms instinctively tightened around her. She let out a short surprised gasp. It shot straight into his core. Her heart pounded in the same frenzied rhythm as his own. And yet it was peaceful. Euan had no clue where this notion came from, but in this moment, he would have gladly boxed a mad gorilla to keep her safe.

A stranger. An American. A good girl.

Don't be ridiculous, man.

Behind them, the scuffle continued. The 'usher' and 'best man' each grabbed one of the groom's arms and hauled him up the pub floor. 'That's enough, pal,' the best man said. 'Sarah wouldn't like to see you like that.'

The groom nodded, swaying like reeds in the wind, and the rowdy energy seeped out of the stag party. Even the 'plus one' seemed to understand that his quips had crossed a line.

Slowly, Euan released his hold on April and let his arms sink. The feel of her waist and shoulder lingered on his palms, fingertips prickling. She stepped back, tucking a strand of hair behind her ear, gaze averted. 'Sorry 'bout that.'

'Nothing to be sorry for.' He hesitated a second before he pulled himself away and moved toward the stag party, slipping back into his bartender persona.

'Can't have you wrecking the pub, lads. There's no other for miles. People would be pissed,' he grumbled. With one hand, he righted a fallen barstool, then he picked up a bottle that was still intact.

'Apologies for the disruption, mate,' the best man said, face reddening. 'We'll pay for the damages, awright?'

Euan's stern expression broke into a wry grin. 'Just help me clean up and bring this steamin' sod to bed and we're square,' he clapped the 'best man' on the back with a thud, '...*mate*.'

When he turned around and walked back behind the bar a few minutes later, April was pulling pins out of her messy updo, collecting them in her empty water glass. Strand by strand, wet hair fell over her shoulders. Euan realised what its colour reminded him of: the sand on Saorsa's beaches, a colour he'd seen all his life. Something was roiling inside him. Hardly made sense. He was used to the occasional riot. This was a Scottish pub, not a bouncy castle on a wean's birthday party. What he wasn't used to was this confusion. It slid in and slunk itself into the cracks of his familiar life, widening them.

Luckily, Euan had everything under control.

The pub, himself, and the rest of it.

'So, April', he said as he pushed another water across the counter towards her. 'That was a wild welcome to Saorsa. First time in Scotland?'

She grabbed the glass and necked its contents. 'How can you tell?'

'That's easy. We don't have many wet t-shirt contests here.'

She laughed, and he felt strangely tickled.

'I packed for Mexico. But then…' Her expression changed to sadness and colour climbed onto her cheeks. 'Let's just say I did something extreme, but necessary. An emergency exit.'

Euan didn't want to pry, and he had thirsty customers to serve, but he was curious. With a nod and a wave of his hand, he signalled his colleague Matt to take over the pint-pouring. Matt was Lorna's nephew, a good fifteen years older than Euan. Nice guy, kept to himself. They had an understanding.

'Go on, then. Spill,' Euan said to her and leaned forward.

April hesitated, chewing on her lower lip. But she seemed to burst at the seams. She inhaled and said, 'I fled from my own wedding and jilted my fiancé at the altar. Well, ex-fiancé now, I guess. I'm not proud of it, but I left over two hundred shocked people in a church in Kansas City.'

Euan dropped his tea towel. 'You did *what*? That's ballsy… wow. Okay. Holy shite. Seriously?'

Tears filled her eyes, and the corner of her mouth twitched. 'I came here to hide, so no one could find me after what I did. To him, to everyone. No idea what I was thinking. I'm so, so tired. And cold. And wet.' She buried her face in her hands.

Now he saw the diamond of her engagement ring sparkling in the dim bar lights.

'Gosh, I'm such a stupid cliché,' she mumbled into her palms. 'Pouring my guts out at the bar. Sorry for unloading on you like that.'

Once again, Euan was hit by the sudden compulsion to

wrap her in his arms and shelter her. It felt like a wipe-out, being swept under. 'Hey…' Without thinking, he reached out and touched her wrist. A buzz raced up his arm, sharp and sudden.

'So sorry', she whispered, and Euan noticed she was still trembling. Shaking like a leaf, actually.

'Again, nothing to be sorry for.' With one swift move, he took off his woollen jumper. 'Here, that'll keep you warm. You can leave it at my sister's house later.'

'Really? Oh wow. That's so nice of you…Hugh?'

'It's Eu-*an*.'

'Okay. Hugh-Anne.'

There was that dizzying smile again. He feigned a cough at the mockery of his name. 'Is that the whisky speaking?'

'The whisky, the vodka…I don't know.' She laughed, tears squeezing from her eyes. 'Shoot, I don't know anything anymore. Least of all myself.' She took off her soaked denim jacket and slipped into his hoodie, nearly disappearing in it. 'Oh, this is *cosy*.' She flipped the hood over her sopping hair. 'Mmm, nice. You know what would be even nicer?'

He shook his head.

'A gin and tonic, Hugh-Anne,' she said.

'Call me that again and you'll go home sober every night – May.'

But Euan wasn't sure if he could make good on that threat. She wasn't his type, but he had the feeling that it would be hard to say no to those green selkie eyes.

'Another gin, por favor,' she said with a weary look on her face. 'To say it in the words of Mary Poppins: people who get their feet wet need their medicine.'

The American was asleep on the counter, head on her forearms, next to three empty glasses and a mountain of hair-pins. It was closing time, most people had left.

'She's staying at Morag's,' Euan said to Matt as he walked around the bar. 'I'll take her to the house.'

Matt nodded and resumed mopping.

'Wake up, sleepyhead.' Euan gently stroked her arm. April turned her head in slow motion and looked at him, eyes dazed. 'Huh?'

'Time to get you to bed, love.'

'Did I pay?'

'Aye, no worries. Now come with me. I'll take you to your place. If that's okay with you?'

'Yeah, sure,' she mumbled. 'Put me in the bed with the captain's daughter.'

'What?'

April lifted her head and slurred, 'Way hay and up she rises!'

She was singing sea shanties with that pirate voice of hers. Euan couldn't prevent a smile. 'Let's put you in the long boat then, ya wee drunken sailor.'

She slid off the stool and clung onto his arm, trustful and heavy. Euan felt two inches taller for no reason.

It was only a one-and-a-half minute walk to Morag's. The studio was cosy and well-appointed, with a small lounge area, a tiny kitchenette, and the queen-sized bed tucked into an alcove by a large window overlooking the sea. Moonlight spilled across the wooden floor.

'Is it okay if I come in?' Euan asked.

'Yeah. You're a good welcome committee, Hugh-Anne,' April mumbled as she flopped onto the mattress.

'Yep. No big deal.' It came out gruffer than he'd intended. He cleared his throat. 'I mean, my pleasure. You're very welcome.'

But she was already fast asleep. He tucked the blankets around her. His jumper was big on her, the sleeves falling over her hands. She looked fragile and exhausted, like a bird that flew too far. He gulped and eased away. What was wrong with him? He didn't do tender. He didn't do sweet. And he sure as hell didn't stand around watching someone sleep. But he wasn't ready to leave yet. So he straightened the maps on the side table, double-checked that the kettle was good to go for the morning. Poured her a large glass of water. Wrote a note.

With a whispered curse, he turned to the door. The blast of cold sea air did nothing to chill the heat in his face.

Chapter Five

The first three seconds were blissful. That was the time it took after waking up before reality punched April in the guts with a mean right hook.

The tumbling bouquet, the expression on Dick's face... It all came back. She let out a muffled grunt. Her heart was beating inside her head and her tongue was furry roadkill. She was in a strange bed, in a strange room, at the end of the world. Hungover and hungry.

The sun shone painfully bright through the window and April blinked, trying to remember what had happened the night before. Her thoughts were hazy and her body ached from the unfamiliar bed and the gruelling power-walk through the rain. She couldn't, for the life of her, recall the details of how she got into this room. Euan must have helped her. There was a glass of water on the nightstand with a post-it next to it:

Morning, May.
Welcome to the first day of your new life.
Hugh-Anne.

April was still wearing his grey sweater, the wool fuzzy against her skin. It was soft and slightly scratchy, just as April imagined the stubble on his face felt. *Euan. What a unique name.*

Truth be told, she couldn't point her finger anywhere, being named after a month herself. The one with notoriously unreliable weather, not even something nice like Summer. Or May. *Thanks Mom and Dad. Thanks for nothing.*

April didn't want to think of her parents. Or anybody else back in KC. Not thinking would be a fabulous thing in general.

She pressed her nose into the sleeve and caught a waft of his scent. It triggered a warm sensation that spread in tender ripples through her body. She took a deeper whiff. It smelled familiar, which was impossible. She'd only met him yesterday. And yet. When he had caught her in his arms and held her, she had felt like both – the tornado *and* the eye of the storm.

But this Scot wasn't even her type. Too hot to be trustworthy and likely self-absorbed to a ridiculous degree. All looks, zero substance. Heck, she didn't have a type! Her type had been Dick for as long as she could remember.

Not anymore.

With a sudden heaviness, another chunk of reality sank in and settled like a rock at the bottom of the Atlantic.

Once April sat up with a groan, the view of the sea through the panoramic window almost cured her hangover. Opal water reached from the horizon towards the clear sky. Closer to shore, each wave tumbled and broke on the rocks into a million tiny jewels. Small birds hopped and flapped across the mossy stones, yellow and purple wildflowers swaying in the wind. Whoever had put this window in had known exactly what they were doing. It was like a living, moving photo-wallpaper. She would have admired it for a while longer, but hunger was pushing her out of bed, spurred on by the seductive smell of bacon and eggs. She had to get to the source of it asap.

With heavy feet, April walked around the outside and opened the door to find an inviting breakfast room. It was homely with a low ceiling. Yet thanks to another enormous window, it gave the impression of expanse. In its centre was a large, rustic table, framed by wooden chairs with tartan cushions. Pans rattled in the background. A woman with a short brown bob, sparkling blue eyes, and an apron, smiled as she peeked through the door to the kitchen. At least that's what the sign above the doorframe said.

'Morning! I'm Morag. You must be April. And hungry! Take a seat at our table, I'll be right with you.'

Before April had the chance to say something, Morag disappeared back into the kitchen. April took a chair next to a man with short white hair in a yellow jumper, who scrutinised her over the rim of his glasses. Facing her was a young couple in proper hiking outfits. Judging by the sound of their language, most likely Norwegian or German. April's head was palpitating, but something about being in this breakfast room in the vicinity of hot food and coffee made her a bit better. Still, was felt out of place amid this group of travellers. She didn't have any hiking gear or touristy plans. Zero gear and zero plans, to be exact.

With a twinge of self-consciousness, April looked down at her outfit: Euan's sweater, a pair of black leggings, and Chucks.

Morag appeared from the kitchen, armed with a small notepad and a pencil. 'What can I get for you this morning?' she asked with a warm smile.

April scanned the laminated menu, but the letters danced in front of her eyes.

'Cooked breakfast is usually before nine, but I can make

you an omelette with Mull cheese, bacon, and a wee bit of tomato on the side. And a strong pot of coffee,' Morag said. 'That should set you straight.'

'Sounds divine', April replied, accompanied by an affirmative rumble in her tummy. 'Do I really look that terrible?'

Morag's smile grew even wider. 'Kind of. But don't worry. There isn't a hangover or heartbreak in the world that this breakfast couldn't cure. Promise.'

April liked her. She made her feel like a guest, not a customer.

When Morag returned with the food ten minutes later, everybody else had already left to get on with their days. 'Here you go, love. Enjoy!'

The omelette was fluffy and golden, the cheese oozing out from the folds. Perfection. April took a sip of coffee, enjoying the warmth spreading through her body. It was so strong, it probably had the capability of waking long-dead relatives. While collecting the empty dishes, Morag gave her a knowing nod. Five minutes later she came back without her apron and sat down in front of April. 'I don't like it when my guests have to eat alone.'

April took a bite of her toast. 'I don't mind.'

'Aye, even so,' Morag said. 'Nice jumper you're wearing. Looks familiar.'

April paused, her fork hovering in front of her mouth. 'It's Euan's. He gave it to me yesterday. Your brother, right?'

'Aye, my brother.' A sliver of doubt appeared on Morag's forehead. 'He gave you his jumper? *Euan* gave you his stuff?' she asked, as if April told her she'd seen a unicorn making out with Nessie.

'Yeah, he did. I was wet and cold from the rain. He said I could keep it and leave it here later.'

'That does *not* sound like my brother.'

'It doesn't? He was so nice and helpful last night. He

saved me from a bar fight, brought me home. He even left a glass of water and a note.'

Now Morag looked like she had to force her jaw from dropping. She shook her head and said, 'He *is* nice and helpful. Just not to strangers. That's…atypical.'

April saw the thoughts working in her head. For whatever reason, Morag seemed sceptical. But April was grateful for his kindness. Which, by the way, was all she was. Grateful.

Morag smiled apologetically. 'Don't get me wrong. He's a good guy – a great guy – he's just…a little restless and loose, I'd say.'

April finished the last of her omelette. 'Not to pry, but what do you mean by restless and loose?'

Morag sighed and leaned back in her chair, folding her arms. 'Nothing. Euan's got that adventurer's spirit. That's all.' Morag scratched her head, looking for the right words. 'My brother has a heart of gold. But he normally doesn't let anyone close enough to see it. He just charms the pants off anyone. A ladies' man. So unless you're into holiday flings, I'd be a bit cautious around him if I were you. Och, and that stupid fanny van of his only makes it worse!'

It took April two seconds to understand, then she felt colour sweep into her face. 'Oh! Oh, no.' She shook her head so vigorously that her brain bumped against her skull. 'No, no. Ain't gonna happen. I'm done.' She coughed and took another swig of coffee.

Morag looked puzzled, and April wanted to explain herself. 'I'm not interested in anybody or anything, except my freedom. Because…two days ago, I left my fiancé. In church.'

'What? Wait, seriously? That *is* a big deal,' Morag said with sympathy.

'Exactly. I'm a hot mess. Not in the right headspace for shenanigans and guys.' *Especially not this kind*. The sort of guy your parents would warn you about, provided they cared. April knew his type, she had seen her friends fall for this kind of dude. Fall and crash. Never ended well. No, those hunky bad boys were only good for inspiring fantasies on rare, quiet evenings with the Rabbit. And she wasn't interested in men, in becoming a player's shiny new toy. She was here to clear her head and decide what to do with her life, how to deal with the fallout. Figure out how to be independent. 'I just want to collect my pieces,' she said, staring into her mug as if it had all the answers.

'I see. Then you relax and enjoy your stay,' Morag said and beamed. 'I hope you're okay with everything. Did you like your breakfast?'

'It was amazing.' She finished her coffee and stood up, hangover already improving. 'Thank you so much.'

Morag got up, too, and gave April a genuine hug. 'You're welcome here, love. If you need anything, let me know. Come back in a minute with your credit card and we'll get you officially booked in for the next few days.'

After sorting out the formalities and a satisfying hot shower, April resolved to explore the island with one of Morag's guest bikes.

Nothing like a bit of exercise to exorcise a hangover.

And then, when her head was clearer, she would call Dick. She had to, sooner or later. Even though guilt twisted in her gut like a corkscrew. By now, he'd hopefully had enough time to cool off a bit.

But that was a problem for afternoon-April. Present-April hopped on the hybrid bike and distracted herself by trying to remember when she had last ridden one. Probably in high school. She couldn't pinpoint the exact memory, her childhood and youth were a fog with very few lampposts in it.

I guess riding a bike is like riding a bike.

As if yesterday's torrent never happened, the sun shone over this windswept green island that was speckled with sheep, white stone cottages, and rocks with tufts of sea thrift in their crevices. The tang of the ocean filled April's nostrils. It did her good. The emotional hangover was harder to get rid of, though. But the repetitive motion of pedalling, the wide and treeless landscape, the wind in her hair, and the sun on her face were enough to give her a bit of peace.

Her mind drifted back to what Morag had said about her brother. There was something that didn't quite fit together, as if there were more layers to Euan than the charming façade she had met yesterday. In that regard, he was the opposite of Dick, who'd always been an open book – only there wasn't much written on the page. And the closer April had tried to look to decipher him, the blurrier the letters got. Much like the menu this morning.

April had no clue how long she had been cycling for. It must have been a while, though, since her thighs were burning. She noticed a bird flying next to her, parallel to the road, on her right side. It was black and white and looked like a magpie, but with a swooping crest of feathers on its head. The bird chirped and chatted, as if it were trying to get her attention. It didn't fly away, instead it kept pace with her for minutes. Intentionally, like a little winged island guide. April felt a simple, unexpected joy; this shared journey with a wild creature seemed like a hint from the universe that she was on the right path.

When she turned her head, her gaze landed on a blue camper van parked on the sandy section next to the road. The scene was picturesque, a perfect blend of freedom and adventure. The side door of the van opened.

And out came Euan. Wearing nothing but tight, black briefs.

Yep. He was half-naked.

April's breath caught in her throat. Within a split second, she saw it all: his sculpted chest, the suggestion of a six-pack, and the contours of his biceps and triceps, highlighted by the sun. He had the arms of someone who'd thrown a ball on the beach or held a surfboard – capable, but without the stiffness of a man who lives for the gym. Used to physical work, but not trying to prove anything. Euan was tall and naturally fit. Involuntarily, her glance dropped lower, taking in the unmistakable outline of his masculinity. His tight briefs left nothing to the imagination. Was this a morning semi or was he just a very lucky guy?

Everything about him screamed, 'Look at me, I'm sex on legs!' A hungry throbbing vibrated in April, and she wrestled the impossible impulse to lick his abs like an ice lolly.

Said sex on legs yawned, opened his eyes…and spotted her. 'Oi, May! Nice surprise! Want a coffee?'

Her feet slipped off the pedals with a scrape, and she fought to realign her centre of gravity. Too late. Clinging onto her handlebars for dear life, April was plunging towards the ditch on the side of the road. The ground rushed up to meet her as she careened forward. With a heavy thud, she landed in the grass, the bike awkwardly sprawled beneath her.

It took her a moment to untangle her feet. Euan was rushing towards her – still scantily clad and outrageously hot – and April simply couldn't deal. As he approached her, her face flared up in embarrassment. Euan stopped in front of her just as she got on her knees, his package glaring at her close to eye level.

Nope, not a semi. Holy mother of God.

She lifted her head. Concern was etched on his face. 'Hey, you okay?'

April struggled to steady herself, tripping over the wheels, and fumbled with her words as she was picking up the bike. 'Yeah, yeah, I'm fine. I-I'm sorry, I didn't mean to…I was just cycling. Bit out of practice. Turning around now. See ya!'

'Wait! April!'

But she was already ferociously kicking the pedals as if it was the final stage of the Tour de France. Until she could no longer hear his voice or feel his stare burning holes into her back.

April stumbled into her room, cheeks burning, eyes stinging. She sank on the bed and tucked her knees up. Nothing made sense. It took a while for her breathing to slow. How could a shirtless stranger throw her off like that? As if she was a four-teen-year-old teenager. Pathetic. Euan had to think she was an absolute klutz.

She let herself slide sideways onto the bed. Lying there, crumpled together like a dust ball, April realised she must have bottled up loads of feelings for a decade. She might have been accumulating a boundless mass of oppressed, unmet needs over the past ten passionless years with Dick. Was it possible to have emo-sexual, metaphorical blue balls?

At least that would explain her cringey reaction.

If she truly wanted to start over, or even remotely consider moving on with her life, she had to get to the root of this chaos. Unravel the knots on her inside. Face the past.

Ugh.

She had to call Dick.

April got up, legs wobbly with the weight of the impending conversation. This was about more than confronting Dick. It was about confronting herself.

She went looking for Morag, to ask if she could use her phone. Because talking to Dick about this disaster was one thing. Talking to parents, family, friends was a whole different story. April wasn't ready to speak to anyone else yet. She wasn't prepared to read hundreds of texts, brave their questions, accusations, and insults.

No, her own phone would remain switched off.

Five minutes later, April sat hunched at the desk in the studio. Her heart pulsed in her ears while she listened to the dial tone and waited for Dick to pick up. It took ages. He didn't know the number, and it was still early in Kansas City, barely seven in the morning. The monotonous ring seemed to get louder each time.

Oh God. What if he doesn't want to speak to me ever again? What if he hates me?

She braced herself for impact.

'Hello?'

That was him. April's heart squeezed like a sponge. Her tongue was suddenly made of lead.

'Hello? Who's there?'

She inhaled shakily and whispered. 'Dick…it's me.'

There was a painful pause that pulled like a tightrope, a tension so prolonged it broke into two layers.

'April?'

Chapter Six

With a trembling hand, April pressed Morag's phone against her ear. 'I know you don't want to hear from me. But I had to call. I owe you an explanation…' Her voice faltered, the words dissolving into the stillness. She could almost picture him, his expression a mix of confusion and pain.

'An explanation? Are you being serious?' Dick's voice was cold, edged with hurt. 'Jesus, you left me at the altar, April! You made me look like a fool. And then you disappeared. I won't even pretend to understand what you did. Do you have any idea how that felt?'

She took a shaky breath, her words loaded with regret. 'No, of course not. How could I? And I'm so sorry. Yell at me all you like. I deserve it. And more.'

'I don't yell. You know that.'

Her eyes misted over. 'Yeah. I do.' She sometimes wished he would.

'So where are you?' He sounded worried now.

'In Scotland. But that's not important. The important thing is…' She paused. 'I'm sorry that I ran away like that. I panicked, Dick. I realised I wasn't ready. It wasn't fair to you, to us, to go through with it.'

'Not ready? That's it? After all these years? You couldn't have figured that out before the wedding day?' His tone was laced with disbelief, a stinging sharpness to his words.

April steeled herself for what she was about to say next, the words dangling in the back of her mouth. 'Dick...I'm sorry how I did it. But I'm not sorry that I left. I don't think we were a good match. We've always been friends, and we were so used to each other's company. Everyone expected us to get married, and we went along with it. But deep down, I was struggling. It wasn't so much about you. It was about not being honest with myself. I-I wasn't happy. And I don't believe you were, either.' Her voice turned into a whisper, as if admitting a secret.

Dick paused, a long, heavy silence. 'I've thought about it a lot these past days.'

'Oh. Okay. Of course. And? Do you hate me?' April bit her finger, an attempt to channel the tension.

'No. I don't hate you. And I think you're right.'

The room was spinning and the ground beneath her was shifting.

'You know, part of me wishes I had the courage to do what you did,' he continued. 'To stop everything when it didn't feel right.'

'Wait... Are you saying...seriously?'

His sigh, weary and disillusioned, echoed through the phone. 'Seriously. Up to that moment, I wasn't aware of how *not* happy I was. Not unhappy, just not truly happy. It's so easy to get stuck in a routine. Especially if you like the other person. It's not that I don't love you, April. But I'm not in love with you anymore. Haven't been for a while, I think.' His voice became softer, contemplative. 'It's such a dumb cliché, but we've grown up and grown apart in the process.'

The irrefutability of this simple truth sent loss, powerlessness, and relief coursing through her. 'You know, Dickie...I believe you're right.'

'Maybe this is a wake-up call for both of us, honey. To figure ourselves out.' He paused. 'And part of me knows I haven't given you what you deserve. We have different needs in that respect. So I don't really blame you. Although it *was* pretty messed-up. Mom is not getting out of bed. Dad's not talking to anyone. Your parents were so upset, I thought they'd strangle each other.'

April let out a groan. 'Oh God. But honestly, that doesn't take much.'

'Yeah.' He let out a dry laugh. 'At least everybody got hammered at the bar. I thought you'd like to hear that.'

He was right. She squeezed her eyes shut, trying to keep the tears in. 'I hate that I hurt you, Dick.'

'I hate that I hurt you, too.' Dick's voice carried a resigned pain. 'Still not sure how we ended up here. It's a mess. But it's for the best. Maybe one day we'll understand this better. One day. God, this is hard.'

'Yeah.' April nodded, her gaze drifting to the sea outside the window. 'One day. Thank you, Dickie. I hope we will find our way through this.'

'We will. And we'll talk about what we're gonna do with the house and all that when you come back. When will that be, by the way?'

'No idea. But rather sooner than later,' she said. 'Although I'm not ready to face it all yet.'

'For good reasons. There's definitely not gonna be a welcome committee for you here. Just saying.' There was a trace of a sad smile in Dick's voice. 'Take care, April. And...I guess, thanks for having the guts to stop it. Even in such a dramatic, humiliating, expensive, and completely fucked-up way.'

April ended the call, hesitating before setting the phone down. The cheery daylight streaming through the studio window contrasted harshly with the roaring confusion inside her. She leaned back, getting used to a strange emptiness where her identity used to be. The room was both oppressively silent and full of echoes from their words. April understood the enormity of what she had done, and what she had yet to face. Her thoughts drifted to the future, a frighteningly empty canvas before her. She needed a direction, a way to rediscover who she was beyond the confines of her past relationship.

She could think of one thing that would help right now.

Writing a list.

It was the only way to make sense of all these whirling thoughts and feelings. Her go-to method to clear her head. Journalling and writing calmed her, getting thoughts on paper helped her to feel in control and sort the chaos.

Grabbing a pen and notepad from the desk, April decided to write a bucket list, a short and tangible plan for her journey. This list would consist of more than activities. It was a roadmap to finding herself again. A guide to living life on her own terms.

Her mind exploded with a myriad of ideas. She started jotting down everything, from the mundane to the extravagant. 'Learn to surf,' she wrote. 'Visit the Great Barrier Reef. Go bungee jumping. Get a tattoo. Drink the mezcal with a worm in the bottle.' All the things she had missed out on because she had spent her twenties being Dick's nice, mousy girlfriend. 'Teach again. Take a Krav Maga class. Learn to knit. Carpentry. Carnival in Rio.'

The list went on and on until she had filled two pages.

It still didn't satisfy her. April was missing something important. It was writhing inside her just below the surface.

But a part of her knew.

With impulsive boldness, April wrote 'sex' onto the paper, then quickly crossed it off again. Her heart was thumping against her ribcage.

'Have a one-night stand.' Didn't feel right either.

'Have orgasms and enjoy sex. With someone who isn't Dick.' That sounded better, but not perfect.

She nibbled on the end of the pen until the words formed in her head.

'Get laid like a goddamn queen.'

Yes, that was it. And the pulsing between her legs confirmed it. Time to explore that slumbering, burning thing inside of her. The only question now was – how and with whom?

Euan, his sister, and the rest of her family gathered around their upstairs kitchen table for lunch. Morag, seated at its head with a smile, watched her husband tossing together spaghetti with meatballs. Euan's niece and two nephews swarmed around their only and favourite uncle like bees in a flowerbed.

'Uncle Euan, look at my Lego thingy!'

'Uncle Euan, look at my race car!'

'Okay, okay. Sit down and look at your plates,' he said, and sent a knowing wink at his sister, who had been watching him with an amused expression.

As the adults continued their meal, the kids finished eating quickly and darted off to the garden, their voices fading as they raced outside. Euan tried to keep up a conversation with his sister and Allan, but his mind wouldn't cooperate. His thoughts kept drifting back to April. The way she had clung to him at the pub last night. Her pink cheeks and wide eyes when she'd ridden her bike into the ditch this morning and stared at his boaby. The way she had hurried away from him. April was strange, uncategorisable. But even if he'd wanted to figure her out, he wouldn't know how to start. He had never bothered with anyone.

Euan barely noticed when Morag nudged him with her elbow.

'I asked you a question,' she said.

'Eh, sorry. What was that?'

'Why did you give April your jumper?'

That threw him off balance. 'The American? Poor thing was cold and wet. Had nothing to wear.'

Morag eyed him askance. 'She said you brought her here and *tucked her in*, leaving a note? That's not like you, baby brother. You're not the knight in shining armour.'

'Must have felt a touch of compassion. Is that so odd?' Euan pushed his cutlery around the plate. Something was nagging him. Morag wasn't wrong. He wasn't used to being someone's saviour. He was the good-time guy.

'For you it is. What's going on, Euan? Tell me.'

'Nothing,' he said, a bit too hastily.

'It's probably because you haven't had a girlfriend since uni,' Morag teased.

'Lilly? That's over twelve years ago,' Euan huffed. 'I don't want or need a girlfriend.'

'You can't just have meaningless sex with a new lady every night in your lust limousine for the rest of your life,' Morag stated.

'I don't want anything serious. As you well know. We've been through that a thousand times, sis. Give it a rest.'

Och, Morag and her ideas. Euan didn't believe in this whole 'happily ever after' thing. He wanted nothing serious because 'serious' wouldn't last. That was simply a fact of life. At nineteen, he had left Saorsa to study at Glasgow Uni with Lilly; within six months, Lilly had left him to be with someone else. A stupid, naïve teenage romance. His only one. He was long over it.

'I prefer no strings, no trouble. Simple as that,' he said.

Allan had cleared the dishes and came back to the table. 'I

get it, Euan. It's fun for a while, aye. But no strings means you'll never truly connect.'

'Oh, I *connect* all right.' Euan laughed, but it came out defensive, almost bitter.

'I mean with your heart,' his brother-in-law said. 'Not just your body.'

Euan snorted. 'Don't be daft, Allan. And when did you become an agony aunt?'

'Agony Allan, if you don't mind.' He grinned. 'That's why you're still single. You haven't found the right woman.'

'I'm single because I choose to be.' Euan sneered cynically. 'There's no such thing as the one right person for someone. That's an invention by Hollywood.'

'My wife for almost fifteen years might disagree,' Allan said, and looked at Morag with tenderness and admiration.

'Doesn't she always?' Euan teased.

'Oi! I'm right here,' Morag said, and flicked her finger against Euan's cheek. He rubbed the spot and laughed. The banter around the table always made him comfortable, no matter how personal it got.

'Is she here?' Euan asked.

Morag pushed her chair closer to the table. 'Who?'

'The American.'

'Oh, do you want your jumper back?' Morag joked. 'Did you only give it to her so you'd have a reason to talk to her again?'

'You're talking shite. I saw her earlier today. She drove her bike into the ditch. Just wanted to check if she's okay.'

'She did? What happened?' Morag asked.

Euan remembered the flustered expression on April's face. And how she'd tried very hard not to look at him. 'Don't know. Must have lost her balance for some reason.'

Morag tilted her head. 'I haven't seen her in a while. Last time she mentioned something about buying snacks.'

'I met her when I came home for lunch, on the road to Tràighmhòr,' Allan said. 'Came towards me on a bike.'

Euan nodded with relief. 'She's okay then.'

Morag squeezed his hand. 'You *like* her, don't you?'

Euan pulled his hand away in a flare of annoyance. 'Don't be a bampot. I'm sorry for her. That's all.'

Allan's eyes narrowed in curiosity. 'Why's that?'

'She had a rough couple of days. With her wedding and all that,' Euan said.

Morag nodded. 'I heard she left her fiancé only days ago. Awful.'

'At the altar, no less.' Euan raked his fingers through his hair. 'Walking away from your own wedding in front of all the guests and your fiancé – can you imagine that set of balls? Impressive.'

'Good grief. Couldn't have been easy.' Morag took Euan's hand again. 'I'm worried about you, brother mine. And I don't believe that living in this rusty fanny van of yours is doing you any good.'

'Aye. If nothing else, that piece of junk is a death trap,' Allan agreed.

'But it's *my* piece of junk. Pun intended. It just needs a new motor, and all will be grand.'

'Okay then.' Morag's eyes twinkled mischievously. 'I'll make you a bet.' She took a breath and said solemnly, 'I bet you won't be able to *not* sleep with April while she's here.'

Euan grunted. 'That's easy. She's not my type.'

'Wait for it. If you don't sleep with her, we'll buy you a new motor for your wham-bam camper van. But'—Morag wiggled her eyebrows—'if you *do*, you sell that monstrosity. Get rid of it, once and for all.'

Allan laughed. 'That's so inappropriate and insane, I'm in. And it actually makes this house a *bet* and breakfast.'

'You and your dad jokes.' Morag sighed in feigned indignation and kissed her husband.

'Are you guys serious?' The prospect of getting a new motor for free was more tempting than any set of boobs or bum could ever be. April was cute, maybe interesting. But she truly wasn't his type. And she would be gone soon. His van, however, was his home. His refuge from the world. Part of his identity. An extension of himself. Euan grinned widely as he took his sister's hand to seal the deal.

That new motor was as good as his.

Chapter Seven

April's heart did a little somersault as she approached the small surf school nestled between the grassy dunes and the ocean's edge. Today was the day to cross the first thing off her list; Morag had given her the address so April could take a lesson. She placed her bike in the grass and strolled along the sand path to the surf school.

Step one.

The building had walls of pine wooden planks and a pitched metal roof. A simple deck area provided covered space for changing and storing gear. Boards of various sizes leaned against the walls, wetsuits hanging over the railing to dry. 'Aonghas Watersports' said a yellow sign in the shape of a surfboard. Next to the school was a gravel parking area.

There was only one vehicle in it.

A blue camper van.

April's heart plummeted. Him? After her graceless plunge into the ditch yesterday, she wasn't keen on facing Euan again. For a second, she thought about turning around. But this was her new life, and she didn't want to start it by throwing in the towel at the slightest inconvenience. With an inhale that tasted of artificial courage, she ascended the three wooden steps, and gripped the door handle with a bravado she didn't feel.

The first thing she noticed was the scent. Over time, the pungent sea air had seeped deep into the wooden walls and mingled with pine, wax, and sunscreen.

The second was how packed it was. There was barely room to move between shelves and racks filled with surfing equipment, the walls full of boards and bleached posters.

The third thing April noticed was Euan's naked butt.

He was in the process of wriggling into his wetsuit, and the sight took her unawares. But there it was, an impeccably toned, undeniably tight masterpiece that would leave any Italian Baroque sculptor squealing in awe. In a nanosecond, her mouth went as dry as the Great American Desert.

'Hi. You're early. No one else's here yet.' Euan turned around and greeted her with a grin. Utterly carefree and completely chill. As if she hadn't just glimpsed at his bare peach emoji. 'Welcome to Aonghas Watersports!'

'Gosh. So sorry. I—'

He brushed it off and finished putting on his suit. 'Nothing to be sorry for. Ready for your lesson?'

'Absolutely, yes. Totally,' she replied, trying to be cool and confident.

Why do I sound like a schoolgirl?

'Then let's get you sorted.' He zipped up the front and led the way. 'Was surprised to see your name in the booking system this morning,' he said.

'It was a spontaneous decision, and this was the only free two-hour spot this week.'

'A lot of spontaneous decisions going on in your life, eh?'

'What do you… Oh, right. *That.*' April lowered her head. She didn't like to be reminded of the mess that was her life. This was supposed to be her refuge from reality. She fought back a tear. Successfully. A small win.

'Too early? I'm sorry, April. I didn't mean to… My mouth is faster than my brain sometimes,' he said apologetically.

She turned her head away. 'It's all right. Never mind. I'll deal with the consequences eventually. Not now, though.'

'Then put on this suit, you can use our loo for that, and let's go surfing. Waves are the best remedy for any trouble. The ultimate head-clearer.' Euan cracked a winning smile. April almost believed him.

Ten minutes later, they headed out towards the shoreline, each carrying a board. April tried her best to keep her balance and not look too clumsy. Her beginner board was a lot bigger than his. This monstrosity was much heavier than she'd thought.

The ocean extended before them, perpetually sloshing. With well-versed explanations and movements, Euan showed April how to read the waves and how to properly position herself on the board.

'All right, that looks good. Let's try it in the water,' he said, holding out the board. His fingers brushed hers. It was a fleeting touch, but she felt it all the way down to her core. She saw a glimmer of surprise in his eyes before he quickly pulled away, as if burned, his professional mask slipping for a blink. 'Keep your eyes on the board, May,' he said with a scratch in his voice.

The coldness of the ocean penetrated through April's wetsuit. Euan saw her flinch. 'Aye. Might appear like the Bacardi beach, but it's freezing,' he said with an amused look.

'Could have fooled me,' she said extra-lightly and followed Euan's lead, paddling out to where the waves were breaking. As they waited for the right one, April stared at the horizon. Boundless, calling out to her with a promise of free-dom. A smile crept onto her face.

'The trick is to paddle fast and hard to match the speed of

the wave,' he explained. 'Once you're moving with it, pop up on the board and balance. Like we practised. Keep your knees bent, compress your lower body down, upper body straight.'

She inhaled and steadied her nerves. *You can do this*, she told herself. *It's just surfing.*

April took the board and paddled out, trying to ignore the weight of his presence behind her. The water rose and fell around her, and for a moment she was weightless, suspended between sea and sky. No past, no future. Just now.

Surfing is great. I should do this more often.

Several violent waves, wrestling matches with an unruly board, and salty nose rinses later, April was seriously reconsidering her newfound love for water sports. Euan was watching her closely, giving her pointers along the way. It was as if he could sense her frustration mounting.

'Don't give up. Remember to breathe,' he said with a lopsided grin, 'and try to enjoy it.'

'Sadist,' she grumbled. But she nodded and attempted to relax. Which was hard for someone who always had to do everything as perfectly as possible. Anything less wasn't enough. Wasn't acceptable. Wasn't noticed.

Every time she fell, she felt Euan's scrutinising glance on her, like he was daring her to prove herself. And dang it, she wanted to. She was done with being seen as a fragile little woman, out of her element, needing to be told what to do, nicely following the rules.

With fierce determination, she caught hold of a wave. There was an overwhelming rush of accomplishment when she almost stood up, before being plunged back into the water. As she surfaced, breathless and exhilarated, she caught Euan looking at her with a genuine smile. 'Next time, May. You're getting there.'

A larger wave was approaching. Euan's voice came from the beach. 'That's the one. Paddle now.'

For the umpteenth time, April dug her freezing hands into the water and kicked, accelerating to match the building wave.

'Pop up! You got this!' Euan shouted.

April pushed to her feet as the wave lifted her, balance wavering for a heart-stopping second before she steadied.

'Knees bent!' he called as April struggled to maintain her balance.

And then, all of a sudden, she was flying. Ocean spray in her face and wind whipping her hair as the wave carried her shoreward. The rush of adrenaline was like nothing she'd ever known. She let out a whoop of delight, all her focus narrowing to the wave beneath her feet. In that moment, it was her and the sea and the thrill of speed.

For about six seconds. But that was enough.

Heck yeah! I did it!

When April came back on shore, beaming all over, Euan was waiting with an equally wide smile. 'Well done, May. Looked good out there.'

And April's heart rumbled all over again.

'Thanks,' she muttered, cheeks filling with heat despite the cool water. 'I'm done, though,' she groaned and let herself collapse onto the sand.

Euan laughed. 'Aye, let's end on a high. Time's up anyway.'

While she was flooded with endorphins, he peeled off the top half of his wetsuit, revealing that sculpted torso of his, glistening in the sunlight. Then he picked up her board.

Is he…flexing?

How was she supposed to know what flexing looked like? Nobody had ever flexed for her. Not that she remembered. She wasn't exactly the flexed-for kind of gal.

'Enjoying the view?' Euan teased, a smirk crossing his lips.

'Yeah. Saorsa is a beautiful island.' She was pretty sure that his comment had nothing to do with the island's scenery. *Bit cocky. So cocky and ridiculously hot.*

He laughed, that deep sound tickling something inside her that hadn't been tickled for a long time. If ever.

'Aye, that it is. Come on. You need to dry your hair before you get on your bike or you'll catch your death.'

As they made their way back to the surf school, April dragged herself behind him with heavy legs and hungry eyes. There was a prick of sadness that their session was over. Because he wasn't just a good surf teacher and a nice guy. He also had a marvellous butt.

April's bike ride back to Morag's was a whirlwind of turbulent thoughts, each pedal stroke fuelling the replay of her surfing lesson with Euan. The memory of watching him take off his wetsuit played on loop in her mind.

Women surely stumbled over their feet in their hurry to get into his van and drop their panties. He was a magnetic force of nature, oozing sexual energy.

'Alright, alright,' she muttered to herself. 'Pull yourself together. He's a player.'

Then the idea hit April like the waves and the board earlier. Only much harder.

Euan was perfect.

He was easy on the eye, experienced, and apparently used to casual sex. A master of no-strings encounters. A man who embodied freedom and uninhibited desire. The ideal candidate for the last point on her list. Plus, there was no danger of either of them catching feelings. She had always been on the sensible side, and he was far too much of a free spirit. And about twenty-thousand leagues above her. They had nothing in common. Also, the last thing she wanted was a relationship of any kind. She'd just narrowly escaped one.

April peeked at her engagement ring, still snug on her finger. She had entirely forgotten it was there. A gust of defiance swept over her, and she knew that a vacation fling with Euan would be the ultimate act of liberation from her former life.

But as she revved up her confidence, a familiar taunting whisper seeped in. It told her that a guy like him, with his smooth swagger, wouldn't give a girl like her a second glance. She was merely another face in the crowd of tourists. Not someone who could capture his attention. This inner battle between old doubt and newfound boldness raged on.

Was this a fast track to rejection?

Only one way to find out. This reckless thought sent a pulse of adrenaline through her.

She had to have him. Just once.

'Time to break free,' April hummed as she zipped through the picturesque landscape, the mineral-tinged breeze tangling her hair and cooling her flushed face. This wasn't about romance. It was about freedom, about seizing a moment. The new her.

By the time she arrived at the B&B, April had made up her mind and come up with a strategy. Tonight, she would step into the pub – not as the cautious old April from Kansas City, but as a new woman unafraid to chase what she wanted. Even if it was only for a fleeting, passionate moment. Even if it was chancy. This was her opportunity to embrace the unknown, to feel alive in ways she never had.

She would have a drink or two to bolster her courage, and make a move.

What did she have to lose, after all? Ultimately, she would be back in Kansas City, and he would go on to his next conquest. She just had to remember that this was temporary. A vacation rebound. A chance to feel free and desired. To do and try new, forbidden things. April smiled as she unlocked the door to her room, boldness fizzing in her veins. She took off her engagement ring and put it into the drawer, along with her switched-off cell and the rest of her past.

Her subconscious had chosen to start this adventure for a reason. Time to stop playing it safe.

April spent the rest of the day dawdling, something she hadn't had the chance to do in ages. With the binoculars by the window, she peered out for seals and dolphins. But there were only two sailboats gently rocking on the water. After leafing through a gorgeous coffee-table book about Hebridean wildlife and a birdwatching brochure, she crawled between the sheets for an extensive nap. Without having to set an alarm. Pure luxury.

It took a very long shower for her to wake up again. And she shaved everywhere, in case her plans came to fruition. *Best to be prepared.*

The sun hung low in the sky as April was getting ready. She spun around her room, letting her gaze wander over every inch of clothing she brought. Her choice fell on a midnight blue wrap top along with a pair of white skinny jeans and black sandals with block heels.

April lingered in front of the full-length mirror, trailing over her reflection with a critical gaze. The top accentuated her curves, a rare choice that made her feel both daring and self-conscious. She turned slightly, eyeing the jeans that clung to her hips, wondering if they were too much, or maybe not enough. Her fingers traced the roundness of her face. No sign of cheekbones anywhere. Just two dimples.

Focus on the positive, girl.

April glanced down at her body, her breasts and hips fuller than the average. Looked okay. Slightly out of proportion for her height, but okay. Her skin was clear, a hard-won victory against teenage acne.

The outfit was simple but, hopefully, effective. Not that

she had many options in her Tulum-bound suitcase. And not that people often took note of her. She wasn't a wallflower or anything. But she was average, nothing special. Just lil' ol' April. The world couldn't be full of gorgeous, glamorous peacocks only. The world needed sparrows, too.

Yet tonight, as she mustered up the courage for her insane plan, she wished for a touch more of the extraordinary. *Just for once*, she thought, *it would be nice to feel more…noteworthy.*

Resigned, she gave herself a final once-over and decided to let her hair fall over her shoulders. She liked that the ocean air made it wavy.

Before she left her room, she turned around and added a last-minute swipe of ruby-red lipstick to complete her look. 'Alright,' April said to herself, blowing out a slow breath. 'Go get him, tigress.'

If only she were so convinced.

Chapter Eight

E uan wiped down the counter, his mind occupied with thoughts of the surfing lesson earlier.

April had been tossed around by the waves so harshly. More than once he had to stop himself from pulling her out of the water and carrying her to shore. Which was silly. Because that woman was determined. Fierce and resilient. He could tell. And the way her eyes had gleamed when she managed to stand up for a handful of seconds. Like the first sunlight after a storm. How those same eyes had widened when he had taken off his wetsuit... He smiled at the memory. Aye, she was cute as a button. Looked hot in a wetsuit, too.

Nope. Not going there. The bet, remember?

As he was pouring a pint, Euan asked himself how much more appealing she'd become now that he wasn't allowed to hook up with her. The forbidden fruit was always juicier. Would it be so hard to keep himself in check this one time? *You're a grown man. Pull yourself together, ya dawg.*

'Here ye go, pal,' Euan said, sliding a pint across the polished surface to a waiting patron, then holding up the card machine. Sometimes he wondered how long he was going to work here for Lorna. In rare moments, he allowed himself to dream of opening up an artisan gin distillery in Saorsa. But then reality slapped him in the face and laughed. The beep snapped him out of his thoughts. Tonight was a good night, the card machine was working. Wasn't always the case.

Nothing could have prepared him for what happened next.

When he turned his head, April was at the other end of the bar. Thick, sandy-blonde waves cascading over her shoulders. Red lipstick was her only accessory. It was a well-calculated assault. She needed a gun licence for that pout.

Euan dropped a glass into the sink. It shattered, and he startled. That hadn't happened in years. Matt glanced at him and raised a bushy eyebrow.

'I'm good, Matt. Nae worries.'

'Ye sure?'

'Aye. Bit distracted is all.'

Euan's gaze flicked back to April. She looked at him with a shy smile. Was that a hair flip?

Then she walked over to him, swaying hips and all, and perched on a stool. 'Busy night, Hugh-Anne?'

'The usual crowd.' He placed a napkin on the bar. 'What can I get you to celebrate your first surf, May?'

'Surprise me,' she said with that husky voice of hers, giving him a slightly nervous smile. 'I like to try new things.'

Christ, is she flirting with me?

They held a brief gaze, and he thought there was a glint of daring in her green eyes. It shouldn't have ignited a red-hot nudge behind his navel. Definitely not.

'Is that so?' Euan turned away to prepare her a drink. And to take a breath. His mind raced. Part of him was gravitating towards this bewildering fusion of boldness and sweetness. But another part, the part reminding him of the bet and his own rules, demanded caution.

'Well, good for you, May. New experiences can be rewarding.'

'Or dangerously addictive.' Her raspy voice dropped to a purr.

Dammit. She is *flirting. Can't have that.*

Three winks later, Euan placed a vibrant blue cocktail with a straw and an umbrella onto the napkin in front of her. 'There you go. One Electric Beach. Guaranteed to shock your senses.'

'Thanks. That looks, um, radioactive? How exciting.'

It was then he realised that giving her a straw had been a huge mistake.

Because she closed her full, red lips around it and began to suck deliberately slowly. Up and down. A promise of something sinful. All the while she kept staring at him. Cute and tempting and way over the top.

Euan also realised in this exact second that his dick cared a lot less about rules, types, and motors than he did.

A hell of a lot less.

He needed to catch himself on. There was too much at risk. His rolling home, for one.

April's pulse hammered through her entire body. *I'm in a Scottish island pub sucking on a straw trying to seduce a stranger. How did that happen?*

When he turned around, she saw red creeping up his neck. He wasn't as unaffected as he wanted her to believe by the looks of it.

'Mmm… That *is* yummy,' April gushed. 'You're a very talented man.'

'Oh, aye. I have many talents.' There was a glimmer of the Devil in his storm-grey eyes. 'Lucky people get to experience a few of them. The important ones.'

Euan's gaze dropped to her mouth and a low thudding spread through her. So, he was open to flirting, too.

Promising, promising.

'I bet they're extraordinarily lucky.' April traced one finger around the rim of the glass, twisting a strand of her hair with the other. It was a bit like stroking your belly and your head simultaneously in two different directions. Flirting was hard work. 'I'm an adventurous spirit, always eager to discover… more. If you know what I mean…' She finished with a wink, for additional emphasis. Best not to leave anything open to interpretation.

'Oh, are you now? How eager?' Euan leaned closer, his breath soft and warm against her ear. His masculine scent was mesmerising. Primal and intoxicating, shooting straight into her private parts. She didn't dare move.

'As eager as a seagull spotting a fry on the beach. Always seizing the moment, you know?' She gripped her glass so tightly, it should have cracked.

'Uh-hum. See, the only thing is…' he whispered in his melodic Scottish accent, drawing out every syllable and sending a delightful shiver down her spine as his lips almost grazed her ear, '…I don't believe you for a single second, love.'

With an infuriatingly smug grin that stretched across his sexy boyish rebel face, he retreated to the other end of the bar and busied himself pouring pints and drams. April stared at the movement of his broad back as he pulled bottles from the shelf. He probably could have done that blindfolded.

I wouldn't mind blindfolding him…

At this moment, she didn't even question her hormonal thoughts anymore. Was she coming on too strong? But he'd been flirting back, hadn't he? She wasn't good at this game. But she also wasn't ready to let it go.

She watched Euan with a mix of frustration and fascination as he poured and served drinks with well-versed motions. Nimble hands, a half-smile here, a semi-ironic scoff there. He was in his element, giving off intense 'rebel who loves his momma' vibes. Very much James Dean pedigree. And yet there was more to him than met the eye, she reckoned.

April put the straw on her napkin and took a generous gulp of her neon-coloured drink, the citrus burn doing nothing to ease the sting behind her ribs. Her gaze traced the worn wooden bar, noticing the cracks and scratches etched into its surface from decades of use. He wasn't completely disinterested, she could tell by the flicker in his eyes. But he was playing hard to get for some reason. Maybe this was how the game of seduction worked, like chess with certain moves? Too bad she didn't know any of those tactics.

She finished her flashy cocktail in a few gulps, the potent alcohol hitting her system in a warm rush. It wasn't like her to be forward, but she was determined to follow through with her plan. *Getting laid like a goddess*. She was thirty and her sexual experience was abysmal. There was this roaring hunger inside her, the insatiable need for friction and touch and words and whispers. Was she desperate? Admittedly, yes. But she didn't care. She craved this. Something new and exhilarating. It was within her reach, buzzing in the air like electricity. And she was oh so ready for it.

Giving up was not an option. On the contrary.

Time to take it up a notch.

'Where's the lavatory?' April asked Euan with as sultry a voice as she could muster when he returned to her end of the bar.

'Right there to the left, between the bar and the kitchen,' he pointed out, and cleared his throat. He watched her as she stood up from her stool. In that instant, she let her purse slip from her grasp and clatter to the floor.

'Oops!' She turned on her heel, looked back at him, and bent over. As slowly as she could.

Was she flaunting her rear like a baboon in heat during mating season?

Absolutely.

But desperate times called for desperate measures.

She can't be doing that on purpose.

Euan had no clue what was going on. Didn't matter. He couldn't stop gawking anyway. The fabric of her snug white jeans hugged her contours, practically painted onto her curves. That right there was proper bubble bum. Slightly too big for her size, slightly out of proportion. Flawless.

Yes, he liked big butts. No point in lying about that. And his anaconda agreed a bit too enthusiastically.

He forced himself to turn around and do something, anything, before people started staring at him as he was staring at her.

Matt lifted another bushy eyebrow.

Miraculously, Euan succeeded in distracting himself with the routines of his bar job. Cashing, wiping, pouring, mixing... Pints of lager, gin and tonics, the occasional dram, the odd round of schnapps. He even half-heartedly tried to flirt with two ladies who both ordered vodka cranberry and giggled as expected when he took off his knitted beanie and ran his hand through his hair. His signature move.

But he didn't feel it.

Instead, Euan's gaze kept returning to April like the tide rolling back to shore. It annoyed him.

'You alright, lad?' Matt asked.

'Aye, don't worry. Bit stressed is all.'

Matt put a hand on Euan's shoulder. 'Hm. Let me know if anything's up.'

'Will do, Matt.'

That was one of the more intimate personal conversations Euan and Matt had had in their years together in the Old Barn.

When Euan looked around the pub after a short while, he couldn't see April anywhere. She must have gone home. The bite of disappointment took him by surprise. He usually didn't drink on the job, but this called for an exception. So he poured himself a small Harris gin. Even though he came from a family of whisky distillers, Euan had always been more of a gin man himself. And the neighbouring isle produced good stuff, he had to give it to them.

He checked his watch and made his way to the loo, if for no other reason than to take a break from the noise of the pub and sort himself out. Euan didn't feel like himself lately.

He walked right into her trap.

April stood there, leaning against the doorframe in the dimly lit hallway. Before he could say a word, she pushed herself off the wall and stepped close to him. 'Hello, sailor.' She trailed her fingers through her hair and a faint smile curled her lips. 'Fancy seeing you here.'

'April, I thought you went home. Wait. Did you…hang out by the loo?'

'Well, you thought wrong,' she said, ignoring his question, and moved closer to him. Hips undulating. 'I don't usually do this,' she confessed, her voice wavering slightly. 'But I feel like I have to. With you, I can't help myself. Do you mind?'

Her gaze met his, and unspoken intensity crackled in the space between them. As if she was daring him.

'No, I generally don't mind,' he said with a quirked smile. 'But I'm a bit confused here.' He took off his beanie, kneading it between his hands.

April ran her index finger slowly down his arm, and he went hot all over. 'It's simple. You're attractive. You're nice. And you smell really, really good.' She hooked her fingers into his belt loops and pulled him towards her before he could even process what was happening. But happening it was. She was so close, he felt every inch of her. And every inch of him, each treacherous cell of his body, wanted to give in. In his mind, he picked her up, pushed her against the wall and took her mouth with a bruising kiss that would make her forget her own name and moan his instead.

It would have been so easy. So good.

And so wrong.

'Hey, hey…April, wait,' he said. 'Don't go there.'

'Why not? We're both adults,' she murmured, before she started grinding against him.

Christ Almighty. This fearless woman was rubbing up and down his body like there was no tomorrow. This was dangerous. He realised he'd had no one in days. And now that was coming back to bite him in the form of an aching hard-on. If it weren't for that stupid bet, he would have thrown her over his shoulder and carried her to his van to give that perfect ass a good spanking. Do things to her that she hadn't even heard of. Give her and himself some release. But he couldn't. Wouldn't. The bet was one reason for it. But not the only one.

She wasn't ready for this. For him. Which she didn't seem to know or care about. Because now she stood on her tiptoes and licked his neck like a kitten with a bowl of cream. 'One night. Isn't that what you do, tiger?'

Euan groaned at the sensation and tried to focus on reasoning with her. She wanted to use him. But to his astonishment, he didn't want that to happen.

Well, that was a first.

'April. No. You're amazing, but I can't do this. I won't. Sorry, love.' He stepped out of her grip, the spell breaking. 'Hey… Listen, you just ended a serious, long relationship. I don't think you're ready—'

'No, it's all right. I get it. I'm not your type. Don't know why I thought otherwise.' Her face glowed bright red. 'My bad, I shouldn't have…I put on you the spot. That wasn't… Sorry. God. So sorry.'

He saw the vulnerability she had hidden with her flirty

charade. Before he could say anything, she turned and hurried out of the pub.

In the empty space she left behind, that unfamiliar ache surfaced within him again. The crowd and noise closed back in around him, but for Euan nothing could shift the memory of her wounded eyes. Somehow, he needed to make it right.

Chapter Nine

April cowered alone at the breakfast table. She had woken early, before any of the other guests, unable to shake off the mortification from last night. It lingered like a stubborn fog, very much in sync with the dull, leaden clouds outside that were pressing down on land and sea. Hands wrapped around a cup of tea, she made no move to drink it.

It should have been easy. As far as she could tell, Euan was something like the island's Casanova. The trusted expert for Hebridean vacations with benefits. But her gawky try at seduction had backfired, leaving her sore with rejection. He had made her feel like a fool.

No, you did this to yourself.

The very idea that she could seduce someone like Euan was laughable. Flirting had never been her forte. That's why Euan had seemed like the perfect choice. Easy-going, not overly discerning, supposedly open for casual encounters. And he had flexed for her, hadn't he? Although it was possible she was fabricating that in her head, making objectifying assumptions about a stranger. Because of hormones.

She let out an annoyed sigh. It wasn't completely her fault, was it? While her friends and everyone else in their twenties had been practising dating, April had spent this decisive decade on the couch next to Dick. Unsurprising that she didn't have a clue about all this mating stuff.

Inevitably, her thoughts circled back to her failed attempts to seduce Dick. Whatever she'd tried, he hadn't been too interested. It hadn't started like that, though. In their first year together, they had done it more often. But Dick never opened up to her, never looked her in the eye, never said a word. He never even made a sound.

How can you not make a single sound during sex?

Gradually, it happened less and less. Until even Dick's grandparents had more sex than them. She had caught him watching porn twice, which made her feel relieved and hurt at the same time. He was interested in women, he was interested in sex. Just not with her.

April tugged at her earlobe. If nobody truly desired her, if nobody wanted to sleep with her, maybe *she* was the problem.

She shouldn't tie her self-worth to a man's sexual approval. But that wasn't what this was about. Not at all. No, she longed to experience a physical connection and was incapable of finding it. Didn't seem too difficult for most other people. So it must be her.

'Oh, good mornin', April,' Morag greeted as she entered the breakfast room, wiping her hands on her apron. 'You're up bright and early today.'

'Morning, Morag,' April replied weakly, forcing a smile. 'Early yes. Bright not so much. Couldn't sleep.'

'Sorry to hear that. Is the bed okay?'

'Yeah, very much. No worries,' April said. 'Just a lot going on in my head.'

'Ah, well, let me get you food then. A full Scottish breakfast will cheer you up. My tattie scones are famous. Have you ever tried Stornoway black pudding?'

'Thanks, Morag,' she said, even though the mere thought of food made her queasy. 'I'll just have scrambled eggs and toast, if that's okay?'

'Sure, love! Whatever you fancy. Glass of juice?'

'Yes, please.'

As Morag bustled back into the kitchen, April tried to focus on the landscape outside. 'Saorsa, the sunniest place in Scotland!' said one of the flyers on display next to the window. *Poor Scotland*, April thought with a look at the brooding wall of clouds.

The door creaked open, and her heart leaped into her throat as Euan strolled in. Hair ruffled from sleep and wind, sheepish grin on his face. A cool morning breeze followed him, carrying a waft of seaweed.

'Mornin',' he said with a mockingly sexy pre-seven o'clock rasp. 'You're up already.'

'Not much sleep,' she mumbled, staring into her tea as if it contained the secret of creation.

'I see. Suppose that makes two of us,' Euan said.

'Probably for *wildly* different reasons.' April's reply came sharp, laced with bitterness. She imagined him in his van, having an orgy that would make good old Hugh Hefner seem like an innocent choir boy, and she wished she could disappear. Recently the theme of her life.

'Wouldn't be so sure.' Euan pulled out a chair and sat across from her, eyes filled with concern.

April was chagrined by their encounter last night, but she couldn't let that show. She fiddled with her fork, avoiding his gaze. 'So, uh, any plans today? Surf lessons and such?' she asked, desperate to change the subject.

'Surf's not good today. Nothing to do but chill. Thought I'd start with a proper breakfast here.'

April could tell he was trying to be nice to her, to make it less weird. *Polite pity*. Made it even worse.

'Nice place Morag has here, right?' he said and coughed lightly. 'I mean, the food alone…'

'Yeah, definitely. So, so good,' April agreed. 'Her omelettes are to die for.' She flinched inwardly at her own words. But Euan grinned, and she felt a hint of relief.

Morag set down two plates with a clatter. One for April, one for Euan. 'Thought I heard your wheezing van of doom. Here you go. But no bacon today, that's for paying guests.'

April reached for the salt at the same time as Euan, their hands hovering awkwardly over the shaker. The tension from the previous night still hung between them like a veil. 'Sorry,' she said, quickly pulling back.

'No, no, you first.' A smile played at the corners of his mouth.

'Thanks,' April said and took the salt. 'I'm trying to avoid a bland life.'

His smile widened. 'I wouldn't want to be accused of contributing to that.'

'I think last night covered the "not bland" part for a long time,' she mumbled.

Euan leaned back, the corner of his mouth twitching. 'Hundred per cent not bland, May. Hundred per cent.'

Morag scurried back and forth between the kitchen and the table. Her eyes darted from April to Euan with curiosity. She could probably sense the tension. 'Since the waters are too choppy for the surf school today, Euan's surely got time for a wee tour,' Morag said abruptly. 'Why don't you show April around the isle today, brother? The old distillery is lovely this time of year.'

Euan's head jerked up. 'The distillery's derelict. Nothing lovely about it, sister. At no time of year.'

April was keen to explore more of Saorsa. But after last night, she wasn't sure if she could handle much more of this weirdness between them. 'Sounds nice, but I don't want to impose.'

'Ah, nonsense,' Morag insisted. 'Euan has plenty of time. He's the best tour guide. And it'll be good for you to see the isle. Trust me, you won't be imposing. And, as far as I know,' she gave a puckish wink in her brother's direction, 'neither of you has anything else to do today.'

'Have you seen the weather, Mo?' He sounded annoyed. 'It's dreich.'

'Naw, the weather is not a reason. If it were, we wouldn't get anything done round here,' Morag coaxed, with a glint in her eye. 'It'll be good for you to show our guest Saorsa's true history. You know how much it means.'

April glanced at Euan, who squirmed in his seat. 'Fine,' he relented, taking another crunching bite of toast. 'We can go after breakfast.'

He looked like he'd agreed to have his tooth pulled by a medieval quack doctor. Without anaesthesia.

'Fab, that's settled then!' Morag lit up, satisfied with her victory. 'You two will have a great time.'

What just happened?

As April looked into his eyes, she wondered what was going on behind them. Was this simply his way of smoothing over last night's mortification? Then again, a free and private island tour wasn't something she could easily say no to. And maybe she could use it as a form of desensitisation therapy. Hang out in skyscrapers until you get over your fear of heights; cuddle with tarantulas until you laugh at the odd bathroom spider. Spend time with a Scottish sex god until you stop being horny.

'Alright,' April agreed. 'But not too long.'

Euan snatched a forkful of egg from her plate. 'Why? Do you have anywhere else to be, May?'

His jaw tightened as he tried to mask his unease with a smile. The last thing Euan wanted was to revisit that distillery, stoking old resentment. And spending time alone with April? That was playing with fire. He almost heard the humming revving of that new motor he'd win. Provided he didn't get too close to her.

Morag knew what she was doing. *That wee devil.*

Euan sighed. There was still the guilt of turning April down last night. She'd looked so hurt, it was like a thousand tiny needles pricking at his heart. He wanted to atone to her somehow. And visiting that cursed place would make him bitter enough to restrain himself. At least, that's what he hoped.

April offered a small smile. 'Thanks for being my tour guide today. It's a bit…weird.' Her cheeks were cherry-red. 'You know…after…'

'No problem,' he said hastily. 'Don't worry about it. Really. All good.'

Was it, though?

As they finished breakfast, Euan stole a few glances at April. Her sandy-blonde hair was tousled at the back and she had a faint pillow print on her cheek. This delicate morning sleepiness moved something in him. He didn't understand why she was affecting him like this. A crumb of toast lingered on the corner of her mouth.

Damn that mouth. Could bring kings and countries to their knees and she didn't even know it. So kissable. Gave him all sorts of ideas. His thumb grazing over her lips…

Yeah, right. Your thumb… Stop it.

He needed to stay focused, keep his distance. His mind sped in circles with thoughts of how to navigate the situation.

Don't eat the forbidden fruit, MacLeod. Remember the bet. The motor. Vroom, vroom.

'Alright, then,' Morag chimed in, clapping her hands

together. 'Give me your plates and off you go. The Isle of Saorsa awaits.'

Euan drove in silence. The distillery was a sore spot, the decaying stone buildings a reminder of loss and betrayal. But April had looked at him with those guileless eyes, and he'd caved.

Now she turned to him with those same deep greens. 'Okay, so about last night…'

Argh. The inevitable.

'Didn't mean to make you feel bad,' he said as kindly as he could.

'Then… Why?'

'It's complicated.' Euan scrubbed a hand over his jaw. 'But it's not you. You're a lovely woman.'

'Ah. I see. Just not for *that*.' She looked away again. 'Fair enough. I'm sorry if I made you uncomfortable. I just thought—'

'No, not at all. My bad if I did give you the wrong impression. I'm sorry for any confusion. It just didn't seem…like you.'

'How do you know what I'm like?' she said with a tense tone. 'Can we please forget about it? That's probably best.'

'Forget what?' he said in a futile attempt to lighten the mood.

Euan shifted gears with a creak as the VW van wound its way through the Hebridean landscape. Its engine whirred and groaned like the neighing of an Each-Uisge, the fearsome water horse of island mythology. The van's rattling and clattering were uneven bouts of discordant noise in an otherwise serene scenery. Low hills rolled past like waves on the roiling sea. The infinite sky, a theatre of bulging clouds, cast shadows that roamed over the landscape.

Euan eased off the gas as he spied the approaching car on

the narrow, meandering track: a bright red Corsa. He pulled the van into a passing place, its worn brakes sighing in relief as it came to a reluctant stop. The Corsa's window lowered to reveal Lorna, her grey hair tied back and eyes crinkling with an easy smile.

'Fancy meeting you here,' Euan called out, the engine of his van still ticking as it cooled.

'I must say, every time I see this van, I'm convinced it's held together by rust and sheer willpower.'

'It's a classic, Lorna.'

She leaned closer, her glance falling on April. 'Who's your co-pilot this time?'

'This is April. She's a guest at Morag's. April, meet Lorna, my boss, and the queen bee of this island's sweetest empire.'

April waved. 'Nice to meet you.'

'You, too. Where you off to, Euan?'

'The distillery.'

'Ye're taking an American to the distillery? Oh, I wish I had yer sense of humour, lad,' Lorna said with a tortured smile. 'Right, have to crack on. Spent too much time with my beehives as it is. See you, Euan.'

'Bye, boss.'

April stared out the window, her eyes wide with wonder as she took in the magnificent vistas. 'Can you believe this place?' she said, her words filled with awe. 'It's beautiful beyond words. Even on a grim day like this. This island makes you feel like... Not happy or sad, but both. Like being alone but not lonely. It makes you feel small, but also huge. Like the moment between breaths. It's awesome.'

Euan glanced at her, his heart skipping a beat at the spark of joy in her eyes. 'Aye, it's something special,' he admitted, a hint of pride sneaking into his voice. He pointed out various landmarks as they passed, told her stories of local legends. Faeries hidden among the hills, smugglers who used to hide whisky barrels in secret caves, selkies trapped

by local fishermen. Tales of resistance, resilience, perseverance, and magic.

As they rounded a bend, the distillery came into view. Or
rather what was left of it. Eroding walls stood defiantly
against the backdrop of greenery and clouds and water. An
air of melancholy clung to the structure.

'Here we are,' Euan said sharply. 'The dead MacLeod
distillery.'

Chapter Ten

The ruin of the stone buildings sat dramatically on top of a cliff, its silhouette jutting out against the sky. Remnants of a long history that had shaped the island. Of better days. Of loss.

'My great-great-grandfather built the distillery. Three generations of MacLeods made whisky here. Until it was sold to an American company,' Euan huffed. 'They shut it down within a year. Not enough profit. Now the land's just sitting here. Nobody knows what to do with it.'

'I'm sorry it's not in your family anymore.' Compassion softened April's voice. 'That must have been difficult.'

'Yep.' He raised his shoulders, though her empathy disarmed him. 'My grandpa never got over it. Cast a long shadow. Not just over our family. Over the entire isle. But that's history now.'

He remembered the days when his grandda brought him here – a small Euan and a big bottle of uisge beatha – telling him stories of former glory and fresh betrayal. Until he sobbed like a madman, staggering between the rocks, crawling on his knees, wailing and cursing, and Euan's angry dad had to come pick them up. Sometimes followed by a brief fistfight with his old man. Not pretty.

'History forms us,' April stated, 'whether we like it or not.'

Euan slowed the van, turned onto a rutted lane leading to the distillery, and stopped at its end. 'Right, that's us. Not much to see now. But the ruins still stand. A mocking reminder.'

'Oh, shut up. It's incredible,' April said, peering out the windscreen. From up here, the grassland cascaded down to the sea in undulating greens, marked by clusters of rocks and boulders. The small village of Cuanag, a scattering of white dots cradled in the valley, seemed to have grown from the land itself. Clouds rolled across the sky. Brooding giants, broken enough to allow slivers of light to pierce through. 'A bit eerie,' April said, 'but so peaceful.'

'Maybe.' Euan flexed his fingers, trying to ease their stiffness.

'Do you mind if I explore?' she asked, clearly itching to run around and stick her nose into the past.

'Go on. But watch where you go. It's uneven.'

April stepped out of the vehicle, her shoes crunching on the rocks beneath her feet. He shut off the engine and climbed out to follow her. A steel claw clamped down on his heart, an amalgam of pride and resentment he usually kept buried. The MacLeod distillery wasn't just stone and mortar. It used to be the pulse of the island, once vibrant and now silent. Euan knew how this place had looked on its zenith, from photo albums he used to flip through with his gran time and again. Listening to her stories, explaining who was who. Master distiller 'Baldy' MacPherson, distiller 'Crack-o-Dawn' MacKinnon, mashman 'Messy' Mackay, stillman 'The Moose' MacGregor, and 'Sand Shoe' Ross, the warehouse manager. But they could only look at photos when Cian wasn't around. To avoid incurring his wrath.

Each step towards the ruins was like strolling back in time.

April's empathy was a light in the darkness of his family's destroyed legacy. She saw beauty where he saw only ghosts. Her words, 'History forms us,' echoed in his mind.

Ain't that the truth.

Euan watched as she walked along the narrow path that cut through the grass. He followed her. Not that he had much choice. This could be a treacherous place. With each step, a piece of his carefully constructed indifference chipped away. April examined the worn and weathered remnants. Covered in moss, the walls refused to surrender to time. Broken barrels littered the site. The machinery and equipment had been taken away, leaving only a few rusted tools and shattered glass in its place. Her expression showed reverence and sadness.

'Even in this state, it's magical,' she said, edging nearer. 'It feels like time has stopped.'

Euan blinked at the once whitewashed stone buildings decaying into the landscape, at the tangles of wildflowers blurred with thistles. He knew these ruins like the lines of his own palm. But as he saw April's fascination, he felt a zing. Maybe, just maybe, the ruins were more than a relic of sorrow. Perhaps she wasn't wrong. There was a certain beauty here in the stillness that had settled over the place. The kind that came from loss and spoke of the perseverance of Saorsa's people. No matter how hard landlords, their ruthless factors, or corporate capitalists had tried over the centuries, they were still here. Despite everything. At least a few of them.

'Never heard someone describe it as magical,' Euan admitted. 'I guess there's something about the way nature has reclaimed it that makes it calm. But still. Could be a working distillery, if it wasn't for… Och, never mind.'

'Stop being so grim. Let's take a closer look!' April said, reaching out for his hand before pulling back. She quickly turned around and strutted towards the old door. As Euan trailed behind her, his eyes were glued to the slow tick-tock of her hips. Each step she took sent a jarring pulse through him, right down to his gut, making it hard to think about anything else but the tempting jiggle in those tight-ass leggings. A distraction from gloomy thoughts.

Nope. The bet. The motor. The wrong type.

As they entered the distillery, quiet wrapped around them like a woollen blanket. The only sound was the distant slosh of waves against the shore and the faint rustle of wind through the tall grass surrounding the old building. The weight of history pressed down on Euan. But he didn't get a chance to dwell.

April's eyes were bright with interest. 'Show me how the whisky was made,' she requested with palpable excitement.

'All right, all right,' Euan agreed, fully disarmed by her honest curiosity, and pointed to the remnants of old mash tuns and wash backs. Walking at April's side, he told her its stories, and with each one, the anger's hold on him loosened. The ruin seemed different today, the memories clinging to its stones less stinging. As he described the process, April listened intently, asking questions. Euan found himself warming to the task, stories of the distillery's heyday coming to life. He'd never shared any of this with anyone.

'Tell me about your family then,' she asked as she picked her way over cracked stones.

Euan hesitated for a moment before the tale. 'As I said, my great-great-grandfather built this distillery. Back in the late eighteen hundreds,' he said, gesturing at the ruins around them. 'Three generations of MacLeods made Scotch here. Good stuff. Until it was sold to an American corporation. That was a thing in the eighties. But they closed it down within a year, leaving many islanders without jobs. And my grandda with a broken heart. He began to drink. It was tough, although I only remember it faintly. I would say ask my father, but he moved away ages ago.'

'I'm sorry. That sounds awfully sad,' April said, running

her fingers along the moss-covered stones. 'It must have been devastating for your family and the community. I'm truly sorry, Euan.'

'Don't be. It's not your fault.' His lips quirked into a mirthless smile. 'Just the way of the world, I suppose. Nothing lasts forever.'

'That doesn't make it easier. Loss is loss.' April laid her hand on his arm. His muscles tightened instantly. But he didn't pull away. She was being kind. Euan let out a sardonic laugh. 'The brand "Isle of Saorsa Scotch" is still used by the US company. Has nothing to do with us or the isle. Just marketing.' He tried to inject some levity into his voice, but the bitterness lingered.

April gave a sympathetic wince. 'I saw one of those ads at the airport in KC.'

'Aye, that's possible.' Euan maintained his distance, careful not to get too close. Not after last night. Not after noticing that he and his dick had such different opinions about suitable types. And certainly not with the bet hanging over him.

April looked at him with inquisitiveness. 'Do you ever come here, to...I don't know, be alone? To think?'

'Never,' he confessed, exposed under her perceptive stare. 'I try to avoid making myself miserable on purpose.'

'Thank you for bringing me here in spite of that,' she said softly. 'It's an enchanting place. I can see why you love it so much.'

'I don't love...' Euan broke off, searching her eyes for any sign of insincerity. But all he found was genuine appreciation and understanding.

'Not true,' she countered. 'Why would you feel so much anger and misery if you didn't love it?'

And in that moment, Euan knew there was a lot more to April than he'd ever thought. And more to himself than he'd ever been willing to admit.

After April listened to Euan recount the distillery's history, she was sad for him and the people of Saorsa. She saw the love he had for the island, and how the loss of the distillery weighed on him. Yet he seemed more relaxed. At least the grim drawl around his mouth was gone. While she continued to inspect the area, he pulled out a pen and a small notebook from his back pocket, sat down on a rock, and started scribbling.

'Really? You're a writer?' she asked, intrigued.

'Not a successful one. But, aye.'

Splotches of pink appeared on his cheeks. Euan blushing? Two minutes ago, she would have sworn on her best friend Alex's life that such a thing was impossible. But here they were. It evened the field a little. 'So what do you write then?'

'Short stories. Some poetry,' he replied, a hint of shyness creeping into his voice. 'I try to capture the spirit of the island. Its people. The way things used to be. How they could be. The good, the bad, and the ugly.'

'I write, too', April said, not sure why she was telling him that. But he had been sharing parts of his life with her. So maybe that's why she wanted to share something as well. He made her feel like she could, without judgement or criticism. 'Mostly journal stuff for myself. It helps to clear my head. Nothing meaningful at all.' Truth was, she couldn't survive without reading or writing. Words gave her peace, books were her refuge.

He didn't make fun of her or roll his eyes, like Dick used to when she talked about writing. Instead he nodded. 'Don't play it down. Writing does that, sorting your thoughts and feelings.' Euan looked abashed as he continued, 'I also try to write in Gaelic sometimes. You know, the language of the isle. It's so poetic. A language of place and belonging. But I'm not a true native speaker. And Gaelic isn't easy.'

April smiled. There was an unexpected depth to the playboy surfer, an emotional connection to his heritage that she admired. He let her peek behind the curtain and she liked what she saw – the corner of a soft heart.

'You're not? Why's that?' she asked. 'I thought Gaelic was an official language in Scotland?'

'It is, and it's not.' He pinched the bridge of his nose. 'It's complicated. And yes, it's on road signs. But still…the number of people who speak it is dwindling. Short version: Gaelic was suppressed after the last Jacobite rising that ended in 1746. Of course, people spoke it in the Highlands and islands. Was their language. In the late nineteenth century, many crofters round here asked for Gaelic schools. Didn't get them. For a long time, Gaelic was associated with poverty, social deprivation, backwardness. There was a stigma.' Euan sighed. 'My parents barely spoke it. Gaelic was considered useless. Wouldn't get you anywhere in life. In my grandda's time, the children in Saorsa's school were even punished by the teacher for speaking Gaelic in class. Today, my niece and nephews learn it in school. But there's a gap. People between thirty and sixty aren't very good at it. Shame, really. Cause it's beautiful and important. Not just in films.'

'I had no idea,' April said, baffled. 'That was unjust and messed-up and cruel.'

'Yeah, Scottish history is complex. Makes you pure raging most of the time.'

She twisted her hair into a bun. 'You know, it's awesome that you're working on your Gaelic. As long as we learn, we're alive. And as long as it's in English, I'd love to read your writing someday. Or I'll learn Gaelic.'

Euan seemed taken aback by her words, but his expression eased. 'Maybe one day, I'll let you.'

She wouldn't be here long enough for 'one day'. But it still made a smile flit across her lips and her insides fuzzy.

April continued to pick her way through the uneven

terrain. The weight of her ignorance pressed upon her and she was lost in thought as she navigated her way over the scattered rocks, some larger than her feet and some much smaller. The rugged surfaces wobbled as she climbed over them to reach the edge of the distillery grounds. She was so clueless. Beyond whisky, kilts, and bagpipes – what did she know about Scotland? Its culture and history? Not a darn thing.

Maybe Euan could teach her a bit. If he could bear it, that was.

But being so distracted was a grave mistake.

April's Chucks met a loose rock and slipped off. She stumbled, sprawling to the ground as her foot twisted and gave way under her weight. The thud of her body hitting the earth was followed by a harsh gasp. Searing pain shot through her ankle.

'You okay?' Euan asked, his voice laced with concern as he rushed over.

'Don't think so.' April's voice trembled as she fought back tears, not from the pain alone, but from the indignity of her repeated clumsiness. Her ankle felt like it was burning. But she didn't want to be the damsel in distress. With gritted teeth, she pulled herself together and tried to stand up.

Another grave mistake.

She yelped with pain as her foot buckled, sending her crumpling back to the ground. 'Damn!'

Euan crouched down beside her, brushing a stray lock of hair away from her face. 'You have to stop throwing yourself on the ground, woman. Let's have a look.' He was so gentle as he examined her ankle. 'It's swelling,' he said with a hint of worry and moved her into a more comfortable position.

'I guess I sprained it,' April admitted. 'Can't put any weight on it.'

'That much is obvious, daftie. Let's hope you haven't torn

a ligament.' Euan hesitated briefly and said, 'I'll carry you back to the van.'

'No! That's not… No. Out of the question.'

'Don't think we have a choice, love. Unless you prefer to crawl on your belly.'

Not a tempting prospect. 'You sure?' April asked. She didn't want him to be uncomfortable after the unsolicited overload of physical contact last night.

But before she could raise any further objections, he had already lifted her. With impressive ease. His grip was firm and steady, her body securely cradled against his. Being held by him made her feel calm and comforted. The warmth of his body was reassuring. And, well, sexy, too. As he carried her, she felt his muscles move beneath his shirt. Despite the throbbing pain in her ankle, heat spread through her with each step they took together.

April rested her head in the crook of his neck. She could have sworn his pulse was racing as fast as hers.

Chapter Eleven

The evening sun cast amber light through the window, bathing the studio in a comforting glow. 'Hey, little clubfoot,' Euan said as he set down the grocery bag on the desk in April's room. 'Got you some painkillers and ice, sandwiches, and two bottles of water.'

'Thanks, knight in knitted armour.' April smiled at him, her lips parting in a way that made Euan's heart play xylophone on his ribs. He forced himself to look away before his mind wandered any further down that path. *Can't let that happen.*

Euan opened the mini fridge to put the ice away. He could navigate this room blindfolded, it was his hibernation cave. Eight steps from the fridge to the desk. He opened the drawer to search for one of the phone chargers that were always lying around here for guests. His mobile battery was low. Considering how antsy he was getting, it was better to make sure that he had enough juice. For later tonight. To find a distraction on the app should he need it. From this nagging confusion inside his guts.

He spotted her phone lying dormant in the drawer's

corner. 'You haven't turned it on?' Euan asked, waving April's phone in the air.

She let out a weary sigh, rubbing at her swollen ankle. 'I'm not ready to face the music. I bolted right before I was about to be chained to someone for life. It felt like a prison sentence. I left Dick at the altar because I couldn't imagine a lifetime without…*it*.'

'Dick is his name?'

'The irony is not lost on me', she said with a sad smile. 'His full name is Richard.'

'Sorry if that was inappropriate.' But what she had just said sounded too ominous not to ask. 'A lifetime without what, May?'

'I mean…well, you know, *that*…' Flames climbed her face. 'Without, um, sex.'

'You serious? What does that… I don't… Didn't you and…' Euan was stunned by what he heard and not sure he understood.

A pained expression flitted across her face before she nodded, avoiding eye contact. 'I don't want to talk about it.'

'That's okay.' He put her phone back into the drawer and closed it. Safer to keep things light and casual between them. That was his vibe, after all. His MO. His DNA. 'I get that. Let's not dive into the mess. You need time to heal.'

But now Euan seriously wondered what had brought April to Saorsa, of all places. Straight from the altar to a remote Scottish isle wasn't the most logical route. Her eyes, when she looked out on the ocean, spoke volumes about how much she revelled in this escape. He had noticed that.

She turned and asked, 'Why did you come here tonight?'

Euan shoved his hands into his pockets. 'Just helping a lass out,' he replied nonchalantly. But her question had caught him unawares. 'Making sure you're doing alright with your ankle and all that. I know there's no food here in the evening.

It's a bed and breakfast. Not a bed and breakfast and lunch and dinner. Didn't want you to starve.'

'Oh,' she said quietly as she washed down a paracetamol. 'Thank you. That's incredibly nice and neighbourly.'

'Course. Nae bother. Right, best get going then.'

'Shift at the pub?'

'No, not tonight. I promised Morag to come to the weekly ceilidh in the community hall.' It wasn't as packed with tourists as the Old Barn, but if he really wanted to, he could surely find some diversion there. Or on the app. 'It's a group dance of sorts.'

'Sounds like fun. I think?'

'Aye, it can be. Every other Wednesday, the isle's community gathers like this. Meeting, sharing stories, hanging out. It's a way of staying connected.'

'Then have a good time,' she said.

Euan saw the loneliness blink in her eyes and something bent inside him. *Och, for fuck's sake.* Despite his reservations, he felt compelled to include her. The idea of her sitting alone in this room, all sad and lonely? Unacceptable.

'Wanna come with me to the ball, princess?' he asked.

Why did I say that? Who am I anymore?

'With my clubfoot? I can't walk, let alone dance, on this ankle.'

'Tell you what,' he said. 'I'll give you a piggyback ride. And you don't have to dance. Just enjoy the atmosphere. See it as part of your Saorsa experience.'

She laughed this warm, hoarse, honey-like chuckle. 'You're nuts, Hugh-Anne!'

'Agreed. But it's no trouble at all. I'm getting used to carrying you around. Come on, May. Let's go.'

'Don't know why I'm doing this, but okay. Getting out of this room might be a good thing.'

Euan crouched, feeling April's weight settle onto his back, her arms looping around his neck. There was an unexpected rightness to it. Her body pressing close to his, warm and alive, her breath soft against his ear. He straightened up, she was an easy burden to carry. There was something about this – her trust, her closeness – that filled him with a quiet gratitude. He was glad to be her support. As they made their way down the road in the evening twilight, her giggles against his neck, Euan was filled with a strange contentment and joy.

This felt better than it should. A different kind of kick.

Don't get used to it, man.

April didn't want to be alone. Neither with herself and her thoughts nor with Euan. This dance was the ideal middle ground. With her body draped around his broad back, the rush of air against her face, and their shared laughter sparking an electric current through her, she felt freedom. When she was with Euan, she didn't dwell on her past. Or fear her future. There was only now.

They arrived at the community hall, and he placed her down onto the grass outside. Disappointment nipped at her – as silly as it was – for the loss of connection, of weightlessness.

'Your carriage has arrived, milady,' he said with a sideways grin.

'Thank you, kind sir.'

The community hall was a contemporary building, one storey, with a tiered sloping roof supported by wooden beams. A modern take on a large traditional barn. Large black letters spelled 'An talla' on the shorter side of its white walls.

'An talla, what does that mean?' April asked.

Euan snorted. 'The hall. Gaelic is a language about place. Well, and a hall is a hall, after all. Shall we?'

The dance was already underway. Along with lively folk tunes, the sound of chat and laughter drifted out from the open doors. Entering, April and Euan were wrapped in the stuffiness of the bustling room. The high ceiling, with its exposed wooden beams, added the right amount of rustic charm to the modern space. Tables lined the edges, adorned with plaid tablecloths and simple floral arrangements. In the centre, dancers whirled and stomped in sync with the folk music that filled the air. As Euan guided her through the open doors, April noticed several heads turning in their direction, their curious glances making her self-conscious. A ripple of unease shot through April, her limp more pronounced as she leaned on Euan for support. She wasn't accustomed to being the focus of so many eyes. Euan, sensing her discomfort, leaned in slightly and gave her a reassuring smile that seemed to say, 'I got you.' They navigated through the crowd, finding a corner where the energy was less intense.

'Here, you take a seat while I make my rounds and get you a drink.' Euan manoeuvred her to one of the few free chairs. 'I'll be back soon. Relax and enjoy the spectacle.'

April sat down and observed. Spectacle was the correct word. On the dance floor in the middle, an enthusiastic crowd churned and moved in various patterns and shapes. Sometimes in pairs, sometimes in groups. There was a lot of spinning and clapping and laughing. It reminded April of a line dance, only a good deal more turbulent.

At the tables laden with cakes and savouries along the walls, people were chatting and laughing, enjoying themselves and each other. She spotted Morag, Allan, and their three kids. As April watched the dancers twirling around the room, envy filled her. They all looked so happy, comfortable. At home. She wished she could at least try to dance, but the ache in her swollen ankle made it impossible.

Probably best. You'd make a fool of yourself anyway.

Yeah, her self-esteem had seen better days. She couldn't remember them, but they must have happened.

The sight of Euan sashaying around the hall with his

sunny smile, sent April's heart into a soft, rhythmic swirl. Every woman, from nine to ninety, seemed to pass through his grasp, bathing in the glow of his charm – including a group of elderly ladies whom he attended to with drinks, smiles, and kisses on their cheeks. April sniggered. It was so obvious that they were all drawn to him.

Not because he was handsome, which he was.

But because he was genuinely kind. That was what was so confounding about him. A guy with his looks could've been an absolute jerk and still got his itch scratched by a different person every night. But that wasn't him. He had a good heart. And he cared for his community.

Even though they seemed to enjoy gossiping about him. April didn't understand a word of Gaelic, but she could interpret the faces and pointing fingers of the people around her and responded with a brief, stern stare that said, 'I see what you're doing. Not okay.'

Oh dear. Protective much?

Euan occupied a bigger chunk of her thoughts than he should. Part of her was grateful for the distraction. But another part screamed bloody murder. She wasn't the girl guys like that went for. Dick was the only one who'd ever picked her. Sadly, he had also been the wrong one.

April's mind drifted to her parents' loveless marriage and their little fake family in which nobody cared for one another. Gary and Nora Smith had been married for over three decades. When they weren't making each other miserable, they tried their best to avoid the other. God knew how they managed to produce four children. No, security and stability didn't guarantee happiness. With Dick, April had tried to create a stable relationship, sacrificing passion for security. But it left her empty and unfulfilled. Now, she craved the opposite. Big time.

April sighed. She wanted to find out if she could have satisfying sex without a relationship. Maybe it was her thing, maybe it wasn't. How could she know if she never tried?

She shouldn't have let her thoughts wander in this direction. Her breath hitched as the hot pressure of arousal pooled between her legs and she shifted in the seat. It was painfully clear. Every molecule of her was yearning for a monumental shag.

But Euan didn't see her that way. And she would rather pull out her toenails with rusty pliers than disgrace herself again.

Maybe some people could never have it all – the loving, stable relationship plus the earth-shattering sex. *Maybe I'm one of those people.*

Euan was just being friendly, humouring his sister's runaway bride guest. Probably all part of the full tourist package.

Speaking of packages… April was hot and cold at the memory of what had shown in his tight black briefs the other morning. If it looked like that when it was…how might look when it was…

For feck's sake, April Virginia Smith, take a cold shower!

Suddenly, and to her relief, her thoughts were interrupted by rumbling laughter that permeated the room in tidal sound waves.

Scottish Santa?

There he was. Angus, the guy from the airport, next to a lovely woman with beautiful long, grey hair. The one with the red Corsa. Lorna was it?

In that instant, Euan dropped into the chair next to her and handed her a paper cup. 'Here, got you a cider.' He followed her gaze. 'Ah, have you met Angus?'

'He was the one who gave me Morag's address at the airport. Super nice guy.'

'True. He owns the surf school, his wife Lorna owns the pub. So together, they own me.' Euan laughed.

April liked the sound of it, warm and deep and a little dirty. As she took a sip of the cider, she couldn't shake a tinge of disappointment that he wasn't into her. He would have made a glorious first one-night stand. She was sure of it. Too bad. Too fricking bad.

Euan's heart leaped as he caught sight of an old friend. Duncan and he had grown up together; they used to play fitbaw, running about in the hills, talking shite. He hadn't seen Duncan in years, not since he had moved to Edinburgh for a job. Euan turned to April. 'Would you excuse me for a moment? Just spotted an old friend. Haven't talked to him in ages. Be right back.'

April's lips curved into a smile. 'Sure. Off you go!'

Euan made his way through the crowd until he stood before Duncan, giving him a tight hug. Duncan responded with three loud, hearty slaps on Euan's back.

'Awright mate?'

'Aye, now that the prodigal son's returned! What's brought you home, ya bawbag?' Euan asked.

'Just checkin' on our old house. Been too long after Pop's funeral in February. Might flip it and rent it out as a holiday let. Need the extra pennies. Edinburgh is expensive. And you, ya numpty? Still the isle's heartbreaker?'

'I never break any hearts, you know the rule,' Euan replied, feeling a slight sting at Duncan's jibe.

'Just taking the pish, man. I envy you, pretty boy. Always have, to be honest.' Duncan grinned.

While they caught up with each other's lives, Euan's head kept turning back to April. Gaze distant, she sat alone in the corner.

Until she didn't.

While Duncan told him about his job, Euan watched this

guy sliding into the seat next to April, starting to talk to her. He knew Rory, of course he did. Everybody knew everyone in Saorsa. Rory was two years older and had gone to school with him. He'd left to study in London, had come back all business-like, and opened a 'glamping' site on his father's land. Always rambling about investment and opportunities.

Pompous prick in his fucking tweed jacket.

Euan cleared his throat, no longer able to pay attention to Duncan's tales of dates and bars and whatnot in the capital. He tried, but his focus kept veering off course, landing on April. Now Rory leaned towards her and whispered something in her ear. Her head tipped back, and she laughed. Euan felt a weird clench in his gut, a reflex he didn't expect. He looked away, gripping his pint too tightly. He chatted along with Duncan, but his laugh sounded hollow even to his own ears. Euan's gaze, traitorous, snapped back to April, catching her smiling at Rory. Easy and bright. He shifted from one foot to the other, the glass cold and slippery in his hand.

He told himself it was nothing. Just an odd moment. He was used to enjoying the company of women, the kick of the chase, the excitement of the moment. Not being racked by searing, acrid edginess. *Maybe it's the novelty of her*, Euan reasoned with himself.

He was unable to peel his eyes away from April. There was a sharp tug on his solar plexus every time she smiled. And not with him.

Man, that's not you. You barely know her.

That was the thing, though.

He *wanted* to know her better. A lot better. And not only the sounds that she would make in bed or how deep and fast he had to go to make her scream his name. He wanted to know what made her laugh out loud like that. Her favourite ice cream. What she sang in the shower. Which books made her cry and how she liked her coffee in the morning. Every morning.

Fuck.

That was a problem.

This American had snuck up on him, and he couldn't have that.

As he stole another glance at April and Rory, Euan knew this could only go in one direction.

Nowhere.

Because of Morag's bet, yes. He needed a new engine. But also because April would leave. Sooner rather than later. This wasn't her life. It was his. She would go back to Kansas City and he'd remain here. He hadn't built a life of safe connections and contained pleasure only to get attached and discarded. Deeper connections only lead to pain. For everyone involved. Promises would be broken, hearts would be shattered, tears would be shed.

You're not the lovey-dovey relationship kind and you know it.

No, whatever was in the process of beginning – it had to stop.

And April deserved to enjoy herself, especially after everything she'd been through recently.

When he looked again, Rory was gone and April alone on her chair.

With a determined sip, Euan downed the rest of his beer, gave Duncan one last loud and loving slap on the back, and made his way back to the corner of the room to rip off the plaster.

Chapter Twelve

'Hey,' Euan said, slipping into the chair next to April with guarded ease. He caught a glimpse of his watch, using it as an excuse. 'It's getting late. I should head back.'

'Already?' April's face reflected a touch of let-down. 'But it's still in full swing! Don't tell me you're getting tired. I haven't even seen you dance, not once.'

He shook his head. 'Early start for me. Full surf calendar tomorrow. And I'm not much of a dancer.'

'Stay a bit longer? Half an hour? I'm enjoying myself, if you believe it. Even without participating.'

'Aye. I saw that.' He plastered on a smile. 'Sorry. Duty calls my name in five languages.' Euan crossed his legs. 'Besides, I had my fair share of chat for the night. I'm all talked out.'

April squinted her eyes and seemed confused. He would be, too.

'About getting back to the B&B… I don't want to be a burden, but my foot…' She gave an exasperated gesture to her injured leg. 'Not sure how I'll get home without my carriage.'

'Why don't you ask Rory?'

Ouch. That came out spiteful. Her reaction was immediate, surprise and a touch of hurt crossing her features. Resentment welled up in him. He wasn't sure what or who he resented – Rory, April, the situation, or himself for being that way. It wasn't like him at all. He quickly collected himself. 'What I mean is that there will be someone here who can get you back.'

She nodded, but her smile couldn't hide the uncertainty in her eyes. 'Are you sure? I don't want to impose on anyone. I don't know them like you do.'

'You know Morag, right? And trust me on this one: we islanders might seem peculiar, but helping each other? Second nature. I'll make sure you get back to Morag's.'

After all, it wasn't her fault he had to keep his distance. She didn't know it, but it was ultimately for her own good. Euan went over to his sister and Allan, and the matter was settled in a minute.

'They'll take you home in their car whenever you're ready to leave,' he said as he stood in front of her again, Morag and Allan waving in the background. 'It takes two minutes. No trouble at all.'

'Thanks, Hugh-Anne. Much appreciated. You're a good caretaker. Now, go on, Mister Responsible, and get your beauty sleep. I mean…not that you need it.' Pink climbed up her face as she gave him a shy smile that made him feel as if he were standing on a shifting dune. Nobody had ever called him a good caretaker. What the hell did this woman see in him?

It was a near thing, though, almost had him wanting to stay, to be the one taking her home. He brushed it off with an insouciant wave. 'Night, May.'

Euan turned away, wondering why he felt like he was leaving something important behind.

❀

The sky was a smudge of graphite, smeared across the horizon. April sat on the beach in front of the bed and breakfast, head on her knees, fingers brushing against the stones beneath her. She was lost in the coarse beauty of the Hebridean landscape that expanded before her. It wasn't mild, gentle, or sweet. Little here was soft. It was lead-grey and harsh. The air smelled of salt and seaweed and wet stone. This island ruffled the hair and the heart. Today, the ocean was rustling impatiently, as if it had something important to say. It matched the floating restlessness inside April.

Is this how it feels to be on your own for the first time?

Moisture hung heavy in the atmosphere, and the wind picked up. April wasn't cold, thanks to Euan's sweater. Her ankle was healing nicely, too, no more piggyback rides necessary. She hadn't seen him in two days. Not even for breakfast. In his absence, April realised how accustomed she'd grown to his cheeky grin, the banter they shared, and the way his eyes lit up with a story or a teasing comment. *What has he been up to?* she wondered, curiosity tinged with concern. She probably could have gone to the pub to check on him. But she didn't want to come across as clingy or, worse, like a weird stalker who couldn't take a hint. Only ever having been with one guy meant she hadn't learned how to navigate these murky men waters.

April had spent her past two days on the beach thinking, chatting with Morag, reading, sleeping, healing. And sitting at the desk in her room gnawing on a pen, trying to write her thoughts down. They were like ash in her head.

She tore her glance away from the mesmerising sea and stood up, brushed the sand off, and meandered back along the short, narrow path to the B&B, barely limping anymore.

The aroma of tea filled the breakfast room, mingling with the sea breeze drifting through the open window. Morag was leaning against the wooden counter, hands wrapped around a steaming mug.

'Can I use your laptop for a minute?' April asked. 'I have to check my bank account.'

'Sure. On you go, hen.'

April opened Morag's computer. But before logging into her bank account, she made a minor detour and opened Instagram. It was too tempting. The first dip of the toe into the acid bath that was her old life. She checked Dick's account.

And almost dropped her biscuit.

There was a new photo of Dick, posted yesterday. But he wasn't alone on it. It was the sweaty faces of him and his colleague Sheryl, both in fitness gear, slurping what looked like protein shakes. The caption read, 'CrossFit Buddies Crushing It! #WorkoutGoals #FitLife #StartingOver'.

Starting over all right. Since when did Dick do CrossFit? Or drink protein shakes? He hit the gym occasionally. But most of his rare spare time was either spent golfing or in his 'man cave', gaming or whatever he did down there. The picture left April with a strange blend of emotions. Relief, because he seemed okay. But also consternation. Sheryl? They'd known each other since kindergarten and had reconnected when Sheryl began working for Dick's dad a year ago. She was the carbon copy of Lauren, Dick's mom, down to the twinset and pearls she wore. Except during CrossFit, naturally.

April would rather shave her head with a blunt flint stone than wear pearls and twinsets.

She startled when Morag put her hand on her shoulder. 'Darlin', I got some news that you're not going to like,' she said. 'It's a shame, but you have to move out of the studio tomorrow. We've got new guests coming, the McCarrons from the mainland. And with the Taigh nan Sgeulachdan Literature and Culture festival happening, the other rooms are fully booked for the next three nights. I wanted to tell you earlier, but I wasn't sure they'd really show up. They're sailing round the Hebrides and apparently, she gets seasick.' Morag shook her head. 'I'm so sorry, love. However, I can offer you a two-day break after that.'

'Oh. Okay.' April's belly flopped at the thought of being without a place to stay. She didn't want to go back to be pelted with rotten eggs or tarred and feathered. Not yet. She wasn't ready.

'I already asked around on your behalf – I hope you don't mind – but everywhere's full. Tis the season.' Morag's usually sunny face showed a shadow of contrition.

'Shit. I can't go back yet. Where am I gonna sleep?' April asked, more herself than anyone else.

Morag blew breath into her hot tea. 'Well…you *could* ask Euan if he'll let you sleep in his van,' she said in a casual tone, 'It's old and musty. But it has walls, and it's an option. He could park it here and you could use our bathrooms. He often does that anyway.'

April sat at the wooden table, her fingers tapping nervously on its surface. 'I'm not sure. I don't think that's a good idea.'

'Why not? I'm sure he'd be happy to help. Like with his jumper,' Morag said. 'I see you're still wearing it.'

April contemplated her suggestion. Being in close confinement with Euan, in his – what had Morag called it? – 'shag mobile' was a very, very bad idea. Rationally speaking.

Her sex, on the other hand, was strongly in favour. Judging by the treacherous tingle between her thighs at the thought of it.

Shush, vag. I'm in charge. Not you.

Was she seriously having internal vagina dialogues right now?

April gave a small cough. 'Is there anywhere else? A couch, a shed? Anything?'

An inexplicable trace of disillusionment seemed to scamper across Morag's face. 'If you don't mind the hassle, you could use our family tent. It's sturdy enough and I'll give you the air mattress and all the gear.'

Memories of camping trips with her dad and three brothers invaded her mind. Often enough, April's father wanted to get away from his wife by any means necessary. And they only took April with them so her mom could be alone, to do God knows what with the Devil knows who. The boys and her dad went fishing, made fire, and mostly ignored her. April spent those weekends with a book in the tent. She could do that again for three nights. After all, she was a free and independent woman on an isle where people didn't even lock their doors. What could possibly go wrong?

'A tent it is then,' April said, conjuring up a smile. 'Thank you, Morag. I appreciate you helping me out.'

'Of course, nae bother! Do you want a cinnamon bun?'

April clicked her tongue. 'Has anyone ever said no to a cinnamon bun?'

'Not if they're sane.'

They both laughed. April liked Morag's warmheartedness. Although, and that much was clear, she also had a good head for business and a strong will. As well as a great sense of humour. *An all-around cool Scottish gal.*

'Morag, can I ask you something?' April began, nibbling on her pastry.

'Shoot.'

'Is it always this beautiful here? The island, I mean.' April glanced out the window at the wildflowers nodding in the gust, their purple and yellow vivid against the backdrop of rock-shaped clouds.

Morag's face brightened. 'Ah, well, Saorsa can be a moody beauty at times. And I'm not gonnae lie to you, winter is grim. You only know island life once you've survived a full winter here,' she admitted. 'But when she shows her true colours, there's no place more enchanting. I feel blessed that this is our home.'

April let out a sigh. 'Do you think it's possible to fall in love with a place?'

'Aye, it is. And Saorsa is good at that. People fall for her all the time.'

'Like they do for Euan?' April asked before she could stop the words tumbling out. *Where the heck did that come from?*

'Aye, he's been a wee charmer since he was a toddler.' Morag's expression softened. 'I was ten and a half when he was born and I adored him. So did everybody else. Ha, you should have seen the old ladies whenever they got near him. Such a fuss!' A brief smile shone on her face. 'He was so incredibly cute, always happy. My youngest, Kieran, takes after his uncle in that regard.'

Her eyes glossed over. 'But our parents…they weren't happy. Not on this isle, not together. It's a long, complicated, painful story. They tried, but they got a divorce and moved away to start over. Both of them. Neither wanted to take Euan out of his school, away from his friends. So,' she absently brushed a strand of hair behind her ear, 'they left him with me. I just got back from uni. He was thirteen, and I was barely twenty-four. I basically raised the bugger,' she said, her fingers tracing circles on the edge of the table. 'It was hard, you know? I could see he was in pain. But he didn't talk to me. He sorted it all out with himself. And he still barely speaks to our parents. I guess some wounds never heal. But he's alright, don't worry. Euan loves this island. And us.'

April put her hand on Morag's. 'I'm so, so sorry. That was an unfair burden on you. Parents can really stink sometimes.'

'They do. But he's my wee brother, you know? I'd do anything for him. Absolutely anything to see him happy.'

April's heart contracted sharply at Morag's protective words. There was so much love here. She had no idea such a thing was possible between siblings. Since adulthood, April and her three brothers were like strangers, friendly indifference mostly.

'Mummy, Mummy! Look what we found!' Little Isla and the two boys burst into the kitchen like a pack of puppies, demanding Morag's immediate attention.

With a smile, she observed how Morag's focus shifted seamlessly from the conversation to her young ones. April longed for the kind of bond between Morag, her family, and Euan; a connection built on unwavering support and unconditional love. Her mind whirled with the newfound knowledge about Euan's past. The layers of his personality were starting to make more sense, and she felt a rush of empathy for him. Being left by your parents was even worse than being ignored by them. Shitty childhoods, they definitely had that in common. It wasn't just sympathy, it was kinship. And that only deepened this irritating pull she kept feeling towards him.

An unhealthy pull. Because at this point in her life, April didn't need someone who wasn't able to feel or express his emotions. In truth, she didn't know what she needed at all. But certainly not that. Right?

Chapter Thirteen

'Last call, folks!' Euan announced as he wiped a wet cloth over the countertop and ran it along the edges to gather any leftover beer puddles. His tired eyes shifted around the pub's diminishing crowd, watching as his patrons downed their drinks.

The past two days had been full of activity. Catching up with Duncan, teaching surf lessons, and tending to his job at the pub. Yet amidst it all, he'd carved out time for writing, a passion that had taken a backseat recently. Even so, he couldn't shake off a certain unease. It kept returning, like a tenacious fly.

'Alright, alright,' slurred a red-faced man near the door, lurching on his feet with some difficulty. 'A'm goin', nighty-night.'

'Night. Take care, Calum,' Euan said, nodding as the man stumbled out into the cool night air. Matt was putting up chairs and stools.

Under the soft amber glow of the pub's lights, Euan poured one drink for himself, his fingers idly playing with the rim of the glass. He had the nagging feeling that something was missing. His routine was hollow, like a worn-out song that had lost its charm. A hole that refused to be filled.

His head turned to the left. Two women were still here, sitting at a table, smiling at him. A redhead and a brunette, the only two people left. He knew what it meant. Of course he did. Euan grabbed a bottle of gin from one of the shelves behind the bar, along with two extra glasses, and made his way over.

Duty called. Twice.

When he lay sprawled on the mattress of his camper two hours later, sleep didn't want to come.

Strangely, the same was true for Euan.

For the first time since he cared to remember, he had said no to the rare opportunity of a threesome. He had gone home alone, even though they'd made their interest blatantly clear.

Problem was that his interest was anything but.

The usual rush had vanished. The thrill of the chase, the anticipation of connection, the triumph, the fun…it had all faded. Tossing from one side to another, Euan tried to get to grips with his sudden lack of interest in the game he'd played for so long. Whatever the reason – his mojo had handed in its notice.

It's not just physical anymore, is it?

Euan tried to recapture and revel in past pleasures. But there were only faint memories. Staring at the ceiling of his van, his thoughts wandered through a maze of faceless encounters. He had liked to think that he gave them nice memories of their vacation here. But what if, in truth, they forgot about him as quickly and thoroughly as he forgot about them?

His mouth was parched, and he hit his elbow as he reached for the water bottle. 'Dammit,' he cursed and punched his pillow, irritation mounting as he tried to grasp the images of past lovers. The wind outside was laughing at him, mocking his sudden loss of self-assuredness. For so long, he had prided himself on his ability to charm and seduce, to give and take. To have the best of both worlds, the pleasure without the pain. But now, he felt like a sailor adrift at sea in a starless night, unsure which way was home. Waiting for the swell that never came.

Why does everything feel like a void now?

Euan wondered if this emptiness had always been there, provisionally patched by fleeting connections. Instead of the moans he had elicited from a never-ending string of delightful women, all he could remember clear as day was April's fucking heart-melting smile, her infectious laugh, and those huge, green selkie eyes. And all he wanted to imagine was the taste of her lips, the swell of her ass in his hands, her legs wound around him. Her head on his chest.

Great. Now you're waking up? Wee arsehole, he thought as his traitorous dick pressed against his briefs. The prospect of a hot threesome couldn't get him going, but the notion of April's buccaneer giggle could?

There was a deep, gnawing ache that echoed in the hollows of his soul. Euan chastised himself for being such a sentimental fool. Something was seriously off. She'd somehow crept under his skin, in a way he couldn't make sense of.

When he fell asleep, it was in the uncomfortable notion of clinging onto a piece of driftwood in the middle of the roaring sea.

The clank of metal against metal punctured the silence of the landscape and echoed off the cliffs under the midday sun. April's muscles tightened with each swing as she hammered the tent stakes into the ground. It had been a while since she had last done that. Seventeen years?

She paused and surveyed her surroundings. This valley was paradise. Which was likely the reason it was so aptly named Paradise Valley. Green hills surrounded her on three sites, their slopes covered in carpet-thick grass, broken up by grey rocks, and sprinkled with millions of white daisies. A few sheep grazed on the hillsides under the wispy grey clouds. In front of her, the vast expanse of the Hebridean sea, where waves rolled in and broke against the rocks with rhythmic hisses. The brisk wind whipped through her hair as it blew off the nearby crags. Here, the elements conspired to create something spectacular.

It was April's first time camping alone, in the middle of nowhere, with nothing but the sounds of nature to keep her company. This wasn't what she had imagined.

But then again, nothing was.

Just over a week ago, she had imagined herself Mrs Williams by now, guzzling honeymoon margaritas in Mexico, sleeping in the only quiet cabaña among nocturnally randy newlyweds.

She wiped the sweat from her brow. Life was full of surprises.

April looked at her tent. Solid enough for a few nights. It wasn't too cold at the moment and Morag had given April all her equipment. She'd even driven and walked her here.

Yet April couldn't shake some mixed feelings about sleeping out here. On the one hand, this secluded valley was glorious. A Hebridean Eden. On the other, she had never been on her own for more than a day. Out here, she only had her thoughts to keep her company. Vulnerability flooded her, and she shivered. But she had to face her fears if she ever wanted to grow and expand her horizons. All part of the journey. And so she pushed the worries aside.

Tent's done. What now?

On the plus side, there was no one else to answer to or please. She smiled to herself as she stretched her arms, the muscles in her back loosening. April scurried towards the cliffs overlooking the ocean, her Chucks crunching on the sharp pebbles underfoot. And then stepping into a pile of sheep shit. Was to be expected, this was their turf. She cleaned her sole on the damp, thick grass. The wind picked up and brushed against her face. There was a lot to untangle and to work through. This right here, however, was freedom and peace.

She closed her eyes. It was as if her soul was expanding, weaving invisible tendrils into the land.

So quiet.

Until there was a noise in the distance. Stuttering and wheezing. The rattling and clanking of metal got louder.

She recognised that sound.

When she turned around, she spotted the sky-blue van with the white hard top as a tiny dot on the dirt road in the distance.

Her heart jumped.

What does Euan want here?

Quickly, April pulled out her scrunchie and combed her fingers through her hair. Then she returned to her tent and busied herself with tidying up the bags. It's not that she had been waiting for him. Not in her life, not today, not at all. He didn't want her, that was fine. Moving on now.

When Euan walked up to her, she saw concerned creases around his eyes and mouth. 'April, what the hell do you think you're doing out here?' he asked with a stern voice.

'Enjoying nature and solitude. Until thirty seconds ago,' she said, climbing out the tent. 'Why are *you* here?'

Euan scratched the back of his neck, looking like a model in an outdoor catalogue, with his windbreaker clinging to his strong shoulders. 'The weather's turning. There's going to be a rainstorm tonight.'

April let out a dismissive grunt. 'We have tornados in the Midwest. Like I can't cope with a little Scottish rain and wind.'

'You wouldn't weather one of those in a tent, would you now?' Euan shook his head. 'This isn't Oz. And not just a little Scottish rain, April. Heavy rain. Comes down in sheets. There could be landslides. Morag is mental to let you camp here. Told her as much. You have to come with me.'

April bristled at the suggestion. 'Thanks for your concern, but I'm not made of paper, Euan. I can handle myself.'

He stepped closer. 'I'm not saying you can't handle yourself, April. I know you can. Anyone who fearlessly breaks up a bar fight like a playground squabble can. But nature is unpredictable. Especially here. You won't stand a chance against that kind of force.'

April chewed on her lip, considering his words.

'And also… You can't sleep out here all alone,' he said with conviction. 'Out of the question.'

'Can't I? And why might that be?'

'Could be dangerous.'

She pulled her bottom lip through her teeth. 'I don't believe I'm gonna be torn to pieces by seals or birds.'

'No, but—'

'People here even don't lock their doors, Hugh-Anne. I'll be fine. Don't worry.'

Perhaps she wanted to assert her newfound independence. Or pay him back for rejecting her the other night. Whatever it was, she wouldn't let him or anyone tell her what to do. Not anymore. She was her own free woman. With her own tiny tent.

Euan stared at her with darkening eyes. 'Fine,' he hissed through gritted teeth. 'If you insist. But at least let me help you secure your tent properly.'

'I did that five minutes ago.' April stuffed her hands into

her pockets. 'But feel free. You're already here anyway and double-checking can't hurt.'

He examined each corner as if he were an archaeologist, searching for prehistoric artifacts. April watched him silently, arms wrapped around her body.

When he was satisfied enough, he stepped away from the tent and turned towards her. 'Right. I would give you my mobile number, so you could phone me if shit's going down. But you don't use your phone. Stupid, by the way.' Euan's voice crackled with annoyance.

'Just consider me off the grid. That's a thing nowadays.' She waved. 'Bye now, Hugh-Anne. And thanks for checking on me.'

'You're such a bloody idiot,' he grumbled in response and stomped off. Back to his van.

Chapter Fourteen

I t shouldn't have been as dark as it was.

Although April had spent little more than a week in Saorsa, she knew its rhythm. She loved the way the sun took its time to disappear, prolonging the twilight until past ten. But it wasn't even eight, and the sky looked like gunpowder.

That can't be good.

Then the first drops were drumming on the fabric of her tent. A menacing rumble of thunder echoed through the air. Within minutes, the skies opened. April cursed under her breath. Maybe she should have listened to Euan. The rain lashed at her tent and she burrowed into her sleeping bag. It seemed like God was angry-crying, unleashing her wrath into the world. April didn't mind the rain in general. But imagining spending the night in it made her hands jitter. She jerked as lightning lit the sky.

With a grating rustle, the zipper tore open. Euan poked into the tent and barked, 'You're coming with me. Don't even try. I'll throw you over my shoulder and carry you if I have to. I mean it.'

'Euan, what—'

'Now, April!'

She tumbled out of her sleeping bag, grabbed her suitcase, and latched onto his hand.

His strong, rough, warm hand.

And she saw her tent stood no chance against the torrent. It poured down from all hillsides, turning the valley into a soggy lump. April would have been sitting in a river within ten minutes.

They stumbled towards Euan's van at the entrance to the valley. Gripping his hand, April following him and his torch. It wasn't that she was scared of the rainstorm – although, to be fair, it assaulted them from all directions – but rather of what she craved more than anything in this moment: an anchor.

Him holding her.

The wrongest person for that job.

He opened the door of his van and helped April inside. She sighed in relief as she collapsed into the passenger seat, trying not to think about what would have happened if he hadn't showed up when he did.

Euan glowered at April as he plopped down beside her. 'Are you out of your goddamn mind, woman?' he bit out. 'I get that you're strong and independent. You don't need a saviour. Love that. Wouldn't dream of fighting you on that. But you sure as hell should've listened to a local!'

April's chin jutted into the air. 'Okay, yeah. I was wrong. And I'm sorry for being so childish.'

'You have no idea how fucking mad I am at you right now! Do you ever think before acting?'

She crossed her arms and made a face at him. 'Normally, yes. Most of the time. But recently…'

Euan's voice rose in exasperation. 'You could have got hurt. Or worse. I'm not keen on retrieving your body out of some gorge because you've got a point to prove!'

She nodded and the feeling of being caught prickled on her cheeks. He was right. She didn't know the land and the weather as he did. Euan relaxed slightly as understanding seemed to settle between them. Despite the storm blustering outside and even though he was cross with her, April felt protected with him.

'Wait. Why were you even here?' she asked. 'I thought you'd left.'

'Because I'm not an arsehole? You don't have a phone to call for help. And I wouldn't let you drown.'

Did she imagine a glint of tenderness in his eyes?

'So you waited here? For me?' April tried to make sure this wasn't all in her head.

Euan averted his gaze. 'Obviously.'

Waited for her. This beautiful, cool-ass, sexy surfer, who could have his pick of women, wanted to keep her safe.

Hold your horses, missy. The more likely scenario was that he was keeping tabs on his sister's guest. For insurance reasons or something.

The rataplan of the downpour on the roof of his camper was a soothing backdrop to the charged gravity that pulsed between them. The thought of April getting caught in a landslide strangled his windpipe. He couldn't have lived with himself if anything had happened to her. Morag was insane.

Euan cast a sideways glance at April, who was staring out of the rain-streaked window. Her fingers played nervously with the frayed edge of her soaked jumper.

Actually, *his* soaked jumper.

'Thank you.' She cleared her throat and broke the silence. 'Euan, about the other night…'

He took off his beanie and crunched it in his fist, not sure what to say.

'I don't blame you for saying no,' she continued, her eyes

closed. 'I was rash. It was just a moment of rebellion. And poor judgement.'

Euan furrowed his brow, curiosity piqued. 'Rebellion? Against what?'

April's lips curled into a self-deprecating smile. 'Against myself, I guess. I've always been so controlled. Predictable. And now…I wanted to try something new. Something spontaneous and daring.'

He was humbled that she opened up to him like that. Although he couldn't see why anyone would want to do that. If women opened anything to him, it was usually their legs. Which was his own doing, he never let them close enough to be comfortable with anything more. But this was better. He was here to listen to whatever April had to say. Or sing or rap for all he cared.

The way April clung to his jumper, as if it was a lifeline, tugged at a part of him he'd buried deep, beneath the layers of cynical armour and his casual hang-loose mentality. The beanie in his hand became a buoy to hold on to. There was a soft, strange stirring against his ribs – and he realised it was relief flowing through him, knowing she was okay.

Without thinking, Euan reached over and tucked a wet strand of April's hair behind her ear, fighting the urge to kiss those rebellious curls the rain had coaxed in her temples.

Little rebel.

The droplets that remained on her skin glistened in the faint light of the van.

'And what about me made you think I was the right choice for that spontaneity?' he asked.

April laughed softly, her shoulders relaxing. 'You are freedom personified. You live in your van, do whatever you like. I wanted to break out of my shell with you, have you take me along for the ride. Just for a night.'

Euan's thumb brushed gently against her cheek, tracing the path of a raindrop. By now, he was well aware there was a lot more to April than he'd thought when he first saw her walking through the pub door. How wrong he had been about her. Tame and sweet? Only on the outside. There was a depth and a perilous undercurrent beneath her kindness and cuteness. Untapped. He saw it burning in her eyes, felt it emanating from her skin. Vast and vibrating. So ready to be unleashed.

All he needed to do was to let his thumb glide over her lips, dip it softly into her mouth, whisper into her ear how beautiful she was, graze his tongue over her neck, and she would melt like butter in his arms. And only God Almighty knew why, but he was yearning to experience that.

'I see,' he said instead and moved his hand to the steering wheel, the other still holding his beanie. 'And here I thought you couldn't resist my charm.'

April's husky laughter filled the van, and Euan smiled in response. There she was, the wee pirate.

'That might have played a part,' she admitted. 'But it wasn't all.'

A deep sigh escaped her lips before she continued. 'To fully understand it, you need to know more about me.' She was kneading her fingers. 'Dick and I barely ever slept together. And when we did it was...not good. As if he wasn't really there with me. He never said anything to me. He didn't even make a sound, other than breathing. I mean, when we...' She inhaled slowly. 'Whenever I tried to talk about it, he pretended there was no problem. Like it was all in my head. We just weren't a good match in the sack, I suppose. And I think I do like sex.' She bit her lower lip, and he saw her pain and how difficult this was for her. 'It's dumb, but I thought you would be the perfect candidate to try things. I wanted my first one-night stand to be with you.' Her voice was almost drowned out by the hail and rain.

Euan took a sharp breath to suppress the surging storm of tenderness and this humbled feeling that constricted his chest.

It was laced with anger, though. He couldn't help but feel pathetically protective over her, this sweet and wild American girl who'd flown halfway across the world to hide from the ruins of her life, to find herself. Hell, he would have pulled her out of any flood with his bare hands without even blinking.

He reached out and entangled his fingers with hers. 'So to be clear: you only ever had sex with one guy and it wasn't good?'

'That's right.'

'So sorry to hear that, love. Not your fault. There's nothing wrong with a healthy sex drive. Did you come, ever?'

'Not with him, no.'

'Do you when you wank?'

'I do, yeah.' Her face glowed as she glanced at him.

She looked so sad and small. So goddamn fucking beautiful with flushed cheeks and trembling lips, breaking his heart with her every shuddering breath.

Whatever his resistance or reason, the last bit of it vaporised the instant she turned her head, faced him, and said with tears in those sea-deep eyes, 'I think something must be really, really wrong with me.'

That took the air right out of his lungs, and his heart imploded. He squeezed her hand, so tightly it almost hurt him. 'No, April. Hundred per cent no.'

'You're only saying that to make me feel better.'

Euan saw the years of hurt, rejection, and insecurity she'd been carrying, and he couldn't leave her with this belief. He couldn't let that stand.

Something snapped.

It didn't make any sense, but he felt drawn towards her like a moth to a flame and he was just about ready for the funeral pyre. He wanted her to know that. She needed to know that. Even though he couldn't explain it, even though he wouldn't act on it. For the bet and a million other reasons.

But if it would make her feel better, he was ready to let down his metaphorical trousers and tell her.

'The truth, April? I'm aching to have you. To taste you. Every night since you got here, I've been alone in this van. When all I can think of, all I fucking *crave,* is to be with you. No. *Inside* you. I want your goddamn nails on my back and your teeth in my neck, April. There's nothing, absolutely nothing, wrong with you. You hear me?'

He didn't expect it to come out so agonised. Maybe he hadn't been aware of the intensity of his longing for her. There was a charged pause, punctuated only by his panting.

And what did she do?

Grabbed his head with both hands, slipping them through the strands of his hair, pulled him in, and kissed him. Lightly at first, as if unsure of herself. Then harder, her tongue searching his mouth, teasing, exploring.

And God, oh God…she tasted like nothing and no one he'd ever tasted before. Sweet and sharp, like the last sip of a perfectly mixed drink, like sin. Instinctively, he leaned in to kiss her deeper. And when their tongues found their rhythm, she let out tiny mews of delight that ran through him like high voltage, raising every hair on his body. She sucked on his lower lip with a fervent hunger, and his heart wanted to jump out of his ribcage. He choked out a surrendering groan. Couldn't help it.

Bloody hell, he was in trouble. Deep as the sea. And he didn't have the faintest idea of how to find his way out.

How dare she?

She was taking his mouth like he was her birthright. Like she was born to do this, to draw out his soul, leaving nothing but a happy, empty shell. The sensation of her soft tongue sent currents from the top of his head into his belly, and his cock hardened so much he thought he might have been able to drive nails with it.

God and holy hell. He was being pulled into her current, never to get out again.

But then something stopped him.

This wasn't right.

She said she wanted the fleeting connection, the fire, the fucking.

Did she though?

And what did he want?

He didn't want her to use him for sex. Or vice versa.

With sheer superhuman power, he collected his last shreds of strength and broke free from her devouring, soul-smashing, cock-bursting, heart-shattering siren kiss.

'This is not how it's going down with us, April. Not here, not now.'

Chapter Fifteen

Aprl was ablaze, and nothing could ever douse her. Not the deluge of Hebridean rain outside, not all the water of the Earth's oceans. She burned so hot for his touch, it made her see little dancing points behind her eyes. And oh, those kisses! How he responded to her, as if he was tasting life for the first time.

Euan groaned and put his hand on the back of her head, pulling her against him, like a drowning man gasping for air. He tasted so masculine, like whisky and wind. The roughness of his scruff against her skin fuelled the flames inside her. She wanted to be scratched, to be marked by him. And do the same. His tongue ignited sparks that sent her blood boiling. It was addicting, the most amazing feeling in the world. And it wasn't enough. She needed more. *More*. Her core clenched at the mere thought of it. She was ready to let go of all inhibitions and embrace that feral thing coursing through her veins.

God. Oh God. It's happening.

'This is not how it's going down with us, April. Not here, not now.'

Wait. What?

A storm was raging in his eyes. 'This is killing me right now. But not like this.'

April stopped breathing at his words. Heat radiated from her skin, a gush of arousal that hadn't yet received the memo about the abrupt stop. 'Not like this? What do you mean?'

The hunger in his eyes belied his words. He was conflicted, torn between restraint and the raw need that mirrored her own. She reached up, tracing the line of his jaw, feeling the tension coiled in his muscles.

'Tell me, Euan.' April's voice held a plea and a challenge. 'Why not? Give me one good reason. One.' Her heart pummelled against her ribs, each beat echoing her longing.

He hesitated, a silent battle within him. 'April, it's not that I don't want you,' he said, tense with the effort of holding back, 'as you can tell. But this,' he motioned between them, 'it's not what *you* want. Not really. You deserve more than a quick rain-soaked shag with a random stranger who you'll never see again.'

'I'm so darn sick of people telling me what I should and shouldn't want,' she spat out, frustration boiling over.

'I get it.' His hand gently cupped her cheek, a tender contrast to the riot outside and inside herself. It felt like resting against a tree and snuggling into a favourite pillow at the same time. 'If this ever happens,' he leaned in, his breath warm against her skin, 'it should be right for you. But let's face it, it's probably best if it never does.' There was something in his voice, a hidden weight beneath the words.

'Excuse me if I'm the one who's a tad confused now.' April's anger flared at his change of heart. 'Didn't you just say you were dying to have me, like, less than three minutes ago? Something about nails and teeth?' She watched his expression closely as he struggled to explain himself.

'Aye, I did. And it's the truth. You're weird. Captivating. Yes, captivating, April. A goddamn mystery. Can't seem to stay away from you. Does it make sense? No. Still happening.

But you're gonna leave, at some point anyway. And then what, hm?' His hand dropped to the gear.

April raised one shoulder, feigning indifference, but inside she was burning with fever and dissatisfaction. 'Then nothing. You move on, I move on. A vacation fling thing. Has it ever bothered you?'

He faltered. 'Naw. Not really.'

'So it *is* me, then. I *am* the problem.' She couldn't shake the feeling that she wasn't what he was looking for. Not his typical conquest. Substandard. Not cool enough, not gorgeous, not interesting. Just a plain midwestern bundle of boredom. Human tumbleweed.

His eyes softened. 'No, love. You are most definitely not the problem.'

Liar, liar, pants on fire.

But if any pants were on fire in this van right now, it was hers. The pulsing resonated through her, aching for friction and release. *Dammit!*

The air between them was loaded, the windows as fogged-up as April's thoughts. Her mind boiled over with insecurities as she tried to decipher his intentions. So he wanted her, but he also didn't want her? Nothing about this added up.

While the intensity of the moment subsided, they both sat in silence, the rain and the wind outside a backdrop to their breathing.

Perhaps he'd only tried to give her a compliment, to make her feel better about her underwhelming, tear-jerkingly miserable sex CV. In an extremely confusing way. Or not. One thing was painfully clear, though. She shouldn't have sucked his face like a sailor on leave. Something was seriously broken with her impulse control recently. Especially when it came to Euan MacLeod.

What now? How do you go back from that kind of tide-stopping kiss?

Opening the van door and running away was not an

option. Not in that kind of downpour. She was stuck with him in his sex van for the time being.

Without the sex. Congratulations.

April fidgeted with the glove compartment latch, desperate for a distraction from the tension between them. On impulse, she lifted her hand – and with the tip of her index finger, she drew the outline of a penis on the steamed-up windscreen.

Then she crossed it out.

Euan tipped back his head and let out a deep laugh. The tenseness slid away like a chunk of hill in the rain. In response, he lifted his finger and drew a vulva.

'You forgot the clit, you amateur', April said and added the crucial point to his artwork.

Euan's smile lasted as he watched April's frisky retort. Something about her candidness, her master-blend of vulnerability and humour, struck a chord in him. He'd been with an abundance of fabulous women, but none had ever disarmed him like she did. He leaned back against his seat. 'You know,' he began, his voice more subdued, 'I might be good at drawing a laugh, but I've never been great at…this.'

April's finger paused on the foggy glass. 'This what? Painting genitals on van windows?'

Euan laughed, but he felt the weight of seriousness on the back of his tongue. 'Naw, not that. I mean, opening up. Talking about stuff. The messy bits.'

'What's stopping you?'

'I've been around for a while. Had some great times with some amazing people. But I've never met anyone like you. You're not someone I picked up at the bar, not a one-night stand.' He let out a short laugh. 'I don't know what the hell you are. But not that. And I don't know how to navigate this thing.'

What are you doing, ya eejit? Bad enough that you'd let that kiss happen. Now spilling your guts?

But April listened intently to his ramblings. 'Sometimes it's okay not to have all the answers,' she said. 'We're two imperfect humans trying to figure things out.'

'Come again, Yoda?'

'See? You're deflecting now.'

'Oh, like you with your penis painting?' Euan asked with faint ironic smile. 'No, you're right. Bad habit.' He exhaled audibly. 'Okay then, May,' he said to his own astonishment, the idea forming as he spoke. 'Let's go in the back of the van. To talk. It's gonna be a long, chilly night and we'll have to sleep at some point. Bit nicer back there than here.' He gestured at the steamed-up windows and the cramped front of the van. When he saw the frown on her face, he quickly added, 'We can stay on different sides.'

'Fear not,' she said with a grin. 'I'm not gonna jump you. Not a third time.'

Oh Lord. How the naughty part of him wished she did just that. And a fourth, and a fifth... The bet and the motor? Mere memories. Giving in to April, to this tightly packed fire-cracker of pent-up sexual energy, meant the real possibility of losing his prized van. How could he have forgotten the bet? It was as if she had scrambled his brain, rewiring his priorities.

As they moved to the back of the camper and took off their wet shoes, Euan set up a small, cosy space with cushions and a dim light.

'Is this a memory foam mattress?' April asked as she sat down and leaned against the wall.

'Course. I sleep in a van, but I'm not opposed to comfort.'

A corner of her mouth quirked up as she stretched her legs out. 'I bet it's been traumatised a thousand times over and unable to forget. Poor thing.'

That got a laugh out of him again. *Cheeky*. He wasn't used to this. Having conversations that delved deeper than surface-level banter and a laugh at the same time. This seemed like a dance to him, one with no set rhythm or steps. But he was dancing with a partner who was willing to lower their guard. It was a strange comfort. Bizarrely liberating *and* terrifying.

Euan sat on the opposite site, their legs touching. 'So, tell me about your life Kansas City,' he said, forcing a smile to mask his nervousness. This was usually the part where he brought up contraception and protection between moans and kisses. Where he asked for consent, boundaries, desires, and all the delicious sins that made the pulse race. *How hard? How fast? How deep?*

Astoundingly, his old routine didn't make his palms nearly as clammy as the simple, 'Tell me about yourself.'

Aye, I might actually be a bit fucked-up.

'About what, specifically?' she asked.

'You. Your life. Everything. I want to know more about you.' He meant it.

'All right, Hugh-Anne.' She looked at him through half-closed eyelids. 'My full name is April Virginia Smith, because my dad's from Richmond and I was supposed to be born in late April, but I dawdled until the first of May. Yeah, don't ask.' She let out an indignant scoff. 'Other than that? Born and raised in Kansas, Overland Park. Youngest of four children. Only girl, three brothers. English major. Fourth grade teacher. Star sign Taurus. Favourite dish spaghetti with meatballs. Favourite film *Mary Poppins*, the original.'

Euan grinned. 'Practically perfect in every way. That all?'

April nodded. 'Wait, no. I'm also afraid of horses, and I utterly despise Brussels sprouts.'

'You skipped the important stuff.'

There was an impish glimmer in her eyes there that made him smile.

'What's the important stuff in the world according to Euan MacLeod?'

'Like… Why did you agree to marry him?'

He saw her tense up, pulling her knees towards her chest.

'Phew. Okay. I've been asking myself the same question. Believe me.' She wrapped her arms around her knees. 'Not sure. There wasn't any reason *not* to get married. He was a solid choice. A straight-laced guy. We've been together since college. Dick was the only guy who was ever into me. He's handsome and nice. Funny, too. And I thought when the price of having a good man is having bad or no sex, then that's a price worth paying,' she explained. 'Perhaps the person who gives you security can't be the same person who gives you excitement. I thought maybe I can't have it all and Dick was good as it's gonna get for me.'

'Load of crap, May.'

'Yeah. I realised that when I saw him at the altar. Little late. But better late than never.' She nibbled on the nail of her thumb. 'I have a question for you, too.'

'Go on.'

'Why do you only have one-night stands? Don't you ever want to fall in love?'

Euan swallowed. 'Look, I'm a realist and I don't do relationships. Love is a complicated, fickle thing. Inevitably leads to disappointment.' His gaze flickered away for a moment before returning to April's. 'Take Eilidh – Lilly, to most. Sweet girl from round here. We were kids, really. Thought she was the be-all and end-all at seventeen. We moved to Glasgow together to study when we were nineteen. Bright-eyed and stupid.'

April watched him closely. 'What happened in Glasgow?'

'She found someone else. A guy "more aligned with her life's trajectory" or some bull like that. Left me with an empty bed and half the rent. Couldn't stand seeing them, so I came back.'

She leaned forward. 'That must've hurt a lot.'

'Kid's stuff.' He paused. 'Wasn't the first time someone decided to leave. My mother wore that path pretty well six years before Lilly.'

'Oh, Euan—'

'Naw, it's fine,' he interjected, waving off her concern with a flick of his hand. 'My maw loved her freedom more than she loved playing house. Who can blame her?'

She sighed. 'Still not okay.'

A corner of his mouth lifted in appreciation at her understanding. 'It's easier to keep things light. No risk, all the fun. People come, people go. So, aye, one night only it is,' he said. 'That's usually more than enough, though.'

'You are a bit full of yourself, you know?' Her husky pirate giggles filled his insides with warmth.

'Euan, you're more than a surfer with a retro van and a knack for pouring drinks. You care so much about this place and its history, your sister and family, the people here. You're not just some lame island fuck-boy.'

Her words hit closer to home than he cared to admit. 'Dunno. I'm not the kind of guy people stick around for. Good for a laugh, a drink, a fun night. That's okay. Simply the way it is,' he replied laconically, leaning forward with his elbows on his knees. 'I'm a Don Euan. What can I do?'

'Good God,' she said on a laugh, mirroring his cross-legged position. 'That physically hurts.' Her hand reached out, resting on his arm. 'But that's where you're wrong. You've got more to offer than you think. You're a writer, a poet, a storyteller. No. Don't contradict me. I listened to you.' She lifted one shoulder. 'And you're an all-round nice guy. Don't wince. I've seen you with your people. Cider for the old ladies? That's not a good-time-only guy move. And you carried me. Twice! Plus bringing me food and painkillers. All that gives you heaps of nice-guy brownie points in my book.'

Euan looked away, fingers digging into his thighs. Part of

him wanted to believe her, to see himself through her eyes. But years of keeping people at arm's length made it hard to accept that he might be more than a fun, fleeting moment. He quickly snuffed out that stupid spark of hope before it had the chance to turn into a bog fire.

But the smouldering wouldn't die down.

And somehow – during the following hours, to the sound-track of splattering rain – his rusty old shag mobile became an emotional safe space.

As April continued to talk, Euan listened, truly listened. Her words painted a picture of a life so different from his own. He found himself pulled in. Her laughter, her insights, her dreams…they all wove a tapestry that was uniquely April. She talked about her distant parents and her three rowdy brothers. About how much she loved teaching. Her fear of returning and her love for the Kansas City Chiefs.

'Football is just rugby for people with no health insur-ance,' he quipped, to which she responded by slamming a pillow onto his head.

He reciprocated by telling her things he'd never told anyone. Not even Morag. His fear of flying. Shared his pipe dream of opening Saorsa's first artisan gin distillery. Told her more about how his parents divorced and both moved away when he was thirteen.

'That wasn't right, you know? Hugely unfair on both you and Morag. I mean, a divorce is a divorce. Geez, I wish my parents would save themselves and others the misery and get one already. But a divorce doesn't relieve you from the responsibility of being a parent,' she said and snuggled up next to him, resting her head on his shoulder. He inhaled the sweet scent of her hair. 'It's not your fault, Euan. Your parents were selfish assholes. They really were. Would get along with mine, I suppose.'

He couldn't believe he was laying it all out there for her. But he had never felt so secure and at ease with someone.

April offered trust and support without judgement or expectations. She showed compassion when others saw his choices as reckless and nothing else. Part of him wanted to take it all back and stay guarded. But another part of him needed to know what could happen if… *Yeah, what if?*

Single raindrops dribbled onto the roof of his van in a steady rhythm, it was hypnotising. She was quivering. 'Are you cold, love?'

'Mhm,' she murmured with closed eyes.

'Right. Let's go to sleep, May. I'm tired, too. So much talking.'

'I like that you call me May,' she whispered, already half-asleep, as she curled up against him under two blankets. 'It's my birth month. You're smarter than my parents. And cuddlier, too.'

It was in this quiet little moment in the wee hours, when her breath came regularly against his body and the ferocious rain had stopped, that Euan felt like, maybe, he did have something to give after all.

Chapter Sixteen

He woke when a ray of sunrise warmed his face. Euan knew exactly where he was. With April. Memories of last night came back – hearts opening, walls dissolving.

Completely uncharted territory.

Her sweet vanilla and earthy cinnamon scent engulfed him. He lay there, still, savouring the warmth of her body curled against his. The rhythmic rise and fall of her chest gave him an odd sense of peace. Euan moved, his arm tightening around her instinctively. She stirred but didn't wake, nestling closer into his embrace. It surprised him how natural it felt.

His mind wandered to their conversation the night before. The way she had opened up to him, how he had found himself doing the same. This was new. As if on top of a towering wave, there was a rush of adrenaline tinged with a generous dose of fear. He reached out to brush a strand of hair from April's cheek. His stomach knotted with apprehension, longing, the urge to protect and shelter her, and something akin to hope. And he knew, with a certainty that rang in his heart, this was it – the perfect wave, the perfect moment.

What he hadn't known until now was how much he had been waiting for it.

His phone buzzed, breaking the spell. April roused and her eyelids fluttered open, adjusting to the morning light. She yawned so heartily that she granted him a revealing look at her tonsils.

'Oh, hi,' she murmured, her morning voice even huskier than usual. Her gaze drifted to the mobile in his hand. 'Everything okay?'

'Just Duncan,' Euan said, tucking the phone away. 'Mornin', by the way.'

She sat up and stretched her arms above her head with another stout-hearted yawn, showing her navel for a split second. That simple peek sent ripples through him. He wanted to tickle it with his tongue.

What have you become? A Victorian parish priest?

'Duncan's away again and wants me to check on the house.' As he said that, an idea formed. It was ideal. He would take her up to the cottage, make her comfortable. Maybe hang out with her for a while.

'How would you like to sleep in a proper bed again, maybe take a bath?' he asked.

'Seriously? Gosh, Euan! Yes, please!'

Anticipation, excitement, and joy sparkled in her eyes as she clapped her hands together like a seal its fins. If that's what she was like after she'd just woken up, he wouldn't mind having more of that.

'Thought so. But first – how do you like your coffee in the mornings?'

They drove up the winding ribbon of tarmac, through a swaying sea of grass. In the distance, single white cottages ducked between the contours of the land. Sheep grazed on the right side, pristine sands and sparkling turquoise waters to April's left. The smell of wet earth permeated the air. She smiled, ignoring the flurry of nerves. Every minute with Euan would complicate things. Yet she couldn't deny she wanted to explore all the layers of her freedom and this island with him. He was easy to be around, made her forget her problems and her past. It was part of his appeal, his vibe. The way he tapped on the steering wheel; the way he hummed along to a song playing in the cassette deck. 'Don't Wanna Be a Player' by Joe, as the tape sleeve said. Followed by 'Natural Woman' by Mary J. Blige and Shai's 'If I Ever Fall in Love'.

'Wait, "Mo's mix"?' April parted her lips in mock astonishment. 'I didn't take Morag for an R&B type of gal.'

'Oh, aye. Or did you think that we only play fiddles around the peat fire?

'Ha, ha. Course not. I've never even touched a banjo myself.'

He gave her a sideway glance. 'What music *do* you like?'

'All over the place. When I was a teen, mostly Beyoncé and Britney. Then Damien Rice, Neko Case. But as long as it makes me feel something and tells a story, I like it.'

'So you contain multitudes. Love that in a girl.'

Love? As if. April had just made her peace with not having a one-night stand with Euan. He wasn't any less sex on legs, but last night's talk had shown her a different side of him. Vulnerable and soft, lonely, and a bit broken. He'd had shiploads of lovers, sure. But friends? She wasn't so certain about that. Except maybe Duncan, who didn't even live on the island. Euan needed a friend more than a lover, and she was happy to be that friend. Half of what she wanted was better than nothing. A different half that the one she'd aimed for, but still.

'Don't you have anywhere to be today, surf school or pub or something?' she asked.

'Naw, Monday is my Sunday. The only day when the surf school and the pub are closed. But it's too muddy anyway because of yesterday's rainstorm. Which reminds me… We have to tell Morag about the tent.'

April knitted her eyebrows together. 'Uh-oh. She's not going to be happy. Do you think there's anything left of it?'

'Unlikely.' He shook his head. 'Don't worry. That thing was old. And it wasn't your fault. You're not the Cailleach, you don't command the weather. Mo shouldn't have let you camp there in the first place. I'll phone her.'

'Thank you.' He made her feel so at ease, it was ridiculous. She closed her eyes and held her hand out the window, the air streaming through her fingers like velvet ribbons. It could have been idyllic, if it weren't for the incessant rumbling, banging, and sputtering of his camper's motor.

'This thing is clearly on its death bed. Why are you holding on to it?' she asked.

'My freedom, I guess. With my Bulli, I'm independent. Can go and sleep wherever I want.'

'Or with whoever,' she teased. As soon as the words left her mouth, a surprising twinge pinched at her heart. *None of your business.* She masked it with a brisk laugh that came out as a snort. But the words lingered in the air.

Euan sounded glum. 'Um…I guess. If you put it that way.'

While she was fumbling her Chapstick out of her hand-bag, he slammed on the brakes, and they came to an abrupt stop. 'Fucking sheep!'

April burst out laughing as she looked outside and saw a herd of sheep casually crossing their way as if they'd have all the time in the world.

He threw his hands up in defeat. 'Those wee fuckers rule this isle. I don't think I'll ever get used to it.'

'I thought you'd know each of them by name.' April gathered up the contents of her handbag that lay scattered in the van's footwell. Her wallet was nowhere to be seen. Must have slipped under the front seat. 'Do you think sheep count humans when they try to fall asleep?' she asked and leaned forward, stretching her arm out as far as possible to reach deeper under where she sat.

He laughed. 'Sure. If that's what it takes to get a good night's *sheep*.'

She grinned and her hand touched something soft. When she pulled it out, it wasn't her wallet, and her grin disappeared.

It was a woman's panties.

'Oh,' was all she could say. When she turned and faced him, crimson was rising up his neck.

'I don't know how or who—'

'No, I shouldn't have… It's okay. Really,' she hastened to say and with two fingers put the thing next to the gearshift.

But was it?

Simple black cotton, not a slinky, kinky accessory. Rather mundane. Personal. It would have been easier if she had found a fancy red ouvert porn-star slip encrusted with sequins and crystals. This here was the everyday item of a real person. A regular woman. One of Euan's one-night stands. One of many. God knew what else lurked under those seats. This van had a lot of history. And so had he.

'I'm sorry, May.' He tried a crooked smile. 'That's just *a thong* of the past.'

She twisted her face into a smile at his joke. There was no reason to be mad at him. They were just friends. Or beginning to be friends. She didn't want to ruin it by being judgemental. Which she categorically wasn't.

When the sheep had passed and they drove on, Euan suggested April could stay at Duncan's place for the rest of her time in Saorsa. 'The tent's a lost cause. You can crash at the cottage. I'm sure Duncan's fine with it, was his grandda's house. I'll ask him.' Euan briefly turned his head to face her and added, 'Does it bother you?'

'What? The lost tent?'

'Naw. That I'm…promiscuous?' A subtle twitch of his eye

was the only clue that something else was going on inside his head, more than he let on.

April sat there, absentmindedly picking under her nails with distracted precision. 'You're experienced, that's not a bad thing. And it's your personal business. No man-slut shaming from me. All good.'

Then why did her guts still burn, as if somebody had poured a pint of acid into her throat?

'Let's go to that literature festival today,' April suggested as she came out of the shower at Duncan's cottage. Already dressed in jeans and t-shirt because she didn't want to fan the sweltering flames.

She also didn't want part ways yet. She wanted to spend time with him.

'Seriously?' Euan narrowed his eyes. He looked like a schoolboy asked to do something for extra credit. That – and insanely attractive and sexy. April wasn't sure she could ever stop marvelling at his defined jawline, peppered with his honey-coloured bristle.

'Yeah, why not?'

'It's not that exciting. Few stalls, some readings, bit of live music, food, yada yada.'

'That's the most exciting thing that's happened since I got here!' April sniggered and slipped into his sweater.

'Is it, aye?' He eyed her up and down. 'I should charge you rent for that thing, considering you're basically living in it.'

She had to laugh so loudly that it startled her. Probably because she hadn't heard herself like that in a decade.

Mere minutes later, they'd climbed into his van. The light of the morning sun was dwindling, giving way to a grey blanket of clouds that hung in the sky like a heavy curtain. *A small island in the Atlantic is like a big ship*, April thought, *always exposed to the fickle weather*.

When Euan parked the van next to the village hall, he turned towards her and asked, 'Ready for Saorsa's cultural highlight of overpriced food, musty books, and pretentious poets?'

'Don't make it sound too tempting,' she gibed as she climbed out the van. 'Why don't you read your stuff here? You're a writer.'

'I'm not ready to share it yet. Maybe never.'

The grass was slick underfoot and April was careful to watch her steps. 'Maybe in the future?'

Euan grunted. 'What future? This is Saorsa. Nothing ever changes. Tomorrow is like today is like yesterday.'

A heavy mist hung in the air as festival-goers wandered the grounds, programmes in hand. 'Not true', April countered. 'Two weeks ago I wasn't here. Now I am. So there's that.'

He gave a jovial laugh. 'Good point. What about your future? Have you thought about it?' There was a hint of tension in his tone, like ice that was about to crack.

'Not yet. But I will soon. No idea what it's going to look like, but I have to return to KC to clean up my mess.' Her throat constricted like a vice at the thought. 'Although I wish I could stay. This place is magical. Not just this isle. Its people, too. But I'm almost ready to face the music,' she continued. 'Even though it's going to sound like a high school band's debut death metal album.'

Euan nodded and said nothing.

Over the din of gentle sea in the distance, snippets of readings carried on the breeze as the hubbub around the village hall swelled parallel to the morning tide turning towards noon. April was surprised to see so many people gathered there. The island usually felt vast and empty. Now, locals and tourists browsed the pop-up stalls scattered across the field, perusing handcrafted items, artisan foods, and boxes of books beneath colourful canopies.

'Look, there's Morag and Allan,' Euan said.

Morag looked as content as a cat after gobbling up a bucket of cream. 'Didn't expect you here, brother. Haven't seen you in a while, now I think about it.' She hugged Euan, then turned to April with a bright smile. 'But you brought lovely company. How are you, April?'

'Dry and alive,' she said. 'I know Euan explained every-thing earlier, but I wanted to say it to your face: I'm so, so sorry about your tent. Of course, I'll pay for the loss.'

'Och, don't be daft, love. That thing was age old. And this will give Allan an excuse to splurge on new camping gear. Right, darlin'?'

Allan, nibbling on a sausage roll, nodded. 'Bout time, babe. It's been too long since I swept you away to our favourite remote bay.' Morag laughed. April noticed the spark between those two. They seemed genuinely content, enjoying each other's company. *Good for them.*

Morag linked arms with Allan. 'We're here for the story-teller's competition. It's important to keep Saorsa's oral stories and traditions alive,' she explained. 'Oh, before I forget,' Morag said in April's direction. 'As of this morning, the McCarrons are back on their boat. You can come back to the B&B.' She paused. 'That is, if you want to.'

But April didn't get the chance to say anything.

'We better get going. So much to see and hear. Stories and all that,' Euan said and pulled on her elbow.

'Isn't it nice of Euan to show you around and let you keep his favourite jumper?' Morag asked with saccharine sweetness.

'Bye, sister.'

'Bye, Morag!' April said as Euan tugged her away towards the tents on the green.

As she hooked her arm into his, April saw how women's –

and some men's – heads turned. *This is how it must be like to go to the mall with Liam Hemsworth.* It wasn't Euan's fault that he looked as absurdly attractive as he did. He was wearing blue jeans and a white shirt, tight enough to subtly draw the eye to his toned arms as he moved. He was the kind of guy songs were written about. Sad songs, mostly.

Just a friend, remember?

A ridiculously hot Scot as a friend who made her nipples pucker purely by looking at her. Could that seriously work? To distract herself, April browsed through some books at a second-hand stall. Reading had always been a part of her. She bought two classics: *Tropic of Cancer* by Henry Miller and Benoîte Groult's *Salt on Our Skin*.

When she turned around, Euan was chatting with a pretty woman with the most incredible hair. Flaming red curls cascaded down her shoulders. She touched his arm and smiled. They were too far away and the green too busy for April to hear a thing. But she saw the redhead's eyes lighting up like a Christmas tree. A bolt of envy shot through April and she instantly scolded herself.

Of course, he has several irons in the fire. He's Don Euan, remember?

True that he needed a friend more than a lover. And she still wanted to be that for him. But she also began to see that she might need both, the lover and the friend. That she might *want* both. But was that even an option for a girl like her?

'Hey! April, right?'

A voice broke through her consciousness, and she turned her head. It was the guy from the dance the other night.

'It's Rory,' he said, and his lips lifted in an easy grin. 'From the ceilidh?'

'Oh, yeah. Hi. Nice to meet you again. How are you?'

'Can't complain, thanks. But the more important questions is: how's your ankle?'

'Much better, thanks for asking.' April was on autopilot.

Her head darted back to Euan and the redhead, who subtly moved closer to him, tilting her head and exposing her neck. In response, Euan raked a hand through his hair, oozing oodles of irresistible, casual sexiness.

Rory followed her gaze. 'Aye, that's Euan in action. Our very own island gigolo. Some even call him "the tourist trap".' There was a hint of rancour in his tone. 'He's always been like this.' Rory barked a laugh. 'His dad was the same, according to my mum's stories. It's the magnetic MacLeod charm.'

'I obviously don't know anything about that,' April said sternly and put on her most serious teacher frown. 'And I'm not sure if *you* know anything about Euan. Because if you did, you'd know that he's a decent guy. And you wouldn't talk shit about him to his friends like an absolute ass.'

'You're friends? Interesting.' Rory tipped his index finger against the tip of his nose. 'Anyway, I didn't come here to talk about Euan. Would you like to have coffee sometime?'

'Huh?' April straightened her shoulders. 'What? No. I'm not sure how long I'm gonna be here.'

Rory pulled out his phone. 'That's all right. Just drop me a message and if it happens, it happens.'

'No. It won't happen,' she said and watched how Euan whispered something into that woman's ear to make her laugh. 'Have a nice day, Rory.'

'Okay. Well, then I guess I'll see you around,' he said with a sour face and walked away.

'Bye now.' April turned and moved on to the next stall. *He didn't seem like such an idiot the other night. But Jesus, no.*

She moved to Lorna's stall with a selection of local artisan honeys and had a little chat with her about bees. Beams of sunlight fought their way through the closing cloud cover. As April examined gorgeous earrings made from sea glass and shells at the stall next to Lorna's, she heard a low hiss at her ear.

His voice. She would have recognised it anywhere, anytime. The clouds had thickened to a drizzle, cooling her hot cheeks.

'Follow me behind the hall and meet me at the back. Three minutes.'

Chapter Seventeen

Wehn she turned around the corner of the village hall, away from the festival, Euan was leaning against the wall, hands in his pockets. April dithered. 'What's going on? You seemed busy five minutes ago.' She despised how she came across. But with him, she didn't have a filter.

'Come here. Please, April.' His voice made her heart send out a pulse through her body. She stepped towards him, as if drawn by a string.

He let out a sigh, relief maybe. 'That was a lass I met at the pub the other night. She and her friend want to schedule a surf lesson before they leave next week.'

'Cool,' was all April could say and sounded anything but.

'Let's not worry about other people,' he said in a ragged tone.

Her eyes locked onto Euan's – intense, desperate. His hand shot out, palm up, and she hesitated for a moment before slipping hers into his. 'What are you doing?' she asked as he pulled her close. Although that was a superfluous question if ever there was one.

His lips brushed over her ear. 'Letting you know what it's like to be wanted, desired,' he whispered. 'I'm here with you, aren't I? With *you*.' His voice was hoarse. 'April…' He broke off.

Her body was flush against his, and oh God, this closeness was her undoing.

Heat was radiating from him, and it was hellfire and heaven. His grip on her fingers was painfully tight, but it only increased the burning in her veins. She was convinced he could feel her heart pounding, screaming for him to take her. His other hand tenderly caressed her cheek, his thumb grazing over her lower lip.

'I love your lips. They're like little pillows. Haven't been thinking about anything else since yesterday,' he murmured. 'Can I kiss them? Your choice, always your choice.'

But it wasn't really a choice, was it? The wildness inside April threatened to overtake any semblance of control. Behind the An Talla, hidden from view and protected by a tall hedge of blackberry bushes, she gave in to her lust, let her eyelids fall, and gave a small nod.

Right then and there, Euan's lips crashed against hers like waves onto the shore.

Oh. My. God.

He consumed her, ravaging her tongue with his, and April's whole body responded by opening up to him, a flower to the sun. She couldn't stop the moan escaping into his mouth as he grabbed at her waist and pulled her closer still. With a sigh, she rose onto her tiptoes to melt into him. She felt his hardness pressing against her. Wrapping her arms around his neck, she lost herself in this kiss.

This floodgate-opening, ship-wrecking kiss.

His friend. Yeah, right.

His lips plundered down her neck. 'Don't go back, April.'

'Mhm?'

'Don't go back to Morag's. Stay with me at Duncan's tonight.'

Euan's expert hands – warm and a bit rough from all the

surfboard-holding and van-steering and pint-pouring –
slipped under her sweater and shirt and trailed the small of
her back, making her tremble like seagrass in the breeze.

'Why?' she gasped out between kisses, fingers tangled in
his hair. She needed something to hold on to or she would
lose her grip on reality. By now, the mist was turning into
droplets on her face, but she barely noticed. She was on fire.

Without warning, Euan grabbed her, flipped her around,
and lifted her up in one swift motion, pinning her against the
wall with his hips. 'Because I want you. Bad. I want you so
fucking bad, April. Can't you feel it?'

He gripped her ass tightly, pressing against her, and her
limbs liquefied. And yeah, she felt him through her jeans, so
hard, pushing right on her sensitive spot. *Oh, yes. God, yes.*

The rain came down now, soaking them both, and April
clutched onto him. He groaned into her skin, the vibration
enough to make her let out a whimper.

'I want to give you what you need, baby. Everything you
missed. Let me show you pleasure. I can make you come a
hundred times, a hundred ways.'

She quivered as his lips trailed down her jawline, nipping
at her neck. Instinctively, her legs wrapped around him.
April's body responded to his every skilled manoeuvre with
an unprecedented surge of heat and wetness.

Yes. Yes, I need this. Need him.

And he knew it.

His breath scorched her skin as he caressed her earlobe
with well-versed kisses, expertly teasing and tasting.

Too well-versed. Too expertly.

'By God, April. I want to be the first man to make you
scream your lungs out when you take all of me. And you
will.' Her heart leaped into her throat when he whispered
against her ear, 'Let me be your one-night stand. I'll make it
good for you, so good.' His words were like a dangerous

secret. Tempting with unpredictable consequences. 'Do you want me to make you come, April?'

No.

Not like this.

This thought was a shock to her. She was about to deny herself a taste of something spectacular. Yes, she wanted to scream it, to let this entire island be a witness to her desire. But she didn't want to be a statistic. A one-night stand. Weirdly, it wasn't enough anymore.

When did that happen?

She inhaled sharply, her body betraying her mind's decision as it kept arching into his touch. 'Euan… No.'

Her words were barely audible. But he listened. With a low groan, he moved back just enough to meet her gaze, revealing the raving greed in his eyes. The rain pattered against the rough stone wall and April's pulse beat like a slow drum in her ears.

'That's okay, baby. But what's going on, April? I thought… Talk to me,' he said as he let her down along the wall, pulling her into his arms, hugging her. She put her head to his chest, his heart roared under her ear. April's own body vibrated so furiously with dammed lust and frustration that she had to fight back a sob. But this wasn't about what she needed or wanted. Not entirely, at least. This was about Euan. He was using sex as a mask or an armour. Not for intimacy, but for distance. She recognised the pain underneath. He was hiding something. Burying something. Closing off. That was what bothered her. It felt like playing an entrancing melody on an untuned piano.

'We can't. Not like this.' She looked up to him, his hair wet with rain, drops on his eyelashes.

'Why?' he asked hoarsely.

'I don't think you're ready for it, Euan. Not sure I am.' April bit her lip, her body still flush against his. 'I honestly believe you need a friend much more than another notch on your bedpost.'

'I can be your friend *and* fuck you senseless,' he grumbled low in his throat. 'Try me. I'll show you.'

'That's the thing. I'm not sure you can. I'm not sure I can,' she said and tried to steady her breathing. 'No idea how long I'm going to stay in Saorsa, but definitely longer than one night. And I couldn't stop after that. I just know it. So one night isn't enough for me. But that's all you're offering. So…no.'

'That's all right, love.' He lifted her chin up, so that she had to look into his eyes, a need emanating from them that made April feel like precious treasure. 'Look at you,' he said softly, 'my little firecracker. Rain running down your cheeks. Wild and free and strong. You're so beautiful right now.'

She buried her face in his shoulder. Nobody had ever called her that. Pretty? Occasionally. Lovely? That, too. But beautiful and wild and free and strong? Not once. Then again, no one had ever seen her as Euan had. And he held her, just held her, sheltering her from the rain.

She wanted to grow roots in his arms.

'Better take you back to the cottage. We're drenched and I don't want you to catch a cold.' He took her by the hand and walked back to the van with her. Shoulders slumped, feet heavy.

Had she seriously just said no to the world's uncontested leading expert in female orgasms?

Yep. Insane.

A guy like him making out with a girl like her behind the village hall? April's high school self would have wanted to print that on a t-shirt. But maybe it was time to grow up.

Euan kept his grip firm on the steering wheel. The rain-slicked road demanded his attention, but it was April that consumed his thoughts. April, with her fiery spirit and vulnerability, was unlike anyone he'd ever met.

He sneaked a furtive peek at her, her profile silhouetted by the afternoon sun breaking through the clouds. Raindrops raced across the window, blurring the world outside much like his own turbid mind.

What have you done to me?

Euan sensed this wasn't just lust or the thrill of connection. And yet a part of him tried to push down the swell of emotions. This was a fling, right? Physical attraction based on certain pheromones. Merely two adults drawn together in a swirl of desire and loneliness. That was it.

Bullshit. He couldn't keep lying to himself.

Desire hadn't made his heart beat in concert with hers. Loneliness hadn't prompted him to hold her so tightly and tenderly in the rain. To want to keep her there. She'd said she wouldn't be able to stop after one night. What he hadn't told her was: neither would he. The more he had of her, the more he wanted.

Fuck.

He stole another look at April, her wet hair plastered against her neck. His mind screamed at him to confess everything: his fears, his cravings, the way she made him feel like more than an island playboy or a holiday shag. She made him feel like a man capable of being completely undone by a woman who saw past his exterior – and be better for it.

But as he turned the wheezing van onto the narrow bit of dirt road that led to the cottage, Euan's courage shrunk with each second. He may have been an expert in all things fucking, but emotional vulnerability was a frightening unknown. What now?

April huddled next to him, wrapped up in her own

thoughts. Her fingers traced the condensation on the windowpane on her side.

'We're almost here. There's a fireplace at the cottage,' he said and punctured the charged air between them. 'We can get you warm and dry there.'

'That's nice,' she said tonelessly.

He brought the van to a halt and switched off the engine. 'C'mon, May. Let's have a bite to eat.'

'Sounds good.' She got out, making her way to the front door. The rain had stopped, and the sun was breaking through again. When Euan reached back to grab his beanie, he saw it.

She had sketched two halves of a broken heart on the pane.

Duncan's family's cottage had been standing on this spot of the windswept Isle of Saorsa for ages. Euan had spent a lot of time here as a lad. Good memories. Before his world had collapsed. A massive wooden beam reached across from one corner of the ceiling to another. Euan remembered from stories that Duncan's ancestors had brought it with them a good 170 years ago when they were cleared by their land-lord from an even smaller neighbouring isle. To make room for sheep. Its lengthy trunk was the centrepiece of the house. An anchor to their history, a reminder of their resilience. Euan watched as the flames in the wood-burning stove danced and leaped, their light playing across the room.

It must have been the hissing fire in front of them that gave April the idea.

'I want to burn my dress,' she suddenly stated in a stern tone.

'Say what?'

She crossed her arms with resolve. 'My wedding dress. I want to burn it on the beach. Do you think that's possible?'

He rubbed the back of his neck. 'Theoretically, yes. Probably not legal. Environmentally not great. But, aye. Why would you do that? Isn't that stuff crazy expensive?'

'Don't care. I didn't pay for it. Dick's mother did. And to be honest, I can't stand that woman. Never could.'

'So she is a cow then, okay. But think this through. You could sell the dress online and cash in.'

'Nope, it's too crumpled,' she said. 'It's also cursed. No one wants to buy a dress from a runaway bride.'

That made him smile. 'Silly girl.'

'Seriously, Euan. I want to get rid of it. Of my past. And fire is very cleansing. At least that's what the witches on Instagram say.'

'And we're listening to them because…?'

'Because they know things.' Her eyes sparkled and she grinned.

'Okay, May. Whatever you wish. I do have an extra petrol can in the van. I doubt that a dress like that burns easily, for safety reasons. Hey, are there candles on a wedding cake?'

'No clue,' she said. 'Never got to that part.'

As they strolled across the road and then down the worn-out path to the beach in the twilight, wedding dress in tow, Euan was walking on air. He realised he hadn't been out surfing for days. Why didn't he miss it?

Complete mystery.

All he knew was that right now, he didn't miss a thing in the world.

The notion scared the shit out of him.

Euan watched as April splashed petrol all over her old wedding dress. He still thought this was mental, but he wanted to support her. She had been through a lot, and if burning that dress would give her closure, then so be it.

The liquid soaked into the delicate lace, tulle and taffeta. 'You're sure about this?' he asked. 'Seems a shame. It's a beautiful dress.'

April nodded firmly, her jaw set. 'Very sure. It represents a future that's dead and gone. And a broken past. I want it destroyed.' She looked him dead in the eyes. 'I want to watch that shit burn.'

Man, this girl.

April struck a match and tossed it onto the pile of wet fabric with a flick of her wrist. Sassy. Movie-like. It whooshed into flames, the fire sizzling as it consumed the dress in a dancing inferno of oranges and yellows and blues, the skies above mirroring with their own fiery hues.

Euan watched as April smiled at the growing fire, her hair blowing in the breeze, the dancing flames reflected in her eyes.

She's a hell of a wild child.

After a while, the fire subsided, leaving a pile of charred and blackened remains. April let out a long exhale and sat next to him on the blanket.

'How do you feel?' Euan put a comforting arm around her shoulders.

'Free.' She laughed. 'The Instagram witches were right.'

'So…you're done with your past now?'

'I don't want to think about the past. Or future. It scares me and I don't want to be scared,' she said. 'Right now, all I want is to hold your hand. That's all I need. That's enough for me.'

No one had ever said that to him.

He took her hand in his. The warmth from the dying fire felt good on his skin; her warmness felt even better in his soul. They leaned back and lay there in silence for a while, side by side, until Euan rolled over to face her. He let out a small cough, willing his pulse to steady. 'I'm not used to this,' he said. 'Not used to feeling…unsettled. You throw me off balance, May.'

'As if anyone ever could, Hugh-Anne. Have you seen you on a surfboard?' She smiled, the dimples on her cheeks playing hide and seek.

He was ready to enjoy whatever time he had with her. One week, maybe two?

Man, this was hard. But he had to say it.

'April, listen… I-I don't want a one-night stand. Not with you.' He paused. 'I want to stay with you. For as long as you're in Saorsa, I want to be by your side. If you let me, sweetheart.'

Jesus. That just slipped out. He had never called anyone sweetheart in his life.

'You do?' she asked cautiously. 'With me?'

Something shifted within her. He could tell. The way she loosened gave her away.

'Aye. With you. Not a one-night stand. But not a friend, either. If you catch my drift.'

'I think I do.'

'Really? Because I haven't even started yet.' Something unstoppable bubbled up from the depths of his soul. 'I want to burn dresses with you on the beach and fuck you against the wall of the community hall. I want to hold your hand under the stars and listen to you moan into my ear. I want to make you coffee in the morning and then make you scream my name. Three times. I want to carry you to every dance and swirl you around the dance floor like the fucking queen you are. I want to fly a kite with you and watch you ride me until your string snaps. All of it, April. All of it.'

There it was. It felt like he'd torn his thorax open and ripped out his heart to serve it to her on a bun.

'Okay,' was all she said as she got up and sat on his lap,

legs to each side. She wrapped her small arms around his neck.

'Euan?'

'Yes, sweetheart?' There, he did it again.

'This feels right to me. I'm ready. Are you?'

'God, baby, yes.'

Chapter Eighteen

April was combusting with anticipation as she pressed against him, feeling the slickness between her thighs and the undeniable, unbearable, unstoppable craving for Euan.

She saw the glint in his eyes, a spark of something new. More than desire. As if he had tapped into a part of him that he had kept hidden from himself. She had seen glimpses of this intensity in him, in the way his gaze would linger a second too long, in the sudden tightness of his jaw at her touch. But this was different. Completely unguarded. He was offering her all of him.

And that's what she wanted. Nothing less.

Euan's fingers traced her spine with a deliberate slowness, teasing and dancing against the small hollows of her back. His steady gaze met hers, a silent acknowledgement that they were both in this, whatever 'this' had evolved into. She saw the determination etched in the lines of his face. No turning back now. There was sizzling energy in the air, an impending thunderstorm that was about to erupt between them and inside them.

Oh, hell yeah.

With both hands, he grabbed her hips tightly, yanking her body against his hard ridge. 'You wee thing,' he murmured, 'I'll break you.'

'Don't think so,' she said with a smile. 'I'm not inexperienced. Just no great experiences.'

'That's gonna change tonight, sweetheart,' he said and kissed her neck.

'You have so much more experience than I have, though.'

'Doesn't matter. It's new with everyone.' Her hair dropped over her face and he brushed it back. 'Where are we on contraception and safety?'

'I've an IUD and I've never had sex with anyone other than Dick, who isn't interested in sex with anybody at all.'

Euan gave a small nod. 'I get a check-up every six months. I also use condoms.'

She rested her hand on the bulge in his jeans, and he groaned into their kiss as she unbuttoned him. 'I'm asking you because this is important. Consent is where it's at. April, do you want to have sex with me?'

'Yes.' She put her lips to his ear. 'A hundred times, yes. Fuck me senseless.'

She felt him inhale sharply. 'You're killing me. My sweet, wild girl,' he said and flipped her over on her back like it was nothing. She liked that.

'Tell me when I do something you enjoy. And tell me to stop if you don't. You're calling the shots, right?' He placed kisses on her chin and the corners of her mouth.

'Oh, you're good.'

'I know. But, April?'

'Yeah?'

'First time is not gonna be gentle.'

Euan took off her shoes and pulled down her jeans and panties. She wasn't cold in the night air. Not when she was near him. He made a rough sound when he saw all of her in the dim starlight. 'Christ, April. You're gorgeous.'

He knelt next to her, tugged down his briefs and guided her hand to grip him. He was hot and velvety and hard. For her.

'Yeah, that's all yours. Do you feel how much you're making me want you? *You*, April. Now let me feel how wet you are for me.'

Her lips parted in a silent gasp as she watched him touch her there. He brushed two fingers between her labia and licked them. 'You taste like the ocean, rain, and sunshine,' he murmured. 'You taste like home. How can you taste like home?' His voice was breaking, as if he couldn't believe it, as if it was too much for him.

That's when she felt her heart crack wide open. Really felt it.

Her eyes rolled back in pleasure as he pushed inside. She couldn't help but part her legs wider for him, and a quiet moan escaped her lips.

'I love when you make this sound.' Euan leaned in to kiss her neck as he whispered, 'Is it nice for you? Say it, April.'

She groaned in response. 'Don't need nice. Need you inside.'

'Then come here,' he rasped and sat down. With a swift move, he put on a condom. Took less than six seconds. 'Come to me, April.'

She would have gladly followed him to Mordor right now.

April let out a muffled sound that came from the depths of her soul as she took him – so easily, he could have been carved for her. And the whole island disappeared for a split second as they first connected. April held onto his shoulders as she moved up and down with helpless abandon. A burst of a new pleasure in her centre rocked her, like a roiling geyser. Almost too much to bear. She let out bursts of air with every exhale.

'I can tell you're holding back. Don't. Not with me. Show me your wild side, April.'

He was talking to her. He was right there with her. He *saw* her.

'Go on,' he panted. 'Be as loud as you want. I want to hear you, sweetheart.'

And she did as he said. Her breathy cries hit like waves, elemental and forceful, surging with her every movement. 'Ooh, it feels so good, Euan. So good… Please… never… stop… fucking… me…'

'If anyone is fucking anyone…it's *you* fucking *me*.'

She moaned deeply. 'And how…does that…feel?'

'Like I never want it to end. Never.'

In response, she rode him harder and faster. Down on him so deep. Not that she had any control, anyway.

'God, fuck, April!' Euan pulled her closer, biting into her shoulder.

She felt unrestrained. She *was* the storm. Unstoppable. Everywhere. Powerful. Free to do or say or feel anything. Heat was building up inside her like a rolling tide. A low, guttural groan escaped her as she called out his name, head lolling back in ecstasy. 'Euan! Please…'

His lips captured hers in a ravenous kiss, depraving her of air. Her fingers dug into his shoulders with a need that had been suppressed and neglected for a decade.

He groaned in response. 'Oh God, you feel incredible…so soft…' His pupils were wide and dark as he looked straight into her soul. 'I want you to come for me. I can't keep… Shit, April… I'm already there.' With that, he pushed his thumb on her clit and circled it. He knew exactly how she needed it there. Who she was. Truly was.

'Yes,' she panted. 'Oh God, yes… OH!'

And then the magic happened. A burst of primal energy shot through her body. She clenched him with all her strength, releasing a guttural scream as she erupted around him.

'April…HOLY FUCK!' Euan roared into the nape of her

neck as he came inside her.

She sagged against him, panting, trembling, and he locked his arms around her. She had never been so alive, free, and herself than in this moment with him. This man made sounds, sounds that she loved. He moaned and talked and whispered. She wanted to hear all of it for eternity.

'Euan?' she asked, sweating and breathless.

'Yes, sweetheart?' He nuzzled her neck.

'That was incredible. Can we repeat that, maybe?'

He laughed out loud. 'Give a man a minute.'

Waves lapped against the shore, grass rustled in the night breeze, and the isle's ancient hills hummed silently as the two of them stared into the night sky, side by side, wrapped into the blanket and post-coital bliss. Euan enjoyed the way April's body moulded so perfectly against his. He didn't care about the rest. An asteroid hitting the isle now? So be it.

'Have you ever seen anything like this?' he asked her as they gazed at the brilliant stars in Saorsa's wide Hebridean skies. A last bright strip of twilight lingered low on the ink-blue horizon. The view was unobstructed, with no city lights to dim the sharp brightness of the stars. Every glint seemed to hold an entire universe. It was a sight that could make even the most hardened heart believe in magic and hope.

'No,' she replied softly. 'But I never really stopped to appreciate things like this. I wonder why it took me so long.'

'We're lucky tonight. It's often too cloudy.' He kissed her hair. It was the colour of Saorsa's sand, her eyes the colour of the ocean. She looked and tasted as if she were made of this isle. The place he loved most in all the world.

And you fancy yourself a writer, ya knobhead.

There was something soothing about being this close to

her, from the way their hearts beat in unison to her breath on his neck every time she exhaled. He had never felt this way before. Satisfied yet wanting more.

How's that possible?

He ran his fingers through her hair as he spoke softly into the quiet of night. 'You're a sensual creature, April. A natural in the sack. Took me less than ten minutes and the last time that happened I was sixteen. You're hot as fuck. Don't let anyone tell you otherwise. Ever.' His words were barely audible. 'Do you believe me? Do you trust me?'

'Mhm. I do.' She stirred slightly then. 'Thank you for my orgasm.'

'The pleasure's all mine.'

Her hand stroked his belly, and she showered his neck with kisses. Euan inhaled sharply, his chest expanding as he took in the cool night air that swirled around them. It carried the scent of saltwater and flowers.

'Euan? Do you think…' She let her hand wander lower, gradually, as if not to impose. But he was already waiting for her. Locked and loaded.

'Yes, sweetheart?'

'More, please.'

He laughed. 'Damn, I created a monster.'

She pulled away the blanket that covered them. 'Wrong. The monster has always been there. You just helped set it free.'

'Uh-hum. But this time, me and the monster are gonna take it slow.'

When he entered her again with reverent care, inch by inch, it was as if his soul was bursting into a million pieces.

Maybe that's how stars are born.

And God, the way she felt around him pushed all the air from his lungs and buckled his heart. She let out a long, deep, throaty moan. Never had someone made such a perfect fucking heat-filled sound as she did right then.

He loved her joy, her lust. He wanted to be careful, as if one thrust would make her crumble and disappear. So he moved slowly, as if she was made of water and sand. His fingers interlocked with hers as he pushed in sync with the rhythm of Saorsa's waves. He held her gaze, murmuring her name like a prayer on his lips, drinking in her scent in, drowning in her moans.

It felt like coming home.

And as she lay on her back and he on top of her, covering her, shielding her from the breeze and all the bad things in the world, he saw the stars and the entire fucking universe in her eyes.

Euan MacLeod – Saorsa's notorious womaniser, master-shagger, seducer of hundreds – was making love for the first time, and it shook him to his core.

Chapter Nineteen

She woke up a new woman.

The cottage was silent except for the distant call of seabirds and the faint creaking of old timber adjusting to the day. The light streamed in through the small window of Duncan's cottage, painting patterns on the walls and linens. April shifted under the duvet, stretching languidly as her muscles remembered the delicious exertions of last night. The smell of salt, sand, and heather lingered on her skin. A remnant of their night under the stars. She grinned as she basked in the afterglow of a sexually very liberating experience.

Feeling Euan's strong, tall body next to hers, she turned towards him. Just to marvel at him, this most ideal possible combination of human genes. His upper body rose and fell in a steady rhythm. The morning shadows played across his gorgeous face, accentuating the strong jawline that always drew her in for a kiss. She was fully prepared to write an epic poem about his collarbones. And there was this one single freckle on his left earlobe… The cutest thing she'd ever seen.

April knew in her heart of hearts that this was more than a lustful fling with a charming, hot Scot. She knew because she never wanted it to end. And because she'd never wanted to write a poem about anyone.

With his arm draped over her waist, she felt secure and invincible. Empowered. And ready to face the music at last.

Today was the day she would switch on her phone and deal with the aftermath of shattering her old life. April understood now that she'd had to do it to become new. She had arrived here like a wretched caterpillar in a bridal gown. Now she was a naked butterfly. And taking responsibility for her escape was the final step in her metamorphosis.

She let her hands glide over her bare breasts, nipples tender from Euan's caresses, from his lips and teeth. It was glorious. She had told him what she liked, how she liked it, and he had given it to her. Everything. Without reserve, without question.

How am I going to live without this ever again? Without him?

She wished she could stay here, on this Scottish island. With Euan. But reality was a persistent whisper, tugging at the corners of her newfound paradise. He wanted to stay with her as long as she stayed here. Those were his words. Not a minute longer. So he obviously took her departure into account whenever that might be. Not a one-night stand, sure, but still a far cry from what she secretly wished for.

Stupid, silly heart.

April's fingers lingered on her skin, tracing patterns as if to memorise the feeling of being so thoroughly worshipped, so she could go back to it when this was over.

Because it would be.

A guy like Euan would never want to spend more than a few days, maybe a couple of weeks, with a girl like her. Yes, the sex was delicious and fun. But that would wear off soon enough. And then he would discover that she was unremarkable, not enough for him. That he'd made a mistake.

April tried to shoo away her insecurities, refusing to let the demons of doubt cloud the beauty of the moment.

Not now, guys. Come back later.

She stood from the bed, careful not to wake him, and tiptoed toward the window. April peered out at the rugged beauty of the island – this palette of green, purple, and grey, the ocean beyond an expanse of opal blue glass. Gazing upon the contours of this land filled her with awe and a humbling sense of scale. Almost as if witnessing the earth as it might have been before humans laid claim to it. She hadn't known such untamed beauty until she came here. Until Euan showed her what it was like to be part of something so unbridled and pure and free. She would enjoy all of it while it lasted. Every bit of it.

But first a shower.

Even before his consciousness became aware of the rushing water in the bathroom next door, Euan sensed her absence. He moved beneath the sheets, his hand reaching out, finding only the cool fabric where April should have been. The tangle of linen was empty without her, like a canvas stripped of its masterpiece. Only her scent lingered like a promise.

As he turned, he felt the marks of her nails on the skin of his back.

Still waters run deep. So damn deep.

Recollections of the previous night flooded his mind, the way her body moved against his. How her eyes rolled back in ecstasy… The way she took him again and again, showed him what she wanted. He couldn't get enough of it. Of her. This woman was in his blood now. It wasn't just the passion they shared, how good it felt to be inside her. No, there was comfort, peace, acceptance.

As Euan opened his eyes, his glance fell on April's open

suitcase in the corner of the room. A sharp sting shot through him like a flame. That piece of luggage thrust him right back to reality. A reminder of the inevitable.

She was only temporary. This – he – was merely an escape for her. April's real life was elsewhere.

Euan had seen an open, half-packed suitcase in his parents' bedroom that day in spring before he went to school. He hadn't thought much of it – boring adult stuff – but when he returned home that day, his mother had left. Him and the isle. For good.

Eventually, April would go back to the States. And he would remain in Saorsa. That wasn't news. That's how it had always been, with all of them. That's how he had wanted it to be.

No, what was new was that it hurt him so much he couldn't breathe. It was as if a massive boulder was crushing his ribs.

April was phenomenal. So much more than a cute doll-face. Fierce and gentle, strong and resilient. Her empathy and kindness. Her infectious laugh, the way her eyes sparkled when she talked, her sexy pirate voice…

He could still try to enjoy every minute of being with her, but he realised there was a certain price to pay. A high price. And according to the fist that tightened around his heart, wringing it out, the first instalments were already being debited.

Euan sighed and rolled out of bed. As he stood up, his legs almost gave in under his weight. Too much intense love-making.

Aye. He had found his match.

But what good was that if she lived on the other side of the world?

'Hello, sailor,' April said as she walked into the small bedroom, wrapped in a towel. Water droplets slid down her collarbone and collected at the corners of the cotton.

'Morning, sweetheart.' How easily that came over his lips by now. Mental.

Her bare feet padded against the wooden floorboards as she came closer. 'How did you sleep?' she asked, rubbing her hair dry.

His body tightened with desire as he watched her. 'Was out like a light. You?'

She stood before him, skin glowing, hair messy, and gave him this generous, bright smile of hers. 'Oh, I slept like a happy slut. Thank you very much.'

That made him laugh. This sweet fucking girl always made him laugh. Even now, despite the pain that flared up with each inhale. He paused.

'April, I—' The words stalled in his throat, tumbling against the blockade of emotions that filled him to the brim.

Before he could say anything else, she pressed a finger against his lips and shushed him gently. 'Don't speak,' she whispered hoarsely. 'Just feel.'

And oh boy, did he feel.

She let her towel fall to the floor. The soft morning light danced through the window and kissed her skin, highlighting every curve. She took his hand and put it onto her heart. He could picture this moment over and over again. The way she looked. Naked. His beautiful selkie.

'You're perfect,' he murmured.

She blushed and leaned in for a kiss that swept him under. The tip of her tongue – tracing the seam of his lips, soft like a brush, smoothly penetrating his mouth – set his whole body ablaze.

He leaned in and captured her full lips with his own. Rough and needy. This was how he was breathing now. April sighed against his mouth, her hand resting on his heart. Euan pulled back slightly and looked at her with half-lidded eyes.

This was what he wanted. Every damn day.

He wanted to ask her to stay.

But he couldn't. He, the writer, was out of words.

There was only one language that would never leave him. It didn't take long before he used it again, rocking her from behind, holding her so tight. And every atom of his being hoped she understood what he was trying to say.

Euan kissed the warm, salty skin of her neck, smelling the sweet scent of her shampoo. He loved being her big spoon. The curves of her body gave his hands and limbs a purpose, like he belonged right there. He could easily lay there like this with her for hours. But he had to get to the surf school.

Like, now.

'Afraid I got to go, sweetheart.'

April turned in his embrace. 'I know,' she sighed, her breath warm on his lips. 'The ocean and the tourists are waiting for the wave tamer.' Her hair was fanned out over the pillow like a golden halo. 'I feel good, Euan. Like new,' she said, and traced a fingertip down his arm, leaving a trail that lingered longer than her touch.

'You do, hm?' He couldn't hide the dash of pride in his voice.

'Mhm. Stronger. More…myself. I think I'm ready to face the music now.'

He tensed up. 'You mean…?'

'I'm switching my phone on. It's time to stop running away and deal with my past. With what I did. To Dick, our friends and family, and everybody back home.'

Her friends and family. *Her* home.

Not him. Not Saorsa.

Euan's grip on her waist tightened involuntarily, his fingertips pressing into her skin. His heart beat frantically in his chest, the dissonant rhythm of his fears. 'April,' he began, the words sticking in his throat like a fishbone. 'You sure? It's not running away if you're not ready to process everything.'

She studied his face with those sea-glassy eyes and placed her hand gently over his. 'I have to deal with it sooner or later.'

He nodded a few times, though each motion was a small betrayal to the dread that was taking root. 'Aye, I get it. You can't run from your life forever. As I can't run from my job.' A sad little attempt to lighten the mood. His mood.

Euan untangled himself from the sheets and the chill of the morning air replaced the temperature of her body against his. He dressed quickly, moving automatically, while his thoughts spiralled in frantic circles. She was leaving. He could sense it in every breath he took, taste it on his tongue.

'I'll write down my number,' he said, pulling on a pair of faded jeans that lay scrunched up by the foot of the bed. 'In case you need anything.'

April nodded, but her gaze was distant, already grappling with the ghosts of her past that were clamouring for attention.

Why don't you ask her to stay, you coward?

But he already knew the answer. Because the one thing that would hurt even more than losing April was knowing it was her conscious decision. To hear her say the words that had been circling around in his skull for two decades.

You're not worth staying for.

Chapter Twenty

April stood at the gate of Duncan's cottage, watching Euan's van drive away. An uneasy feeling spread through her like stinging smoke. Her cheek was still warm from his kiss.

Her cheek.

He had kissed her on the *cheek*.

April watched his camper getting smaller on the road between the fields. Even when he was long out of sight, she still heard the coughing and spitting engine. She turned back to the cottage and trudged inside, fished her phone from the bottom of her suitcase, and sat on the couch, staring blankly at the peeling paint on the walls.

The cursed thing was heavy in her hand. Of course it was. She might have been ready to take responsibility for her actions. That didn't mean she was keen on it.

Her mind drifted back to Euan. He understood her, he didn't judge her for what she had done, for wanting more than a marriage of convenience, for having desires. He saw her for who she was. Accepted her, all of her. Wanted her.

Does he, though?

April closed her eyes, trying to calm her nerves. She had to push those thoughts aside. She had to focus on the immediate task. The inevitable hour of truth.

Her fingers quivered as she switched her phone on. After she'd typed in her passcode, she watched as the screen lit up and the notifications started flowing in. The flood of missed calls and unread texts was overwhelming. April scrolled through the messages, heart clenching as she read each one.

> *MOM (12.20 PM) Where are you??? I need to talk*
> *to you. Can't believe you did that to me. - Mom*

> *DAD (12.20 PM) April, it's Dad. Call me back asap.*
> *We must to discuss what happened and do*
> *damage control.*

> *ALEX (12.23 PM) Boo, what's going on? WTF?*
> *Where are you?? Call me back!!!*

> *LAUREN (12:24) Ungrateful child! Have you NO*
> *SHAME??*

It went on and on. Guilt and hurt crushed April like a monster wave. Pulling her under, drowning her.

And for the first time since her fateful decision, she was ready to let it all in.

Agony rioted in her belly, clawing its way up through her throat, and she finally cried. Properly, no trickles. Hot and unrelenting torrents. Each sob reverberated through her body, releasing everything she'd bottled up. The tang of loss coated her tongue, the cottage walls absorbed the echoes of her weeping.

Because yes, she wanted her freedom. It had been the right

decision to leave before it was too late. But there was loss, too. That was what she had locked out all this time. Loss of Dick. Not her lover, but a nice guy and friend, practically family. Of their life together. Suffocating, yes, but familiar and comfy. Loss of friends and family, people she cared about who – understandably – didn't want to have anything to do with her ever again. Loss of her home because it was Dick's house and she would have to move out. Loss of her identity, of her path. Where her future had been so clear a few weeks ago, there was a colossal and scary void.

April had chosen to start over, to be remade, and the rational corner of her brain knew this was how it was supposed to be. This was healthy. But right now, her emotions were catching up with her at last and it hurt like the depths of the second, no, the ninth circle of hell. She leaned forward, fists tight and shoulders heaving. There was nothing to do but ride it out.

When the billows ebbed, she wiped her snotty nose with the sleeve of her sweater.

His sweater.

It was a bit damp from rain and tears, and yet it still made her feel warm.

April drew in a deep and slow breath. Then another. Still shuddering but getting there. Freedom was fabulous and petrifying. Amidst the emotional tempest inside her, she felt relief. This was the right journey wherever it may lead her.

Time for round two.

She opened her emails. Between eleven (!) from her mother, various authors' and bookshop newsletters and an email from Alex, there was one from Richard Williams III. Dick.

Subject: we need to talk
  Honey,

I hope you're ok. Tried to call you, but your cell seems to be switched off?

Dunno how to put it, so I'll just say it. I'm with Sheryl now. Early days, but I think I've had a thing for her since she started working for my dad. She was the one who picked up the pieces (aka drunken me from the bar after the "wedding") and has been incredible since then.

I would say "don't be mad". But to be fair, I don't think you have the right to be anyway.

So don't worry about me, okay? It's annoying enough that everybody else does. I'll be okay.

I told your mom you're in Scotland, so she doesn't call Interpol. LOL. You come back when you're ready. Don't stay away because of me (maybe because of your mother, haha). I hope you really are okay. And we definitely have to get a lot of things sorted when you get back.

Dickie

And that was a wrap on life as she knew it. Reading it, in black and white, in his words… It wasn't a hazy escape dream anymore. It had happened. She had done it. Fled her wedding. Left him. April slumped back against the couch and let out a groan. Then she reread Dick's email.

Wait.

Twinset-Sheryl? Seriously? Wow.

Talk about moving on at lightning speed.

Her inkling had been right. She had never imagined Dick with anyone else. Then again, she had never imagined herself with anyone else. Yet here she was, tired and aching from her shagathon with the hottest, most gorgeous, and sweetest man who had ever graced the face of the earth.

April stood and paced around the room, trying to collect her thoughts. It was a consolation to know that Dick was all right. Still, the fact that he had moved on within thirty seconds hurt her ego a little.

But so have you, doofus.

In her gut, April knew Sheryl was a better match for Dick. Maybe…this was all exactly as it was meant to be.

Maybe this was destiny. Or fate.

With that, an entire world of possibilities opened in front of her. The future was unwritten. Open. Maybe she, April Virginia Smith, could indeed have it all. If she was brave and willing to take a risk.

She had the irrepressible need to be near Euan. To tell him she wanted to stay. Here in Saorsa. With him. A million thoughts tumbled through her mind. Could she seriously find a way to make this work, visa and all? Would he be willing to try something new – an indefinite-nights stand?

Hands shaking, she searched for the whale-watching flyer, grabbed her phone, and dialled Angus' number for a ride to the pub later. He must know someone with a car, bike, balloon, hoverboard, pony…anything to get her to the Old Barn when it opened later. The adrenaline pulsing through her veins made her feel like anything was possible.

April was about to do something brave. Or insane. Probably both.

The engine of the camper van groaned in protest as Euan navigated the narrow road leading to the surf school. He gripped the wheel, knuckles bleached with strain. The ocean, a slab of blue muscle flexing in the morning light, was eternally indifferent to his turmoil.

His phone chimed, an eruption of electronic chirps that cut through the noise of the van. Duncan's name flashed on the screen.

'Oi, what's up?' Euan answered, hoping his voice didn't betray the heaviness in his limbs.

'Euan, my man! Keeping my house out of trouble?'

'Your cottage's awright,' Euan replied.

'You sound stressed, mate,' Duncan's tone was laced with brotherly concern.

Euan let out a grunt. 'Och, it's nothing. I mean… There's this one girl…'

Duncan laughed. 'Only one? Euan, have ye lost your touch? I remember when—'

'Don't,' Euan cut in, not ready for a trip down that particular memory lane.

'Sorry, sorry,' Duncan said quickly. 'But seriously, what's got ye tied up in knots?'

Euan paused. Even to his own ears, he sounded like a man clinging to the edge of reason. 'She's got this…fire about her.'

Duncan snorted. 'Listen to me, mate. You're out there living the dream. Waves at your doorstep, freedom in your pocket, women queuing at your van. Why change that for one lass? Naw, man.'

Euan's gaze travelled across the sea almost willing it to give him answers. He was searching for a sign, something to sway him one way or the other, but nature was a stoic counsellor this morning, withholding her advice.

'Yeah, well,' he said. But Duncan's words had left their mark. Even though Euan wished he could dismiss them as the ramblings of a man whose heart was more guarded than the Scottish crown jewels. Because it was, that much he knew still to be true about Duncan.

There was a beat of silence before Euan said dryly, 'Listen, I checked the pipes. They're clear. So don't worry about the house.'

'And you stop wasting your time on one girl, pal,' Duncan said. 'You've got too much to offer to all of womankind.

You're a gift that must be shared, man. And you can still settle down when you're a bawdy.'

'Stop with the blethering. I love you, man. Talk to you soon.'

'I love you, too, arsehole. Kisses!'

Euan tossed his phone onto the passenger seat. The horizon was an unbroken line, the point where dreams either sailed away or came crashing onto the shores of reality.

The world shuddered to a halt with the agonised screech of metal and the death rattle of an engine pushed far beyond its limits. Euan quailed as the cacophony reached a crescendo of clanks and hisses, a thick cloud of white smoke belching from the van's failing core.

He wrestled with the wheel, guiding the ailing beast to the side of the road. The van coughed and spluttered its last breath before settling into an uneasy silence.

When he turned the ignition key, there was nothing but a tormented wheeze. Euan cursed, then again for good measure, and gave the dashboard an affectionate thump that betrayed years of shared hardship. The rugged Isle of Saorsa was no place for the faint-hearted – man or machine – and his van had been a stalwart companion for many years.

Fuck.

Euan grabbed his phone and called the mechanic. The ringing seemed to jeer at him as the van hissed another steamy sigh.

'Gloria's Motors. How can I help ye?' The voice at the other end was as rough as the rocks of this isle.

'It's Euan. The old boy's given up the ghost in the middle of nowhere.'

There was a pause, a drag of a cigarette. 'So did ye finally kill it, lad?'

'It's not dead, just…resting. Can you come out?'

A laugh crackled through the line. 'You and that van are like an old married couple. Alright, gimme your coordinates.'

Euan squinted at the road sign ahead. 'Half a mile past the turn for Craggan's Point, near the lighthouse.'

'Gotcha. But, Euan, I can't make it till tomorrow morning. I'm elbow deep in a Land Rover's guts.'

'Tomorrow? Gloria, you can't leave me stranded with the sheep for company.' His tone carried a casual edge, but underlaid with genuine concern. 'I have to get to the surf school and to the pub later.'

'Och, dinnae fash. You know how Angus is. And I'll sort ye out first thing. Awright?'

Euan leaned back on the driver's seat, letting out a disgruntled huff that steamed up the windscreen. 'What am I supposed to do till then? Grow wool and start bleating?'

There was another drag on the other end. 'Call Allan, ye daftie. The petrol station construction site is but a mile away. Bye now!'

Allan.

The bet.

Euan had completely forgotten about it. Until now.

But he needed that bloody new motor. More than ever. This wasn't optional anymore.

Morag and Allan must never find out. Sleeping with April had jeopardised it all. His entire life. Duncan was right. Giving it all up for one woman was lunacy. Even if that woman was…her. She was leaving anyway. It was never going to work, never going to last. How could it? She lived on the other side of the world, for fuck's sake. This was delusional. She had a life to return to. Friends, family, her old job.

He gripped the steering wheel tighter, as if trying to derive some certainty from its worn grooves. There was nothing he could do to make her stay on this remote isle at the end of the world. What did he have to offer her? Hobby poet, pint pourer, surf instructor. What did he have to show for in his life? What had he achieved? Not a damn thing.

She probably wanted kids, a solid house. The thought of

having weans never seriously crossed his mind. Euan loved spending time with his nephews and niece, but that was it. He couldn't imagine himself being responsible for another human being. Too much pressure. What if he messed up? What if he ended up abandoning them? That was practically inevitable.

He was a good-time guy. Irresponsible. The fun-and-fling man. That's where he shone. That was his groove. Not babies and matching windbreakers and all that.

So even if he were going to ask her to stay, even if, he would just cost her precious time in which she would have the chance to meet someone better and more serious than him. A family man. He was only going to weigh her down and hold her back. Sure as night follows day. He was going to let her down. April didn't deserve that. She'd been through enough.

He had to keep his distance. He had to let her go.

It was the right thing to give her space, but that didn't make it any easier. She had glimpsed past his exterior and not shied away. What on earth did she see in him? Part of Euan wanted to reach out to her, hold her close and tell her it was going to be alright. He wished he could give her the happily ever after she wanted and deserved. He wanted to give her everything, so much it twisted his insides. But he couldn't. Not him. Euan cared too for April much to be in her way.

And in her way was all he was ever going to be.

Best to cut her loose before it was too late.

Chapter Twenty-One

'Thanks for driving me, Angus. So kind of you.' April gave the man a grateful smile as she stepped out of his Volvo.

'Told ye that you can call me. I meant it, lass. I heard what happened with you and yer wedding. Shame, really. Ye deserve happiness.'

These people truly knew everything about everyone.

'It's not easy, but I'll be all right,' she said. 'I'm like a weed. Small, but indestructible.'

Angus laughed his thundering laugh again, and it felt like a warm cup of tea. 'Ye're hiding your light under a bushel. I'd say wildflower, not weed.'

April smiled. He was such a good soul. 'Semantics.'

'Take care now, love!' Angus said and drove off.

Anxiety was having a rave in her gut. It was one thing to be brave and resolute in the sanctuary of her own thoughts, but another to face the man who had been occupying her mind and heart and body so incessantly. Unexpectedly. Powerfully. Every fibre of her being was calling out to him.

Euan was on shift tonight, that much she knew. A quick

glance at her reflection in the window revealed a face that was pale but determined.

April entered the dimly lit pub, the wooden floor creaking under her feet like the first time seven days ago. But so much had changed since then. Mostly her. There was no going back from it. The scent of alcohol mixed with sweat and perfume hit her like a wall. The Old Barn was crowded, with people laughing, talking, and drinking. In a corner, April saw Morag and Allan sharing a bowl of crisps and a bottle of wine. Looked like a date night. Morag threw a chip at her husband and laughed, he gave her a kiss on the neck in response. *Those two turtle doves.*

April's gaze roamed the crowded pub, searching for Euan. Found him. He was behind the bar, chatting with some dudes, handing out pints with his barkeeper-smile across his face. God, that man was trouble, with his chiselled jaw, long lashes and mischievous eyes. Not at all surprising that she seemed to be falling for him, against better judgement and all odds.

Euan whipped his head around when he sensed her, his mouth opening in surprise under furrowed brows. His professional smile had made way for concern. By the looks of it, he hadn't expected her. April couldn't tell whether he was happy about it. She walked towards him, as casually as possible. Hand clenched around her purse strap. The noise of the pub faded into the background, leaving only the sound of her pulse in her head. She stopped in front of him, searching for the right words.

'Hey,' she said, her voice shaking slightly.

'Hey,' he replied. He looked at her, his eyes unreadable, before turning back to his customers. 'Guys, I'll catch up with you later.'

'I, um, wanted to talk to you,' she said, her words tumbling out in a rush. 'I know this is probably not the best time, but I had to see you.'

Euan leaned forward. 'What's the matter?'

Her resolve crumbled. Perhaps this was a mistake and she should leave things as they were. But then she looked into his eyes and a spark of courage ignited within her. 'We need to talk. About us,' she said. 'About what we are to each other.'

Euan's expression clouded. 'I thought we were enjoying this for as long as you're here,' he said, his tone cautious.

'I know,' she said, her voice gaining strength. 'But since I met you… It's crazy, but maybe this was meant to be. Do you know why I came here, of all places?' she asked and looked directly at him. 'Because I saw an ad for Saorsa whisky at the airport in KC. I had just climbed out of my wedding dress, no idea what to do or where to go, when I noticed it. "The taste of freedom." Your family's legacy. I can't explain it, but it drew me here, like a calling, and—'

That's when she saw her.

April's insides turned to molten lava and ash as she caught sight of the fiery-haired woman from the festival. Seated at the short end of the bar. Alone, her eyes pinned to Euan.

Oh no. No, no, no.

The ground broke beneath her feet. That woman right there was the embodiment of everything April wasn't. Tall and slender, sexy and confident. Her vibe was seductive, a little wicked. And she was probably sensational at mattress mambo, knowing a trick or two.

Not a clumsy noob like you.

Her being here could only mean one thing. April's heart sunk. Their holiday fling was over. He was already fed up with her. She couldn't believe her timing could be more off. Stabbing abashment crept up her neck.

Did you really think he had feelings for you? You dumb, dumb girl.

Euan hesitated for a moment, his eyes flicking back to the redhead before settling on April. 'What do you want me to say?' he asked, his voice tired and brittle. 'That I'm falling for you? That I want you to stay? That wouldn't be fair to either of us. Sooner or later, you *will* be leaving. Your life isn't here. And I'll stay behind. I have nothing to offer you, April. Nothing!'

Pain was etched into his features. She touched his arm, tears stinging in her eyes.

April gritted her teeth. She needed to say what she wanted, even if it hurt. 'I'm falling for you, Euan. And if you don't feel the same way, then tell me.'

Euan's gaze dropped to where her hand rested on his arm and shook his head.

April found herself struggling to find the words to say what she had to. 'Just to be clear, everything that happened during the past few days was nothing?'

Euan looked away, pushing a hand through his hair. 'Course not, April. I do have feelings for you. But…'

She felt nauseous and wished with all her might that she had not come here. She wanted an answer, and now she had it.

'I'm not the right guy for you,' he continued. 'And deep down, you must know it, too. We come from different worlds, want different things.'

April nodded and let out a shuddering exhale, pushing away the hurt that threatened to roundhouse kick her in the gut any second now. 'I guess that's that, then.' She swallowed hard, wishing desperately for him to scream 'No!' But there was nothing but silence.

It told her everything she needed to know.

'But…I want you to understand that I'll never forget you.' His voice was a whisper. He reached out as if to touch her face, but let his hand fall back to his side.

'Am I supposed to feel honoured now?' She took a step back from the bar, her eyes still unfocused. 'See, the thing is, I don't believe you for a single second.'

With that, she turned around and left.

As she crossed into the fresh evening air, April realised that she had been holding her breath. She was so damn stupid. Early on, he'd told her exactly what to expect and her childish fantasies and post-orgasmic oxytocin brain had tricked her into thinking he… No, she wouldn't go there.

At least she got what she wanted. She'd got laid like a goddess. And she now understood it hadn't been her fault that the sex with Dick had been so abysmal. Knowing that was worth something. A lot, actually.

The image of the drop-dead gorgeous redhead refused to leave her mind, taunting her, and she wondered if Euan had already moved on to her. April's heart felt like a porcelain figure that had been knocked over the edge of a lofty mantle and shattered into jagged shards upon the cold, tiled floor of reality.

Her vision blurred as she stumbled past Morag's B&B, fingertips grazing the rough stone wall. Hadn't Morag said the McCarrons were gone and April could come back to the studio?

For a fleeting moment, April considered walking back all the way to Duncan's cottage and staying there, as planned. But the image of this other woman entwined with Euan, planting a seed of dread in her heart, propelled her towards Morag's B&B. She didn't want to be in a space where she would be circled and strangled by memories of him next to her, on top of her, inside her…

April made her way to the shed on the side and picked one of two e-Bikes, the one with the sturdy porter, to pick up her luggage at Duncan's and cycle back. She hoisted herself onto the seat. The bike hummed beneath her as she rode down the long road, leading away from all that was splintered inside her. The crisp air lashed at her skin, but it was no match for the piercing anguish of humiliation and betrayal scorching every inch of her soul. Each push of the pedals a silent rebuke against her own naivety.

If a guy like Euan would ever fall for anyone – provided that was even possible – then it certainly wouldn't be a girl like her. The very idea was absurd. Against the laws of the universe. She had known it all along. April was hollow, as if someone had carved out her insides with an ice cream scoop and thrown them on a barbecue. Nobody could have it all, passion and love, sex and friendship, excitement and stability. Least of all someone like her. But even if she couldn't have it all, she could have it her way. Whatever that might look like.

And that was the moment April was ready to go back to Kansas City.

Chapter Twenty-Two

The sea was his sanctuary. But even that couldn't wash away the guilt. As Euan paddled out past the break, the waves lapping against his board, his mind drifted towards April. The way she had looked at him in the pub. Crestfallen. He couldn't bear to see the hurt in her face, to know he had caused her pain. Agony ripped through him as he plunged into the waves, splashing and churning, getting a good thrashing from the Atlantic.

It's what you deserve, arsehole.

Euan had always been a lone wolf, content with his own company, certain that he was living his life as he was supposed to. He'd always like the simplicity of it. No fuss. But then she had appeared out of the blue and changed the way he viewed himself. Challenged him. For the first time, Euan was questioning his choices. His life.

As he sat on his surfboard, staring out at the sea, he couldn't evade the nagging feeling that he was missing something. Not just her. Which he did. He missed her skin against his, her laugh in his ear, her taste on his lips, her softness around him. Barely knew the woman and yet had never known anyone that well.

But he also missed something like…meaning. Purpose. Direction. As if somebody had switched off the lighthouse.

Euan closed his eyes for a moment, taking a deep breath to inhale the briny air. He had messed up. He had let his guard down and allowed her to get under his skin. Against his better judgement. Hadn't he known it would lead to trouble? He had. Had it stopped him? Course it hadn't.

Fucking eejit.

His recklessness had hurt her, and he hated himself for it.

Euan paddled hard under the crest of the wave, felt the power build beneath him. He rushed toward shore, wind whipping through his hair. He'd decided to let her go. April, the girl who'd sparked something in him he hadn't been prepared for. She needed to figure her life out as much as he needed to figure out his. He'd met her at the wrong time. A tragedy. Who knew what could've happened, if…

Doesn't matter now.

On top of that, Euan couldn't risk Morag or Allan knowing about what had happened between them. It was suspicious enough that they'd met him in her company. Repeatedly. He'd have some serious explaining to do as it was. And he still needed that motor. Without it, his Bulli was a pile of rusty metal, ready for the scrapyard.

Euan emerged from the surf, drenched and exhausted. As he reached the shore, he got off his board and shuffled along the beach. He couldn't tie April down to a lame surfer's existence on a remote Scottish isle. Nor could he uproot himself from the sea. From Saorsa. He was a shallow nobody with nothing. The only thing he had to give her was space. He bit his fist to stop the nausea.

April straightened her shoulders as she approached Morag at the table in the breakfast room. After spending half the day on the phone, texting and talking, explaining, apologising, and grovelling until she felt as flat as a piece of paper, April didn't have many words left. Her throat was sore and there was a little monkey with a hammer wreaking havoc inside her skull.

But she had made up her mind, and she had to tell her generous host. 'Hey, Morag, do you have a minute?'

She closed her laptop. 'For you, always! What's going on?'

'I'm leaving,' April said. 'On the earliest flight I could get.'

Morag's eyebrows shot up in surprise. 'Leaving where? Saorsa?'

'Yeah. I have to go back, Morag. I need to clean up my mess.'

'What mess, love?'

'I ran away from my own wedding, remember? Leaving two hundred stunned guests and one shocked groom.'

She placed a comforting hand on April's shoulder. 'Aye, right. That is a mess. But on the bright side, you might have avoided a much nastier one. With a divorce and children and all that. Wish that one of my parents had your sense.' Her eyes glazed over.

'Fair point.' April forced a small smile. 'I have to talk to people face to face. Start over. Although I wish I could stay and that things were different. Anyway, I booked the last seat for tomorrow morning.'

'So soon? Oh, man. Well, I guess once you've decided, that's that. Is there anything we can do to help?'

'Not really.' April shook her head. 'Although, maybe you can help me get to the airport? Not looking forward to that walk again.'

'Of course, love! Consider it done.' Morag stood up and pulled April into a tight embrace. 'You're always welcome here, April. Never forget that. The legend says you can't come to Saorsa only once. And when you return, you'll stay forever.'

'Ha, I wish.' April hugged her back. 'Thank you. For

everything. Don't know what I would have done without you.'

'Och, you'd have been all right. You might not see it, but you're a tough one.'

'I'm trying my best not to wilt,' April said. 'I'll pay you before I leave, yeah?'

'Whenever you want, love.'

April went to her room to start packing. Inhaling a deep breath of courage, she grabbed her suitcase off the bed and started tossing clothes inside without care. Light clothes that were meant for a different, much dryer and warmer destination.

But then there it was.

On the chair was Euan's sweater, and the memories came rushing in like a spring storm. His touch, his kisses, his heat. His scent of salt and sunshine. The way he held her, the way his lips burned her skin. The sound of his voice whispering in her ear, teasing her until she was supple with pleasure. She sat on the edge of the bed, pressed the fabric to her face and inhaled, desperate for a hint of him in the weave. Her heart quaked at the thought of never seeing him again.

April shook her head, trying to push those notions out of her mind. This had had temporary stamped on it from the beginning and she couldn't afford to think about Euan now. She needed to focus on leaving. Starting over. Going home.

Home? Where is that even?

She had no home, she would have to move out. No husband or fiancé, only a life she had run away from. Willingly. Thinking of returning to the city filled her with dread.

As she continued to pack, memories of her time on this remote Scottish island occupied her mind. The stunning scenery with its sandy beaches and delicate wildflowers, the tangy air, the elements. This freedom and vastness. But most of all, the lovely, kind people she had met. Morag, who had taken care of her from the moment she arrived. Allan. Angus and Lorna…

And him.

She grabbed Euan's sweater off the chair and faltered for a moment before folding it neatly and placing it on top of her clothes.

I'll take a piece of you with me.

April zipped her suitcase, attempting to ignore the tumult in her belly and the sting in her eyes. It was for the best. This whole thing had been nothing but an escape from reality. Now reality was calling her name.

Euan leaned against fridge, swirling his coffee, while Morag stared at numbers on her laptop on the counter. It was afternoon, the guests were out and about, exploring Saorsa. The steam from the mug wafted around his face, filling his nostrils. He tried to focus on the bitter aroma, to ignore the rock in his belly. Impossible. He had been lost in thought, replaying the days he had spent with April in his head. Fascinating how fast he had grown used to the gloriously dirty sound of her laughter, the weight of her small hand in his. Those captivating green eyes.

'What's on your mind, love?' Morag's voice cut through his reverie.

He looked at her, taking in the faint crinkles at the corners of her mouth. 'Nothing much,' he muttered. But she could read him like a book.

'She's leaving, Euan. Thought you'd like to be informed.'

His shoulders stiffened. It was as if someone had sucked the air right out of the room. 'Who?'

Morag puffed him in the side. 'Don't play daft, brother. You know who.'

Euan's heart contracted. He had suspected as much but hearing it out loud made it all the more real. 'When?'

'First thing tomorrow morning,' Morag said.

'She here?'

'No, she went for a farewell walk to Bàgh an Dòchais.'

'Hm. Nice up there. I hope she enjoyed her stay in Saorsa.'

Morag inclined her head slightly. 'I guess you made extra sure of it.'

That comment startled him. 'What do you mean?'

'Oh, *nothing*,' Morag said slowly and grinned. 'You gave her your jumper, took her to the distillery, brought her to the dance and the festival, saved her from a rainstorm…nothing any solid tour guide wouldn't do, right?'

Euan's neck burned. 'Half of it was your idea. And it's not what it looked like.'

'Enlighten me. What *did* it look like?' Morag seemed to enjoy his squirming a little too much.

He cleared his throat, trying to steady his voice. 'It's just… she's been through a lot recently. I wanted to show her she could still have a good time.'

'I know, mo bhràthair beag.' Morag's expression softened as she poured herself a coffee. 'But I bet that's not all it was.'

Fuck. The bet.

Euan shuffled his weight from one foot to the other, trying to come up with a plausible answer that wouldn't betray the truth. At least not too much. Admitting what happened between him and April would mean giving up his van. So he put on a casual expression and the most disinterested tone he could muster. 'Nothing serious happened between us. Told you, she's not my type.'

He was fibbing. Because that was merely how it was *supposed* to be. Not how it actually was.

Morag froze. 'My God.' She turned around. 'You *did* sleep with her!'

He forced the clump of emotion back down and gave a nervous laugh. 'What? That's daft, even for you.'

How does she always know everything?

Morag took his face into both hands, squeezing his cheeks together. 'Shut up, fish face! I know you. How do you always forget that?'

'Let go of me, you silly cow.'

Morag laughed. 'I knew there was something between you from the moment she sat at my table in your jumper. You've never given anything to a stranger. And then appearing here all the time for *breakfast*…' She threw a conspiratorial look his way.

Euan had never been stellar at keeping secrets from his sister. He pulled away and set down his coffee mug. 'Look, Morag, it's complicated, okay?'

She put on her scary no-bullshit face. 'Euan Cian MacLeod. Talk. Now.'

Euan grunted. He couldn't keep his sister in the dark forever. Morag was always there for him. Even when he didn't deserve it. *Especially* when he didn't deserve it.

That was it for the motor then.

He let out a long, anguished sigh of defeat. 'Okay, yeah. We may have slept together. But—'

'Ha! I knew it! The way you two were staring at each other. So obvious. She's such a sweet, lovely girl. I hope you treated her well.' Her face darkened. 'Otherwise, I—'

'Mo, if you listen to me for a minute, I'll tell you.' She had always been able to get to him, he couldn't let her rile him up now. 'I treated her fine. I always do. It was clear from the beginning that it was temporary, and she agreed. We are both consenting adults who had a few days of grown-up fun. That's it. All right?'

'Really? Don't be surprised if I'm not sold,' she said. 'You have a notorious reputation, brother.'

Euan gritted his teeth, his anger boiling up. 'I'm well aware of my reputation. That's not all there is to me.'

'So, what else is there to you then?' She folded her arms tightly.

'Mo, what do you want? April is a sweet girl. Much too good and lovely for someone with my, as you brought up, notorious reputation. Maybe you're right and there really is nothing else to me.' He angled his head back towards the ceiling, struggling to keep his composure.

'Holy shite,' Morag whispered. 'You're in love with her.'

'What? Christ no! For fuck's sake. Do you hear yourself?'

Morag knew as well as anybody, including himself, that he was incapable of love. But as he spoke the words, something inside him twitched. An ache in his chest, a longing, a tenderness. He tried to shake it off, but it lingered like a nasty smell. He couldn't fall in love. Love was for the weak and naïve, for those who lacked the ability to protect themselves.

Morag gripped his arm. 'I know you, mo bhràthair beag. You can pretend all you want, but I see you. You're terrified. Because you're vulnerable. Means you're at risk of getting hurt. But that doesn't mean you should deny it.' Morag's voice softened and her grip on his arm became gentle. Her genuine concern for him came through in her words, making him both irritated and touched.

'Maybe it's worth exploring these feelings, because they're real,' she said.

Euan dropped his gaze and shook his head. 'Still no clue what you want me to say.'

'I want you to be honest with yourself! To recognise and accept your emotions.'

'I don't think there's anything on the cards for me,' he said. 'I'm a nobody with nothing to show for. No plans, no ambitions, nothing.'

'Oh, Euan. Don't say that. You're breaking my heart,

brother. I've not raised you to be a self-deprecating coward.'
Morag paused. 'Um, but you *do* know you lost our bet, right?'

'Aye, I'll sell the van. The motor is close to death anyway. For real this time. And a deal is a deal.'

'Euan, we're all aware of how much you love that rusty beast,' she said with a wry smile. 'Even though I hate it. But by all means, keep it if it makes you happy.'

That was the thing, though.

He wasn't sure it still did.

Chapter Twenty-Three

April woke up reluctantly. Her face was swollen from sleeplessness, and a heavy weight settled within her. This was it. Goodbye.

She slid from her bed, put on her Chucks, and made her way down to the beach one last time. The sun was rising above the horizon, a soft orange hue in the pale blue sky. The beach behind the bed and breakfast had become a sanctuary for her. The sound of the waves was the only thing that gave her any semblance of peace. She shuffled along the shoreline, focused on the water's rhythm against the sand, ocean air filling her lungs with each breath.

April pressed her lips together to stop the tears. In her short time here, this Scottish island had given her so much. Liberation and joy. So many moments that were burned into her skin and her heart. It had been her refuge, a realm where every day had been like a dream. A place where she could breathe without worry.

Breathe.

It's over now. Nothing lasts forever. Weren't they his exact words?

A stab of longing lanced through her. Despite the sadness

that filled her, the beauty of Saorsa still held the power to calm her soul. She watched the tall grass swaying in the breeze, birds dancing in the air, the sun spreading its morning glow over the beach. A new dawn. Silently, she thanked Saorsa for comforting her when she needed it most.

As the horizon opened up before her, she made out a blue spot in the distance.

An uncomfortably familiar hue of blue.

Euan's van was parked in the tall grass at the beach. For the last time less than five hundred feet between them. Tomorrow, it would be four thousand miles.

Despite her weariness, something inside April softened at the sight of it. Longing overflowed from her heart like a river that burst its banks. The need to knock on his door to say a proper goodbye, to see him one more time, made her knees buckle. She walked closer. After all, it was only polite to say goodbye. It would be good to leave as friends. Only a few yards between her and his van now.

Then the door opened – and out came a woman.

April's heart stopped.

Of course. A woman. What else did you expect?

Fully clothed and not smiling, a good few years older than April or Euan. She pulled a cigarette out of her shirt pocket and lit it up.

Ah, the infamous after-sex smoke.

April was a fool. She'd seen enough. A leopard couldn't change its spots. He would always be Don Euan, Saorsa's tourist trap. Rory had been right. That's what Euan was most comfortable with. He liked who he was. And the stupid thing was he'd been honest with her from the beginning.

The true problem here was that April hadn't been honest with herself. Again.

Because if she had been, she would have noticed much earlier what she was understanding now that she was about to leave Saorsa. That she had been falling for him the second he'd caught her in his arms in the Old Barn. And he hadn't.

Falling for a guy like Euan. Can it get any worse?

April didn't want an answer to that question. She didn't want anything except to disappear. She turned around and ran back.

Time to leave for good.

It had been Morag's idea that he should drive April to the airport. Typical.

April sat at the table, suitcase by her side, staring blankly ahead while Euan hovered nearby. The silence between them was as thick as Cullen skink. She had barely said two words to him.

Euan shuffled his feet. 'We should get going,' he said. 'We don't want you to miss your flight.'

April stood up and shouldered her bag, not meeting his eyes. 'No, we don't want that. I already said goodbye to Morag and Allan. Let's get it over with.'

Euan followed her out to his van. The old vehicle, patched up by Gloria in a makeshift way this morning, sputtered as they drove. Euan knew he'd hurt April by pulling away. He also knew that he couldn't give her what she wanted, what she deserved. It was glaringly obvious.

Why had people such a hard time seeing it?

Stillness unfolded like a scratchy blanket during the drive to the airport. Neither of them was in the mood for conversation. Occasionally, Euan stole glances at her. But she kept staring out the window, her face a blank mask. Sea air filled the van and April inhaled it deeply, as if it were the last time she would ever smell it.

Well, it was. She was leaving. Just as he'd known she would.

She leaned forward as she took in the view of Saorsa's landscape. The rocks rose above the sea, their faces patterned with streaks of verdant green and brown. Gulls soared and cried in the wind, their wings catching the light of the sun as they wheeled in the sky.

The tiny airport tower came into sight. Not long now. Euan wished he could slow time. Or that some sheep would block the road again.

Where are those wee fuckers when you need them?

April moved in her seat and took an agitated breath. Then she turned to him with a fire in her eyes, her hands clenching around her knees. 'I saw a woman leave your van this morning.'

'Did ye, aye? Oh, right,' Euan said. 'That was—'

'Don't bother. I already know what it is. You're just being yourself. I knew from the start that you were never going to be the settling type. Not for someone like me. And that's fine. Believe me, I didn't want this'—she motioned between them —'but it happened anyway. It wasn't nothing. But there's a picture of you next to "commitment-phobe" in the dictionary.'

That was unfair. Or was it? Anger simmered in his stomach. 'Nobody uses dictionaries anymore. Not since we have this thing called the internet,' he commented flatly.

'I do! I use them!' Her face was bright red. 'I'm a teacher and a reader and I like books and dictionaries and your photo is in there!'

'Don't be upset. It's not what it looked like—'

'I bet you say that so often, you could print it on a t-shirt, wear it every day and it would always be true!'

So this is what meeting angry April is like: half adorable, half harpy.

'I tell you something.' She shot him a glare that could have melted steel. 'You take women as easily as you change your socks because you're too scared to get hurt.'

Her acrid words sliced through his defences without mercy. Euan's anger flared inside him. He fisted his hands on the steering wheel. 'You know what? You're right. I'm a man-whore. Never pretended to be anything else. So what?'

'We both knew,' she said, 'and it still happened.'

'What happened, April? What the hell are you talking about?'

'You damn well know what!' She was seriously yelling now.

'Oh, c'mon! As if you were so much better. You only wanted to sleep with me because you thought there were no strings attached. I was a distraction from your real life. Part of your dreamy Scotland experience. Whisky, haggis, and a good shag with a guy with a funny accent.'

'A good shag? How do you know it was good for me?'

It was defiant sarcasm, and yet it hit the bullseye of his sore spot. 'Because you fucking came around my dick, my tongue, and my fingers like there was no tomorrow!'

'But there could have been!' April grunted and buried her face in her hands.

'Be serious, love. I was just part of your little Scottish escape and that's fine. Let's leave it at that. Okay?'

Euan briefly looked into her eyes, but saw only a reflection of his own aching heart. No point in fighting now. He didn't want their last minutes to be like that. 'Look, you deserve better, April. Better than this. Than me. I wish I could change things. Me. But I can't.' He met her gaze. 'I want you to be happy. Truly.'

'Me too,' April said sternly, almost cold now. 'And you bet I will be. One day.'

Euan pulled into the airport car park and stopped at the kerb outside the terminal doors. She climbed out and grabbed her suitcase.

He had to tell her. Euan couldn't let her leave with the wrong image in her mind. He wanted her to remember the glorious moments under the stars and in the rain and every-where. He wanted her to take home good memories, not over-shadowed by all that hurt and anger.

'The woman this morning? Yeah, not what you think,' he blurted out. 'She wasn't a one-night stand. That was Gloria, the mechanic. After towing me yesterday and fixing the engine provisionally, she checked the van again to tell me how much it will cost to get a new motor. Spoiler: a gazillion. And the woman in the pub the other night, from the festival? She is thinking about buying a holiday home here and I put her in touch with Duncan.'

'Oh? Oh… Okay.' Euan watched as April's cheeks blazed scarlet. 'If you say so.'

'I do say so. Cause it's the truth.'

April nodded, her face still flaming. 'Well, then…sorry for the misunderstanding. Going back to KC isn't exactly easy. And…thanks for everything, despite everything.'

She tried to be polite and that hurt like a kick in the balls with a steel-toe boot. Euan cleared his throat and tried to speak, only to find himself tongue-tied as the moment dragged on. He offered the only thing he had left to give: 'You're welcome. And, um, good luck.'

'Goodbye, Euan.'

He watched as she walked away, her suitcase rolling behind her. They would never see each other again. He wanted to follow her, to make sure she was okay, to kiss her one more time. But that wouldn't do anyone any good.

'Bye, May,' he said to himself as she disappeared inside the building, not even looking back once, before she was gone. Euan wanted to rip his heart out and set it on fire to make it stop hurting. Instead, he slammed his fist on the car dashboard. A radio button fell off.

That soul-destroying feeling right there that tore through his entire being? He didn't need that. It was the whole reason he had decided to be a one-night-only event.

The small plane carrying April away from Saorsa was full, but felt oddly empty and heavy with the weight of her sadness and regret. Doubts crept in, mingling with the shame for having let him see how upset and petty she was.

Had she misjudged him? Perhaps. As much as she could tell, he was many things, but not a liar.

As they flew higher, drifting further from the Hebrides towards the mainland, she pressed her head against the wall, trying to memorise the stunning view. Rolling hills, white beaches, and turquoise waters. The inland lochs glittering jewels against the green of the land.

April sighed as a wave of homesickness rolled over her. For Saorsa. For him.

She could almost picture Euan in the pub, surrounded by laughter and music. His roguish smile, the sparkle in his eyes, the sound of his voice. The pain of the memories made April bite her tongue.

Was he really just a good-time guy?

The plane hit a pocket of air, and her stomach dropped.

Despite her best efforts at closure, her heart ached for the man she had left behind. A man she didn't even know existed two weeks ago. A man she definitely hadn't been looking for.

April leaned back in her seat. Was that truly all they'd been? A vacation fling?

In those fleeting moments when everything had seemed so perfect and right… It was like every inch of her body remembered him – moving inside her, whispering to her, his deep groan when he came with her, how tightly he held her. Being with Euan was unlike anything she'd ever experienced.

You don't have much experience, that's why you're so smitten.

But the closer she got to mainland Scotland, the more it felt like a breakup. After only two weeks. Much more than leaving Dick at the altar after ten years. She struggled to draw air into her lungs. This wasn't just goodbye. She'd left her heart in Saorsa.

Damn Euan MacLeod for giving her a glimpse into the possibilities of what could be.

Well, not for her.

She couldn't be mad at him. Not really. She was the one who let herself fall, while he wanted to have a good time.

How could you let this happen?

April leaned back against the headrest and closed her eyes. Never in her entire life had she lusted after someone so badly. Her heart and her vagina were aching in unison. But she had to let him go. He was right, partly at least. She'd had her Scottish escape, and it was time to restart her life. However that might look like. But people had rebuilt Dresden and London after World War Two, so she, April Virginia Smith, could rebuild her privileged, sheltered little life.

As the plane continued its journey, she said a quiet goodbye to Saorsa, to Scotland, chunks of her soul, and to the man who had shown her a thousand kinds of freedom.

Chapter Twenty-Four

E uan sat on the edge of his van's open side door, wind rustling through his hair. Saorsa's beaches were a place where the wildness of nature embraced the untamed parts of the soul. Even in his darkest moments, he had always found solace in this landscape.

Not today.

The waves lapped against the shore, their soothing melody doing little to calm his restless mind. His knee bobbing, he stared ahead at the boundless expanse of pale golden sand spread out before him.

It reminded him of April's hair.

The memories of her laughter, her touch, invaded his mind, and for a moment, he tried to push them away. But like the tides against the shore, they couldn't be stopped. Would he ever be able to look at his isle again without thinking of her?

He jumped up and picked up the towel that lay carelessly crumpled under him. A Chapstick fell out. Vanilla. Hers.

He twisted it open and inhaled in the scent, her scent, mingled with the cloying sweetness of artificial flavours. As if this small gesture would somehow bring her back to him.

Euan tensed his jaw. Then he let it slide into his pocket. It was all he had left of her.

Feeling restless, he walked towards the shoreline, his feet sinking into the sand with each step. The wind grew stronger, tugging at his hair and clothes. Euan's heart sank as he remembered their last conversation. The hurt and anger in her voice. He looked up towards the sky, watching as the clouds drifted across the horizon. Was she still up there now, flying home?

A world away.

He turned to the sound of a car approaching, his eyes widening in surprise as he saw his sister pulling up.

Her short hair whipped around her face in the wind as she came towards him. 'What are you up to, brother? Why are you not at the surf school?'

'Just…thinking,' he replied. 'Angus gave me the day off. Said I looked like a miserable dog. Joan is covering for me.'

'Where's April?' Morag asked with a cheerful smile.

'What do you mean "where's April"?' Euan's brows creased in confusion.

'Didn't you take her to the airport?' Her smile was fading.

'Aye, I did,' he said with a hint of annoyance. 'That's why I'm beginning to wonder if you've lost your marbles.'

Morag pressed on, 'But didn't you two talk?'

'We did,' Euan said. 'And that's relevant how…?'

'I assumed you guys would work it out.'

'Are you nuts, Mo? There was nothing to work out.'

'But that's why I asked you to drive her!' She threw her hands up in perplexity. 'I thought you guys were falling for each other. That's why I sent you to the distillery together, gave her the tent and all that.'

Realisation dawned on Euan. 'Christ's sake. You did *what*? Are you telling me you played matchmaker?'

'Someone had to, since you're woefully incompetent on that front.'

'So you took it upon yourself? Don't you think that's a tad manipulative?' Euan crossed his arms in front of him.

'I'm your big sister, I'm always looking out for you!' she shouted and pointed her finger at him.

'There's nothing to look out for. I'm fine!'

'No, you're not, Euan! I can see that.'

'Mo, shut up!'

Euan saw the hurt in Morag's features. She grabbed his hand. 'I've had it with you. Let's go. High time we had a real talk.'

'What? Where?'

'You'll see. Just get in my car and I'll drive,' she said. 'Wouldn't set foot in that deadly venereal disease van of yours for the life of me.'

Morag's car grumbled as it whirled down the treeless road. The sunlight reflected off the waves and windswept crags. Euan's mind teemed with questions, but he kept silent as she drove, her jaw set. He wasn't going to ask even though he had no idea where they were driving. Not at first, that was.

But when he spotted the three ducked and bent trees on the side of the road, he knew. And everything inside him revolted. 'No,' he said, gripping the side of the seat. 'No. I'm not going back there.'

Morag's voice was heavy. 'This is where it began,' she said. 'We need to talk about what happened.'

Despite the growing unease, he settled into the seat and stared out the window as they drove up the hill. He had spent his entire life forgetting. And now she was taking him here, of all places.

The car pulled into the gravel driveway of their childhood home, and the memories rushed back. The few good ones and all the bad ones. Of Morag teaching him how to ride a bike on their stretch of the road. Of his parents yelling at each other.

Of the family playing Scrabble or Duncan and him playing Bruce's knights in the hills. Of coming home to an empty house.

Morag turned off the engine, and they both sat in silence. The house looked nearly the same as they had left it almost two decades ago. Two storeys, small windows. The leaky roof long replaced with sleek, sturdy shingles, solar panels on one side. It was a holiday let now, like so many of Saorsa's former homes. Fewer and fewer people lived here all year round. Morag opened her door and stepped out, searching the horizon. Euan stayed in the car and stared at the nicely painted stone walls.

'Don't you want to come out, brother?'

'To be honest? Not really.'

'This is where our story begins,' Morag said and came to his side. 'Why do you think I brought you here?'

He shrugged. 'To torment me?'

'No. I brought you here because it's time to stop running from the past and instead face it. No matter how painful. I've shielded you long enough.'

'Fuck's sake, Mo!' he shouted as he got out of her car.

The house was as he remembered it, but now it looked like someone actually cared for it. At least enough to make some money. Euan trudged towards the sage-green front door. 'What if there are guests?' he asked.

'There aren't,' she said. 'I checked. Left yesterday.'

Euan's hand trembled as he reached out to touch the round doorknob. He felt the impulse to turn back and run away. Far, far away. But he pushed the door open, revealing a dim hallway. A faint smell of wood, bleach, and fresh linen wafted through the air. Morag entered behind him, and they stood together in the narrow hall with low ceiling beams. It was barely enough space for two people to walk side by side.

Strange, it didn't seem as small then.

The walls were lined with textured wallpaper now. As he

ran his fingers along the surface, the subtle ridges and bumps felt like scars beneath his touch. But he couldn't get his feet to move.

'Why don't you go in? I haven't raised you to be a coward,' Morag said.

Pain gripped him. 'And why did you have to raise me in the first place, hm? Because our messed-up mother left one day without so much as a note and our fucked-up father followed her example weeks later. Do you know how it felt to come home to a half-empty house? All her things gone? Not even a note. Just gone.' His voice trembled.

Morag put her hand on his shoulder. 'I know, baby brother. I know.'

The memories vibrated in the air around him. 'You didn't even live here anymore!'

She let out a sad sigh. 'No. But I came back, didn't I?'

'Mo, our own mother just left us. Me. And our father, too.' A fist of ice twisted his heart.

'Let's take this one step at a time, aye?' Morag took his hand and led him to their old kitchen. The new wallpaper couldn't hide what happened, what the walls underneath had soaked up. The kitchen was fairly new, too. Generic beech veneer fronts, tartan curtains, photographs of Highland coos and bagpipers to invoke the maximum Scottishness. Typical holiday let.

Morag leaned in closer. 'You know that they weren't happy, don't you?' she asked.

He looked down at his hands. 'Seemed all right to me. With the occasional argument.'

'Because you were young, running around with Duncan all day. But Mum had always wanted to leave Saorsa. Dad kept her here, family ties.' Morag tapped on the counter. 'She claims he wasn't faithful. Still not sure that's true.'

The air was stale. Euan said nothing, so Morag filled the silence. 'I mean, you know him. He's a good-looking man.

That made the rumours easy to believe, but I don't think he ever did anything. He was probably overcompensating with charm and niceness, trying to make up for the loss of the distillery and for Cian's subsequent arseholeness. I guess she was insecure. Plus, he was always busy and not good at talking about feelings.'

'Unlike you, who can't seem to stop,' Euan said sarcastically.

She ignored his remark. 'His life was hard. With grandpa losing the distillery and the drinking and all that.'

'Aye, heard the stories.'

'But do you understand what they mean?'

Euan rubbed his temples. 'I guess you're about to tell me I don't.'

'So you're not too daft after all,' she said. 'Cian was a broken man, he had a lot of suppressed anger and sadness about him. He passed parts of that on to his son. And he to you.'

'Thanks for the lecture in intergenerational trauma. I'd rather listen to your TED talk next time.'

'Stop deflecting! That's exactly what I mean. We MacLeods are not good at talking about feelings. We're not good at feelings, period.' She let out a long sigh. 'That includes me. I just came back from uni, picked up the pieces and carried on. You never spoke about the day when Mum left and I thought it best not to stir anything. I was wrong. And I'm sorry for it.'

Euan noticed the tears in her eyes. His big, strong, confident sister. He'd never seen her cry. Rage, yes, but not a single tear. This side of her was strange to him.

'I failed you,' Morag whispered. 'I didn't teach you how to be happy.'

Tenderness and shock flooded Euan's core. 'Mo? No! You didn't fail me. It wasn't your job to teach me anything.'

'Aye, but it was. I didn't ask for it. But it was. Our parents both thought about taking you with them, you know? Either to Stirling or Edinburgh. But they decided it would be best to leave you in your school. With your friends. Then I fell in love with Allan, we sold this house and moved on. But sometimes I think we didn't. Parts of us stayed here. And I never showed you how I felt about it.'

He could still sense the presence of the past in the walls, like ghosts. 'Then how *do* you feel about it?'

'I'm bloody raging! Fucking shite parents!'

'That's what I've been saying!'

'I love you with all my heart and I would do anything for you. But I was twenty-four. I was supposed to have a youth! Instead, I became the parent of a moody teenager. I had to wash stained sheets long before it was my turn. Egocentric fuckers.'

He laughed, although every bone in him wanted to cry and scream and fall to dust.

Morag continued, 'I brought you here because I need you to understand that the past might be with us still, but it's also over.'

'You're speaking in tongues, sister.'

'What I mean is: we still carry the weight and the wounds, but we mustn't let them dictate our present and future.'

He looked at her, puzzled.

'Jesus, Euan. I see I have to spell it out for you. Just because yer maw was a cow who left you doesn't mean that every woman is. And just because you split up with your teenage girlfriend doesn't mean you can never have another relationship again. Stubborn numpty.'

He felt like he'd been doused with ice water, Morag's words ringing in his ears. Was that it?

'See, it took me years to fully trust Allan. There was always this voice nagging inside me, "What if he's like Dad? What if I end up like Mum?". Years, Euan! But we did the work, and it was worth it.' She exhaled audibly. 'You can't have love without the risk of loss, you know.'

Euan stared at his sister, taking in her words, trying to understand. He remembered the pain and bitterness he had towards their parents for leaving him. It had shaped his worldview. Hardened him, maybe. Scared him, definitely.

Her voice trembled. 'I was wrong to protect you, to pretend like it was nothing. Cause all that taught you was that these emotions should be suppressed. That's not right. And now you can't open your heart to anyone. I'm sorry, baby brother. So sorry.'

He didn't know how to respond to his sister's honesty and vulnerability. Seeing Morag like that...the protective shell he had built began to crack. Euan wanted to reach out and comfort her. But he couldn't. He was frozen, caught between the past and the present.

She wiped away her tears. 'I'm angry, too. And I know it's hard, Euan. But you have to take that step. Trust someone. Take a chance. It's not enough knowing you're broken. You have to do something to fix it. I'm sorry that I didn't show you how.'

As she hugged him, her embrace was like a special form of pressure, urging him to break through all the walls that he had built. For a moment, silence hung in the air. 'I'm sorry too, sis.'

Morag looked up, surprised. 'What are *you* sorry for? The stained sheets?'

'I'm sorry for taking you for granted.'

She smiled. A secret, knowing kind of smile. 'That's okay. You were just a kid. I love you to bits. Just remember that, no matter what. You deserve to live the life you want.'

But what life do I want?

Part of him understood that his sister was right. But another part of him was wrapped in cold dread. 'Nothing lasts forever, Mo.'

'No. It doesn't. But that's part of the beauty of life. If everything were endless, nothing would be precious. You know what you want. Question is: are you willing to do something about it?'

He couldn't keep letting his past dictate his present and future. But what if he ended up like his parents, hurting those he loved the most?

Morag read his mind. Again. 'Aye, it's scary.'

Euan nodded as understanding rose in his chest. Like a sunrise. A tiny spark of optimism grew within him. Only to be crushed by the next thought that shot through his mind. 'She left, Mo. She's gone.' There was a whole world of hopelessness in those five words.

Mo slapped his arm. 'Yeah, how could you let *that* happen, you idiot?'

'She thinks I'm a commitment-phobe.' He scoffed. 'She's right. The thought of being with someone scares the living daylights out of me. Always has.'

Morag grabbed his shoulder. 'I know. Hence the van.'

'Hence the van.' He hung his head. 'She's too good for me. She's the kindest, most honest person I've ever met. She deserves better.'

'Shut up. That's for her to decide. What *did* she say?'

He looked up at his sister sheepishly, tugging at the collar of his t-shirt. 'That she was thinking about staying.'

'Oh, you absolute idiot!'

Euan pulled his phone out of his pocket. But then he remembered that he didn't have her number. He'd never asked any woman for it, so it wasn't part of his routine. But also because April hadn't used her phone in Saorsa. Morag was right in more than one regard. He was an idiot. 'Um, I don't have her number.'

'Unbelievable. Luckily, I have her email,' Morag said.

Relief washed over Euan. He would write to her, explain himself. Even if she never wanted to see him again, at least she'd know that his behaviour had nothing to do with her and everything with him. His past. He needed her to know how amazing she was. How lovable. How loved. And then he would make some serious changes.

He turned around and stormed outside, phone in hand.

'Where are you going, weirdo?' Morag asked, running after him.

'To do something I should've done ages ago.'

Chapter Twenty-Five

He was a crab without its shell. It only took five pictures, one posting in Saorsa's Facebook group, thirty minutes, and Euan's van was gone. No islander would touch that camper with a prong, but there were only two thousand of them in the group, along with about twelve thousand tourists. And for people who didn't live here, who weren't aware of his reputation, it was an opportunity. People with the money to own a second home here, who could afford a new motor and to refurbish an old van to lure their nest-flown kids here for the summer.

The van was more than a vehicle. It had been a part of him for many years. He would have to stay at Morag's or Duncan's until he found his own place. Which was ridiculously difficult, considering Saorsa's property market. There were hundreds of holiday lets and zero long-term rentals.

He'd figure something out.

And he had yet to write that email to April.

Euan let out a defeated grunt and ran a hand through his hair, tugging at the strands. He had to write down his thoughts before he lost his courage, but his notebook was full and without a new one, he was at a loss. What he was about to get off his chest couldn't be typed into a phone. It needed to be done on paper first. Thoughts sorted and structured. Get it all out and then choose the words. He wanted to do right by her.

There's always a notebook in my room at Mo's.

Euan stood and brushed the sand from his jeans before heading back towards the B&B. As he walked up the beach, he felt a piece of him was missing, now that his van was gone. But the much bigger missing piece of him was to board a plane from Glasgow to the States soon.

Entering the room, he remembered the night he'd brought her here, put her to bed. How his heart had already known what he refused to acknowledge. That he'd fallen for her the moment she'd been thrust into his arms, feeling like a lost part clicking into place.

Dammit.

With a swift move, he opened the desk drawer and took out the notebook. There was a rumbling sound, like a pebble rolling over wood. Euan touched something cold and sharp and round.

Her engagement ring.

Euan turned it over in his hand. It was exquisite. With a thin but sturdy band, the cool silver smooth and polished under his fingertips. In the centre sat a sparkling diamond, catching and reflecting stray beams. He was no expert, but even he could tell that it was worth a small fortune.

A more cynical man would have thought that this was his new motor right there. But he didn't need a motor anymore.

He needed her to know how he felt.

Euan couldn't believe she had left such a valuable piece behind. She must have forgotten that she put it there, been distracted. He stared at the glinting rock. He missed her so much it physically hurt.

You're stalling. Write her, man.

Carefully, Euan put the ring on the desk and opened the

notebook. But instead of a blank page, he found a list with the title: 'Things to do before I die'.

Learn to surf
Visit the Great Barrier Reef
Go bungee jumping
Get a tattoo
Drink tequila with a worm
Teach again
Figure out what else I want
Take a Krav Maga class
Learn to knit

It was two pages filled with travel destinations, small and big plans, it was all April. All of her. The silly and the serious parts. The dreamer. Her honesty. At the bottom of page two, the word 'sex' was crossed off. So was 'Have a one-night stand' and 'Have orgasms and enjoy sex. With someone who isn't Dick. No relationship'.

Every word screamed out the desperate desire for a full life, for excitement and joy. God, she deserved it. All of it and so much more.

Then he saw April had ticked off 'Get laid like a goddamn queen' and sketched a heart next to it. Euan smiled, touching the doodle with his fingertip.

Aye, ye have, sweetheart. Or so I hope. Did my best.

He was honoured and humbled. Euan's chest swelled with determination and longing. He had always been a solitary person, content that way. But April had washed his barriers away. He hadn't stood a chance, he knew that now. His heart thudded painfully as he reread April's bucket list. He wanted her to experience all those things.

The crazy thing? He wanted to do them with her. Side by side.

Euan had never felt this way about anyone, never even considered a future with someone else. Not even another morning. His hand shook as he reached for a pen, practically vibrating with the need to write to her. He began and stopped.

What if there was a better way?

With a firm nod, Euan stood up, slipping the engagement ring into his pocket, pushing it against his thigh. He snatched the notebook, closed the drawer, and hurried out of the B&B. He had to act fast if he wanted to have a chance.

'Angus? I know it's spontaneous. But do you still have that Cessna? I need a favour.'

April's heart was a jumbled mess as she got off the Twin Otter plane. She clutched her carry-on bag as she made her way through the packed airport of Glasgow. Everything was loud, overwhelming, shrill. She missed Saorsa already, the lush green hills, the soft rustling of the breeze, the sea spray and the cliffs, the cosy B&B. Even rain couldn't dim the gripping beauty of the place. As if she was leaving behind a piece of her soul.

Which she had.

As she navigated through the crowds, her eyes flickered up at the various screens around the airport. Her connecting flight to London was on time. Even so, it was hours away. She let out a disgruntled huff and the weight of her decision settled in the pit of her stomach.

April looked around, searching for a place to sit and pass the time. She spotted a generic airport café. Beige walls, a hint of cleaning solution in the scent of warmed pastries. The hissing of the espresso machine blended with the countless voices and announcements. April approached the counter with the pre-packaged snacks and ordered a flat white and a lemon poppyseed muffin, trying to ignore the knot in her gut that grew tighter by the minute. She found a small table near the window where she could watch the planes take off and land.

A family arrived across from April's table. A mother, a father, two boys and a little girl, only four or five years old. The parents tried to wrangle their children and carry multiple bags at the same time. One of the boys was throwing a tantrum, the other boy was busy with a tablet. And the little girl sat in the corner playing with two dinosaurs.

As April sipped her coffee, she noticed an advertisement for a photography studio, showcasing idyllic family pictures – two dads and their two kids in a summer field, sun low and warm, smiling faces. A perfect, happy family captured in a moment of joy. Her thoughts lingered on the photo, her mind wandering to the past. She wondered why there were so few photos of her growing up. She could recall only three childhood pictures of herself. All three taken by her paternal grandparents who passed away when April was ten. Her mother didn't have contact with her parents.

But why are there no childhood photos of me?

Maybe her parents were too busy avoiding each other to document her growing up. Or she simply wasn't important enough to be captured on camera. April shook her head, trying to chase the melancholy away.

The sound of plates clanking brought her attention back to the present. She needed five minutes for herself. April rushed towards the washroom and pushed the door open. One of the stalls was occupied. She went into the other one, relieved to have the solitude to process her thoughts.

Pressing the heel of her hand against her forehead, she sat on the toilet seat and pondered.

What now?

Reflexively, she grabbed her cell and called her friend Alex's number. When April remembered it was the middle of the night in KC, the phone was already ringing for the second time. Alex always had their phone at their bedside and this was, well, an emergency. Sort of.

'April? April! Oh my God. Are you okay, girl?' Alex's voice on the other side of the world was sleepy and fuzzy.

'Yeah, sorry. I'm so sorry for waking you up.'

Alex yawned. 'It's okay, honey. What's going on? Are you still in Scotland? Do you need money? Are you in jail?'

'No.'

'Talk to me, April. Thanks for your email by the way, but I had to hear your voice, dummy.'

She smiled, even though Alex couldn't see her. And then a wave built up inside her and everything spilled over. 'I...I met someone here in Scotland.'

'What?' Suddenly, Alex sounded fully awake. 'You didn't! Someone as in...bada-bing, bada-boom?'

'More in bada-didn't look for it. I just wanted to get away. But then... It lasted for a while, and it was good. Like extremely good. I can't stop thinking about it. About him.'

'Honey, you sound flustered. That's so not you. Cute! Tell me more.'

'No, it's late. I should let you sleep. Sorry for—'

'April Virginia Smith! I didn't wake up at three o'clock in the morning for a tease. Make it worth my while. Have mercy, tell me everything.'

And that's what April did. In great detail. She ended with '…just with his tongue. Unbelievable.'

'Oh my God, April. Good for you, girl,' Alex said. 'And I hate to break it to you, but you sound like you're falling in love with that Scottish surfer dude.'

'Maybe. But he's not falling in love with me.' April let out a grunt.

'Sweetie, we've known each other since kindergarten and

you've always hidden your light under a bushel. You could never imagine that anyone would think you were great. Even with Dick it took months.' Alex cleared their throat. 'I always liked Dick, everybody does. But he is a bit dull. No fire. Not to throw a truth bomb at you, but he couldn't hold a candle to you.'

'What? You think? But—'

'Honey, you deserve all those orgasms and the fun. No need to feel guilty. As you said, Dick has moved on. With a woman who looks like his mother no less. Be thankful that you got away. Your life is your own. Just live it already.'

Alex had always been the brave, bold, and outgoing one.

'You know what? You're right, I will—'

A resolute knock on the toilet door interrupted their conversation. A female voice said, 'It's great that ye got yer fanny taken care o' wi' all that hochmagandy, hen. But some o' us really need tae pish noo.'

When April came back to the café, the family's table was empty. Except…the little girl was still sitting next to the cooler on the tiles, absorbed in playing with her dinosaurs. Her brothers and parents were gone, including their bags.

That's odd. Guess they'll come back.

April sat down and kept an eye on the girl. After ten minutes had passed without any signs of her family's return, she decided to do something. She ambled over to the girl and squatted down. 'Hello, I'm April,' she said with her best friendly-teacher-on-your-first-day-in-school face.

'Hello.' The girl didn't look up.

April was careful not to scare her. 'What are you playing?'

'Dinosaurs.'

'That's cool. I like dinosaurs. Do they have names?'

'Aye. T-Rex and Triceratops.'

'Aha, that makes sense. And what's your name?'

'Gracie.'

'Nice to meet you, Gracie. Can you tell me where your parents are?'

The girl shook her head as her dinosaurs were entangled in an epic fight.

'Do you want me to help you find them?'

Now Gracie looked at her. She seemed to consider it for a moment before tilting her head slightly. 'Okay.'

'Would you like to take my hand so we can stay together in the crowd?' April said, standing up.

Gracie nodded but then realised she couldn't carry both dinosaurs in one hand.

'I'll take T-Rex in my bag, okay?' April suggested.

Gracie gave her the dinosaur. 'Aye.'

April took Gracie by the hand, grabbed her own suitcase, and walked the girl to the information desk, from where her parents could be called via the airport system.

While they were waiting, anger welled up inside April. This wasn't about a lost kid. It reminded her of a similar situation in her childhood at the grocery store. Her parents had taken two hours to come and get her. Not to mention all those times they had forgotten to pick her up after school. She pressed her lips together. This constant feeling of being invisible, unimportant, her entire existence merely an afterthought. It echoed throughout April's life.

Shitty fucking catastrophic parents.

April was deep in thought, confronting the realities of her past. She remembered a young girl, desperately vying for attention and affirmation from her miserable parents, only to be overlooked and dismissed.

It hit her like a freight train.

She had been waiting for others to recognise her worth

without ever expressing her needs, because her needs had never mattered. She never asked for more. For anything. Instead of fighting for what she truly wanted, she settled for whatever love or affection was thrown her way.

As this realisation sunk in, April's eyes filled with tears.

No more.

From now on, she would fight for what she truly desired. No more settling, not for anything. No giving up and accepting scraps.

When Gracie's parents showed up at last, April bolted from the scene. She didn't want to accidentally lash out. There could've been any number of reasons why they'd left their child there, an emergency of sorts. April had no clue what was going on with their family. All she knew was that it had cracked open an old wound and now it was up to her to heal it.

It was like a dam had broken inside her. Euan wasn't the only one controlled by fear and ancient wounds. Just like Euan and his fear of commitment, April too was held back by scars from her past. She understood that they were both constrained by emotional barriers.

When April closed her eyes, she saw very clearly what she wanted.

And for the first time ever, she decided to fight for it. Really go for it. She rushed to the DeanAir desk.

Chapter Twenty-Six

As the Cessna soared through the sky, Euan was convinced he was dying. Knuckles white as he gripped his knees, palms sweaty. The roar of the engine drowned out everything else, a constant reminder of his mortality. The smell of fuel filled the small cabin, the air thin and suffocating, making his insides churn. A sour taste rose in his mouth as Angus' plane dipped and swayed. Euan gagged, praying to keep his breakfast down. His body was a tightly coiled spring, his mind struggled to focus on anything other than the sheer terror of being up in the air. Unnatural.

If humans were meant to fly, they would have wings. Simple as that.

'Never thought I'd see ye in the air,' Angus said with a grin. 'Must really like the lass.'

Euan groaned in response.

'Dinnae fash, lad. We'll get there in time.'

'Not my biggest worry now,' Euan said between shallow breaths.

That got a laugh out of Angus, almost as loud as the engine. And then the clouds dispersed. 'Look doon, lad,' Angus said, 'or ye'll miss her.'

'Miss who?' Euan asked in agony.

'Scotland of course, daftie! She's laid out in all her beauty right before yer very eyes. She's truly bonnie.'

Euan, briefly fearing that Angus might break into song and belt out 'Flower of Scotland', did as he told him. As he dared to look down, he gasped. She was exquisite. Like a vibrant quilt, the cliffs and beaches of the Scottish coast unfurled beneath them. So green, with patches of yellow gorse and purple heather, winding roads snaking through the landscape, sweet and harsh. An eternal boundary marked by cliffs and sandy beaches where the huge Atlantic met this wee timeless country. There was a vastness, a feeling of being a part of something much larger and much, much older.

Angus glanced over at him, smiling knowingly. 'Aye, gets me every time. Scotland's like naewhere in the whole world. Can ask anyone.'

Euan was grateful for the brief distraction. But his mind was elsewhere. What if he was too late? What if April was already gone?

What if we're gonna crash and die and I never told her that…I love her?

Angus' voice broke through Euan's thoughts. 'We're approaching Glaschu Airport soon.'

Euan nodded absentmindedly, eyes on the horizon.

Thank God it's almost over.

When he had gone to the mainland, he'd always taken the ferry. That's what they were for. This was his first flight, and he hated each second. He was doing this for her.

And, as he now knew, he would do anything for her. Anything.

Hell, even squeeze himself into a flying tin can.

He could punch himself in the face for taking so long to understand that.

As they landed and taxied towards the terminal, Euan's

heartbeat quickened even more. Angus parked the plane and turned to him. 'Ready?'

'Aye, man,' Euan said, grabbed his backpack, and followed Angus into the airport.

April weaved through the crowd at Glasgow Airport and clutched her carry-on bag, a trace of unease settling in. She had changed her plans on a whim. Again. Fly back to Saorsa to mend things with Euan? Insanity. But she couldn't shake the feeling that the matter wasn't closed yet. The way his body tensed up with, 'I was just part of your little Scottish escape'. The pain in his voice when he had said 'you deserve better'. This hadn't been the tone of someone who felt nothing.

No, it had been the tone of someone who felt *too much*.

April was bursting at the seams, needing to tell him everything *she* felt. It wasn't just physical desire, it was an all-consuming fire, roaring and calm. *Yeah, love probably.* She loved every aspect of him – his silly jokes, his not-so cool side, his giant heart, his vulnerability, his love for his community. He had so much untapped potential that it made her want to scream in frustration. Anyone who underestimated him would have to answer to her. Because he was a lot more than they could ever imagine. He was creative and loving and deserved to be whoever he wanted to be. To be seen and accepted and cherished, all of him. Just like herself.

April felt like she had been forged just to be in his arms. Her soul was whole when he held her, flying and tethered. Home wasn't a place anymore. Home was wherever Euan was.

And that's what she had to tell him. In person. If he still didn't want her, he'd better damn well say it to her face.

Now she had to cancel her flight to KC via London and

Washington and get a ticket back to the isle. But those planes were tiny, only a few passengers at a time, and it was peak season. The chances were abysmal. She had to try anyway. She would never forgive herself otherwise.

If not, I'll get a ferry tomorrow. Or I'll ride a dolphin. I'll get to Saorsa one way or another.

April had never been that determined and laser-focused. It was almost frightening. She made her way to the DeanAir desk. No queue, just a crew member. 'Hi, hello! I need your help,' April said to the woman with the tight ponytail and formidable lashes behind the counter.

'Welcome to DeanAir. What can I do for you?'

'I have to get on the next plane to Saorsa. Is that possible, can I do that here?'

The airline employee frowned, which briefly gave her a mono brow. 'The next plane leaves soon. Let me see if there are any seats,' she said, tapping away at her computer with perfectly manicured long nails.

Each second stretched like an eternity, as April anxiously waited while she checked.

'You're lucky. There's one seat left,' she said. 'Must have been a cancellation. Would you like me to book it for you?'

'Fuck yes!' April exclaimed. 'I mean, yes please, that would be nice.'

She smiled. 'No problem at all.'

The weight slid off April's shoulders like an avalanche. That was one problem sorted. Now all she had to do was cancel her journey to the US and figure out how to retrieve her luggage somehow.

One impossibility at the time.

Euan paced in the airport terminal. Thanks to Angus' clearance and connections, he'd been able to slip into the departure area. It was probable that April hadn't left yet. She was most likely flying via London. He glanced at the departure board. The only direct international flights from Glasgow today were all to Europe, Dubai, and Canada. There was a flight to London leaving in less than thirty minutes. He checked the time on his phone, anxiety mounting. The chance was tiny, but he still had to take it.

'I'm gonna go to the gate. See if I catch her there,' Euan said to Angus, who patted his belly three times in response.

'Ye get the girl, I'll get a burger. At last, the good stuff. Sadly nae available at home. But dinnae tell Lorna.'

'You do you, man. Enjoy!'

Euan took off in a sprint towards the gate, dodging travellers. He had to find April before she boarded the flight or she would be gone forever.

Why must airports be so huge and packed?

His eyes scanned every face he passed. He couldn't miss her. Not when he was so close. He pushed his way past a family with two shouting boys and a wee girl holding a dinosaur. He apologised over his shoulder as he continued on.

April was short, that was a bit of a problem. She could easily disappear in this vast crowd of people. No sign of her anywhere.

Fuck.

Euan's heart sank as he arrived at the gate. The flight attendant was already announcing the final boarding call for London. Frantically, Euan stared at the passengers, sitting or standing, searching for any sign of April. A bead of sweat trickled down his temple. Boarding was already in progress. For all he knew, she could be on the plane.

'Excuse me, have you seen a woman, about yay tall, with blonde hair?' he asked, gesturing to the midpoint of his chest to illustrate her height. The passengers shook their heads.

Shite.

Euan tried to tamp down the exasperation that was bubbling up inside him. He turned to the boarding crew, pleading for any information. 'Sorry, I won't be long. I'm not flying,' he explained as he wiggled his way to the desk. 'Excuse me, do you have a passenger named April Smith on board, headed for the US?' he asked the boarding crew member.

She looked at him sympathetically but shook her head. 'Sorry, sir, we can't disclose passenger data.'

Euan ran a hand through his hair, helpless and desperate. He had been so close to finding her. Defeat wanted to crawl up his spine, but he wasn't ready to throw in the towel. Maybe she was on the loo?

April came from the toilet and rushed to the baggage claim area, equipped with a heap of forms and documents. It had taken forever, but now she was on her way to retrieve her suitcase and make her new flight back to Saorsa – before it left without her.

The airport was crowded, making it difficult to navigate through the throngs of people. The minutes were slipping away and panic clawed at her. April groaned inwardly, glancing at her watch. Only fifteen minutes.

'Miss, is this your bag?' A young man with a bright smile and a mop of ginger hair held up a suitcase that looked exactly like hers. Black with a little red bow and a Kansas City Chiefs sticker. 'Yes! Thank you so, so much!' She rushed over to him and grabbed the suitcase with gratitude.

'Ah, not so fast. I'll need to check your paperwork first.'

It took him a while to leaf through the papers. The minutes were ticking away and April's eyes darted anxiously around the crowded baggage claim area.

'Awright, that's you.' He handed her the luggage. She

thanked him as she turned on her heels and ran. Not away, but towards something. Or rather someone. It felt very different from last time.

Now she had her suitcase, but her flight to Saorsa was boarding soon. Like, five minutes ago. She clutched her carry-on as if it held the secrets of the universe as she raced through the crowd. Not even time for apologetic smiles. The people around her seemed to be moving in fast-forward while she was stuck in slow motion. Her surroundings were a blur of faces and colours as she barrelled through the sea of people to her gate on the other side of the airport.

In an attempt to speed past two elderly ladies holding hands, she slammed into a suit, the brief impact knocking her back and causing a scalding liquid to splash all over. The businessman's crisp white shirt darkened with the coffee from his cup. His face contorted in anger as a huge stain formed.

'So sorry,' she muttered, trying to avoid eye contact as she steadied herself.

The suit let out a low grunt of annoyance and shouted, 'Watch where ye're going, ye daft cow!'

Shit happens.

Her hand was damp and sticky as she helped him pick up his scattered belongings. It cost her two precious minutes.

'Final boarding call for April Virginia Smith, flight DN0457 to Saorsa. Please proceed to gate fifteen immediately. The final checks are being completed. This is the final boarding call for April Virginia Smith. Gate fifteen please. Thank you.'

'No, no, no!' April muttered under her breath as she made a mad dash towards the gate of destiny.

Euan stood rigidly at the London flight gate. Every damn passenger had boarded, but he hadn't caught a glimpse of

April. She was either on an earlier flight to London or sitting a few feet away on that plane, tantalisingly out of his grasp. Which meant he had missed her. His heart knotted at the thought of her flying back. Without her engagement ring, but more importantly without hearing what he desperately had to say.

There was one last Hail Mary he could pull. And he was willing to do anything at this point.

He dug out his phone, hands trembling, trying to find out how to have someone called for via the airport's public address system. *There must be a number to phone or something. Why haven't I thought of it before? Fucking stress brain.*

Euan was so focused on his phone that he only vaguely noticed a male voice behind him shouting, 'Watch where ye're going, ye daft cow!'

No time for a riot or a fist fight. He had to find her. But the airport website wasn't helpful. Okay, so now he had to try finding a security person. When Euan lifted his head, he saw a man in a suit with a red face and coffee all over his white shirt stomping past.

Shit happens.

Euan shoved his phone in his pocket and took off running towards the information desk.

And then he heard it. First a crackle, then a monotone voice: 'Final boarding call for April Virginia Smith, flight DN0457 to Saorsa. Please proceed to gate fifteen immediately. The final checks are being completed. This is the final boarding call for April Virginia Smith to Saorsa. Gate fifteen please. Thank you.'

What the hell…?

She was still here, somewhere. Thank heavens!

And she was on her way to…Saorsa?

That couldn't be right. But what if…Maybe she was going back for her ring. The ring that he had in his pocket. Wasn't exactly something you'd want to send via second class mail.

Oh no. Euan bolted towards gate fifteen, dodging and weaving through the crowd of travellers, apologising as he bumped into them. Sweat trickled down his forehead and his heart thundered with adrenaline as he muttered curses about the ridiculousness of it all.

He finally reached gate fifteen, utterly breathless. His heart seized when the last few passengers disappeared through the doorway onto the tarmac. The gate closed. Euan's shoulders slumped.

Where are you, sweetheart?

Well, if she was on the flight, he'd catch her in Saorsa. If not…

He let out a heavy sigh, feeling defeated and foolish.

'Euan?'

Chapter Twenty-Seven

In the expanse of the buzzing airport, April froze. And time froze with her.

Looking like he had been through hell and back, Euan was staring at the gate, his back to her. She would have recognised those shoulders and that ass anywhere. Even though his confident composure was replaced by weariness. For a split second, she couldn't believe what she saw. April blinked. 'Euan?'

He turned around, his gaze reflecting a storm of emotions. Pain and longing. 'April?' he said, his voice rough. 'Thank God I found you!'

Her pulse accelerated to a near life-threatening pace. His mere presence a shock to her system. April tried to steady her breath, to brace herself. 'What are you doing here?' she asked, trying to mask any trace of hope in her words. 'I thought you were—'

Euan wavered, cracking his knuckles. 'I had to find you, April, before... I had to tell you...' His voice trailed off, laden with an emotional weight that made her knees feel like custard.

April searched his eyes for his guardedness. There was

none. She drew in a long inhale, her own fears and doubts swirling inside. 'To tell me what?'

Euan paused, as if gathering the courage to speak his truth. 'Been doing a lot of thinking. About us. About everything. Couldn't let you go without speaking my piece.'

Oh, boy. He was going to tell her she was a great gal and they could be really good pen pals. But why would he do that here, in person?

The most logical answer scared her more than being amongst a herd of wild horses. Luckily, he looked just as panicky. Pale and a little green around the nose.

'I'm not one for grand speeches. Never have been. I thought I knew what I wanted, April. Thought I had it all figured out. But you've shattered every rule I had. Every line I drew in the sand.'

Jesus. This was a speech. He was giving a speech. For her. Right here, right now. April gripped the handle of her suitcase in order to avoid fainting.

'You were damn right. I'm a commitment-phobe. I realised I've been running away from the one thing that ever felt right. You, April.'

'I didn't mean to—'

'Let me finish, sweetheart. Then I'll listen to whatever you throw at me. Hell, slap me and punch me in the gut if that's what you need. Aye?'

His face was flaming now and her skin burned, too. 'Yeah, okay.' A part of her noticed that people were looking at them.

Euan's words kept pouring. 'You've pushed me to dig deeper, be more than surface level. Your struggle for your happiness and purpose…it's lighting a fire inside me. Makes me re-evaluate what I want. Who the hell I want to be. No idea how it happened, but in just a few weeks, you've toppled my world.' He paused, the lines on his face deepening. 'It's madness, the way I feel about you. Like I'm drowning and only you can save me.'

He stepped closer, fervency all over his face. 'And, April, you're a damn revelation. The way you give into your wants... Every small response, every kiss and gasp, keeps me desperate for more. And it's not just sex. It's soul-deep with us. I didn't know I wanted this, how much I *needed* this. You've ruined me for anyone else, baby. I'm yours.'

An awed smile tugged at his lips, and April felt a warm flush at the memories of their passionate moments together.

'And yes, I want to make you come every day. But it's your heart that's taken me. You're so full of love and life and kindness. How can I *not* love you? Fuck, I tried. But you're making it impossible!' Euan's hand flew up to his chest, his fist slamming on his heart. 'That's where you live now. Right here. Rent free.'

April felt the sincerity in his words, his vulnerability and hope laid bare.

He took another step, and his voice was a low, urgent whisper. 'I'm not asking for forever, sweetheart. I'm just asking for today. A moment to prove that this, us, it's worth the risk. I want a chance to be the one who stands by you. The one who drowns in your love and learns to breathe in it. Today, tomorrow, for as long as you'll have me.'

Is this really happening? April's heart hammered in a frantic cadence that mirrored the quiver in his words.

People were now staring in earnest.

Euan inched closer to her, the intensity in his gaze unflinching. 'Your hair is the colour of the sand in Saorsa. Your eyes are the colour of the sea I grew up with. Every time I look at you, I'm home.'

For a moment, the busy airport faded into the background. 'I've never felt like this. It's scary as hell,' he said. 'But I'd rather face that crushing fear and try to make it work with you than let you walk out of my life.'

'Euan,' she started. This was exactly what she had planned on saying to him. What she had wanted to hear. 'We have our fears, our pasts… I'm scared, too. Scared of making a mistake, scared of getting my heart broken.'

'I know, sweetheart. I've been an idiot. I know I hurt you. But I'm here now, standing in front of you, telling you I can't walk away. Not from you. Not without fighting for us, for what we could be.'

Euan grasped her hand. 'I don't know what the future holds. But I know I want you in mine. I love you. And that's the scariest, truest thing I've ever said.'

April looked deep into Euan's eyes, searching for any ounce of deceit or hesitation. But all she found was love. She reached her hand up to his cheek. This stubbled, gorgeous, lovely cheek of his. Her Scot. 'I don't want to walk away either. Why do you think I booked a flight back to Saorsa? Home is where you are. But I need to be my own independent person.'

'I'd never want you to be anything else,' he said, took her hand and kissed her palm. 'That's what I need, too. Let's be independent together.'

She smiled. 'But where are we going to live, smart-ass?'

'Saorsa, Kansas, Missouri, Mars, even Edinburgh. Wherever you fucking want, baby. We'll figure it out.'

Their foreheads touched as they stood amidst the chaotic swirl of people and sounds at the airport. In this moment, they were the centre of the universe. Just them, April and Euan.

'Stay with me,' he whispered. 'Stay with me forever.'

She felt the heat of his breath. 'Yeah, okay,' she murmured, closing her eyes as their lips met in a soft kiss.

When they parted, April's entire being thrummed with certainty. This was the real deal. This was how love was supposed to feel. Euan wasn't perfect – far from it, and neither was she – but he was kind and loving and willing to making things work between them. He saw her, he listened to her. That was all she needed, that was all it took. He was her friend as well as her lover.

And, to her delight, they were a great match in bed.

A small crowd of people had formed around them. It was in this moment that Euan remembered the other thing. The other reason he had come here, despite the danger to life and limb and heart. His pulse was thudding. He had just done a complete emotional striptease. That sort of thing was exhausting, draining, and also wild. Hardly surprising that he'd almost forgotten.

With shaking fingers, he reached into his pocket and pulled out her old engagement ring. All shiny and sparkly. 'You forgot that tiny thing in my drawer,' he said and held it up for her to see.

A few excited whispers rippled through the crowd, and suddenly, there was a buzz of anticipation.

April gasped and clapped her hands over her mouth. 'Oh my God, how stupid can one person be?'

People were filming with their phones.

'Thank you,' she said. 'You thief.'

'Thief? Never! Speaking of thieves…has anybody seen my jumper?'

April laughed. 'I have to give the ring back. It's worth a fortune and I don't want to keep it… Wait. Why are people filming us?'

He pulled her back in and chortled against her neck. 'Best guess? They think it's a proposal.'

'No they don't. Right? Oh no.' She turned almost scarlet, and Euan loved her all the more for it. He didn't care. What he had done had felt like a proposal, anyway. It was true. He couldn't imagine a single day without her.

This was it for him. This was his woman.

His jumper-thieving partner in crime.

So he held her as tight as he could and murmured into her ear, just for the two of them to hear: 'April Virginia Smith. Do you want to get laid like a goddamn queen for the rest of your foreseeable future?'

She jumped into his arms and answered with a kiss that would make the strongest man fall to his knees and forget his name. No words spoke clearer than this kiss, as deep and boundless as Saorsa's seas.

Epilogue

One year later…

When April Virginia Smith got married, it wasn't in a stuffy, suffocating dress in a church. It was in a white t-shirt and a long white skirt on the beach, the fabric catching the sea breeze like a sail.

She could breathe.

April stood barefoot in the sand, toes wriggling with excitement and nerves. And when Euan appeared in his light blue linen suit, he looked every bit the gorgeous man she fell in love with over a year ago.

She had decided to keep her name. Because she wasn't becoming someone else today. With Euan, at last, she was who she had always been.

'You look like a pirate and an angel had a baby,' Euan whispered as he reached her, eyes wide and glistening.

'And you look like a surfer who accidentally stumbled into a wedding,' April teased with a smirk. 'Dashing.' The wildflower bouquet, picked by Euan's niece and nephews, lay light in her hand.

Every bone in April's body hummed in affirmation. From tip to toe, this felt right. Utterly, completely, everlastingly right.

April and Euan had chosen a simple and intimate setting. Wooden folding chairs were arranged on the beach. Each setting had a small gift – a handmade trinket, a piece of local craftsmanship, a token of the isle's soul. Between the chairs, a path in the sand, lined with seashells, led to a wooden arch. It was adorned with a garland of wildflowers and sea grass. Tulle and silk ribbons fluttered like banners in the wind and framed the view. The arch was a thoughtful gift from Morag and Allan. Painted signs, crafted by their kids, directed guests to the ceremony.

As the late afternoon sun cast soft shadows, Saorsa's pristine beach felt more sacred to April than any church or chapel ever could. The calm sky and the sea were as vast and pure as her love for Euan.

When Matt started to play Des'ree's 'Kissing You' on his fiddle, Euan took her hand. 'Ready, sweetheart?'

'*So* ready.'

Together, they walked towards the archway, sharing a wistful glance. They had decided to lead each other to the altar, as they were about to share the path of their lives forever. These were merely the first steps. Their steps.

Angus, in the role of officiant, was waiting for them beneath the arch, a sparkle in his eye.

For this one day, Saorsa paused. Everything stopped in celebration, the entire island halting its daily routine. Just for them. Whoever tried to phone anyone or book anything in Saorsa that day was out of luck. The surf school had shut its doors. Aamer from the bike rental had put up a sign that read 'Closed for Love'. The Old Barn, the buzzing heart of Cuanag's – and, some would say, even Saorsa's – social life, was closed for a private function. That's where the wedding party would venture after the ceremony. And Morag had told all her guests that they could, of course, have a bed. But there was zero breakfast to be expected, since her baby brother was tying the knot and she intended to celebrate with gusto into the wee hours.

It was a day when personal ventures took a back seat to the love story that had captivated everyone's hearts. To her surprise, all three of April's brothers had flown in. Saorsa's entire community had gathered on the beach to share in the joy of April and Euan's wedding. A testament to the island's tight-knit nature. And to the two of them.

The only missing people were their parents. There was still far too much unresolved pain and baggage. Her mom hadn't forgiven April for moving to Scotland; Euan had just started talking to his parents again. These things took time, and that was okay.

But April and Euan didn't want to wait.

Deep gratitude flooded her core. For this, for Euan, for this place, for their future.

Their guests wore whatever they felt pretty and comfortable in. Pragmatically, her brothers put on the suits they had bought over a year ago, Duncan pranced up and down the beach in a kilt, while April's friend Alex from Kansas City had opted for a stunning dinner jacket with a bow tie – and a plaid petticoat.

The violin's notes floated on the breeze, intermingling with the sound of the waves and the hushed murmur of the guests.

'We're gathered here today to witness these two souls find their home in each other,' Angus began. 'This hand-fasting ritual symbolises the binding of two souls in love.' He placed their hands into each other's, their rings in their palms. Then he took the MacLeod tartan ribbon from Duncan and wrapped it around the couple's hands. The woollen fabric brushed against April's skin as they stood facing each other, eyes locked and hearts full of love.

As little Isla recited the Gaelic poem she had practised for weeks, Angus tied the cord. The sea whispered softly in the background. 'Today, we bind April and Euan's lives,' Angus said, his voice steady and warm. As their fingers intertwined, he gently wrapped the cord around their hands. 'With this cord, I bind your lives and spirits. As the sea is to the shore, may your love be constant and eternal,' he said, his words carrying the weight and strength of tradition.

April glanced at Euan, her heart swelling. They had written their own vows, and now it was time.

'I thought I was running away, but I ran to you,' she said, her voice shaking slightly. 'You are my lighthouse in the storm, my adventure in the calm. I promise to laugh at your dad jokes, to surf at dawn with you, and to be your anchor, as you are mine. In good times and in bad. In sickness and in health. Gu sìorraidh is gu bràth.'

Euan's eyes glistened. 'You came into my life and turned everything upside down. You taught me to love in ways I never thought possible. I promise to be your safe harbour, shelter you from the storm, and to love you until the last breath leaves my body. In good times and in bad. In sickness and in health. Gu sìorraidh is gu bràth.'

Angus cleared his throat. 'As you are bound together, so are your lives joined in love and in trust. Above you are the stars, below you is the earth, around you is the ocean. Like the stars, your love will be a source of light. Like the earth, a foundation from which to grow. And like the ocean, it will be vast,' he continued. With the last words spoken, he gently removed the cord, symbolising that, although the physical binding was removed, their union was everlasting.

They exchanged rings, simple bands of gold.

'You are now bound in love and life,' Angus declared, smiling warmly. 'You may seal your vows with a kiss.'

And as April tiptoed to kiss her husband, their guests erupted into cheers and the air was echoed with joy and laughter.

Warm light filled the Old Barn, the glow from string lights and tea lights casting a gentle ambiance. White tablecloths covered the whisky cask tables, and jars with wildflowers were scattered throughout the space. A small stage was set up at one end, where Matt's band was playing. Tonight, the bar was staffed by Allan and Angus.

On the makeshift dance floor, April snuggled up close to Euan. 'Do you remember how it all began?' she said to him.

'Course I do. You basically jumped into my arms!'

'I was pushed!'

'That's what they all say.'

April leaned into Euan, her head on his shoulder as they swayed to a fiddle tune. 'This is perfect,' she whispered.

'Only because you're with me,' he murmured back. 'You really did it,' Euan said with pride. 'Taking over the school. You're an islander.'

Her laughter mingled with the music. 'And you, opening your own gin distillery. Who would've guessed? Euan MacLeod, the entrepreneur. You've come a long way from your van days.' She kissed his neck. 'Surviving the first Saorsa winter wasn't about the weather, the storms, the power outages, or the empty shelves in the shop, was it? It was about finding where I belong. Here, with you. But actually…I knew that the moment you held me for the first time. You made me feel safe.'

Euan kissed her temple, his voice soft. 'And I always will. I'll always protect you, as you will protect me. My strong, amazing wife.'

Euan's hand slipped down her back as they swayed to the music. In that moment, surrounded by their loved ones and lost in each other's embrace, this was exactly where she was meant to be. On this tiny isle in Scotland, married to Saorsa's playboy who turned out to be the love of her life.

She had it all.

'Baby brother, sister-in-law…follow me, we have a surprise for you!' Morag said, and tugged at April's arm. It was getting late and Morag was officially buzzed. She led them to the parking lot outside the pub.

And there stood a shiny vintage Volkswagen camper van.

Euan's jaw dropped. 'What the actual—'

'It's our wedding gift to you!' Morag announced excitedly. 'Don't worry, it's only rented for the weekend.'

Allan scuffed his feet. 'We thought it would be nice if you had a special place for your wedding night.'

Their friends and family had gone all out to transform the vehicle into a romantic hideaway. Twinkling fairy lights cascaded along the van's ceiling, creating a starry canopy. The spacious bed was inviting and soft, with ivory linens, plush cushions, and cosy blankets. A trail of rose petals led to a cooler with bubbly and a platter of strawberries. Nothing was missing. Morag had even hung a 'Love Mobile' sign on the rear-view mirror.

'It's beautiful,' April said, trying not to cry. Euan squeezed her hand, looking at her with nothing but bursting love in his eyes.

And then it was time for their wedding night.

– THE END –

Want to read what happened in the van? Get the extra-steamy bonus scene here: beatricebradshaw.com/wedding-night

Book 3 in the series, *Love on the Scottish Summer Coast*, is available for preorder on Amazon.

Or get Love in the Scottish Winter Highlands on Amazon – book 1 in the series! It's a story about a wintry castle in Scotland, two broken hearts, and the healing power of love and community.

Thank you so much for reading this book. If you enjoyed April and Euan's story, it would be wonderful if you could spare a moment to leave a review on Amazon. It doesn't need to have epic length. Even one or two sentences mean a lot – I'd be eternally grateful. <3

Escape to Scotland and get book 1 today – what are you waiting for?

Glossary

- bampot = foolish person, idiot
- bawbag = scrotum (more often than not used endearingly)
- bawdy = bald person
- braw = great, beautiful
- Cailleach = powerful Celtic goddess of winter, wilderness, and wind; creator of hills and mountains
- ceilidh = Scottish community gathering with a dance; used to be accompanied by storytelling
- croft = agricultural small holding
- daft = silly, foolish, stupid
- dinnae = don't
- dreich = dreary, bleak (mostly weather)
- Each-Uisge = mythological water horse
- eejit = idiot
- factor = agent of the landlord
- fitbaw = football (soccer)
- gonnae = going to
- Gu sìorraidh is gu bràth = forever and always (Gaelic)

- hochmagandy = sex
- nae = no/ not
- naewhere = nowhere
- naw = no
- noo = now
- numpty = idiot
- pish = piss (often used for nonsense)
- selkie = mythical seal, shifts into human form by shedding its skin
- outwith = beyond
- uisge beatha = water of life (whisky)
- wean = child

Resources:

Dictionary of the Scottish Language https://dsl.ac.uk/ and fabulous pals from uni who are native Gaelic speakers <3

Author's Note

Dearest reader,

Authors often pour their hearts into their creations, leaving traces of their soul within the pages. This book emerged not just from my imagination, but from a deeply personal moment.

In 2006, I stood in a beautiful barn converted into a chapel, wearing a gorgeous champagne-coloured wedding dress, about to marry my long-term boyfriend. We had just bought a house; it made sense to get married. But as I stood there, holding my bouquet and clutching my grandpa's arm tightly, I thought, 'This is probably a mistake.' My fiancé was a nice guy, but for a long time, we had been drifting further and further apart. I should have listened to my gut. Because less than two years later, we were divorced.

The idea for this story stems directly from that one moment – the split second before I walked down the aisle. What if I had the courage to leave and run away? That's precisely what April does in this story. It takes tremendous courage. Or, to quote Euan, 'Can you imagine that set of balls?'

This novel is a testament to pursuing your truth, your passion, being unapologetically yourself. And, if necessary, taking a flight to Scotland! Speaking from experience, I can say it's one of the best places in the world to clear your head and heart.

I hope you'll join me for more stories of courage, self-discovery, and the power of embracing one's own truth, set against the stunning and soul-stirring backdrop of bonny Scotland.

With love,

About the Author

Beatrice Bradshaw writes small-town contemporary romances set in Scotland with a bit of heat. Because sex-positivity, ya'll!

Scottish Historian and German journalist/ translator by day and romance author by night, she has escaped from Berlin to Scotland five years ago. And not looked back once.

Beatrice Bradshaw is the pen name/ pseudonym of Jessica Beatrice Wagener – chosen so as not to have German narrative non-fiction confused with her (English) romance books.

She enjoys sharing her love for her adopted home country with others, bringing a sprinkle of the real Scotland into her books.

When she isn't glued to her desk in Glasgow, surrounded by baked goods and coffee, she can be found wandering around in Scottish castles and landscapes, finding peace and stories on cemeteries and in old buildings, or binge-watching romance series online.

Love on the Scottish Spring Isle is her second romance novel, the third is currently being written and will be published in summer 2024.

Connect with Beatrice here:
instagram.com/beatricebradshawauthor
facebook.com/beatricebradshawauthor
www.beatricebradshaw.com

Love on the Scottish Spring Isle
By Beatrice Bradshaw

First published in the UK by Jessica B. Wagener under the pen name Beatrice Bradshaw 2024.

Suite 624
Claymore House
145-149 Kilmarnock Road
Glasgow, G41 3JA

Jessica B. Wagener as Beatrice Bradshaw has asserted her right to be identified as the author of this work.

This book is entirely a work of fiction. Names, characters, businesses, organisations, places, incidents, and events other than those clearly in the public domain, are either the product of the author's imagination or are used fictitiously and are not to be construed as real. Any resemblance to actual persons, living or dead, events or locales is entirely coincidental.

Editing: Aimee Walker

Cover design: Hellie Cory

Print ISBN: 978-1-7395568-3-9
Ebook Edition © March 2024
ISBN: 978-1-7395568-2-2
Version: 2024-03-12

Printed in Great Britain
by Amazon

43558603R00146